AN IMPRUDENT INVESTIGATION

When Lyndhurst pulled Carolyn into his arms, she surrendered with curiosity rather than passion, since the scene had begun just as all her favorite authors were wont to describe such moments.

His arms tightened crushingly, and she felt his tongue pressing against her lips. There had been nothing about tongues in her books. Not one word. She struggled, but he was too strong. Indeed, she realized when she felt one of his hands push her aside, he was imprisoning her easily with only one arm. His hand was beneath the lace now, beneath even the silk, moving over the soft bare skin of her breast.

Carolyn had learned one thing for sure: How much her books had failed to teach her. . . .

SIGNET REGENCY ROMANCE
COMING IN AUGUST 1991

Irene Saunders
Talk Of The Town

Margaret Westhaven
Country Dance

Barbara Allister
A Love Match

Laura Matthews
The Seventh Suitor

BATH
CHARADE

❖━━━━━━━━━━❖

by

Amanda Scott

Ⓞ
A SIGNET BOOK

SIGNET
Published by the Penguin Group
Penguin Books USA Inc., 375 Hudson Street,
New York, New York 10014, U.S.A.
Penguin Books Ltd, 27 Wrights Lane,
London W8 5TZ, England
Penguin Books Australia Ltd, Ringwood,
Victoria, Australia
Penguin Books Canada Ltd, 2801 John Street,
Markham, Ontario, Canada L3R 1B4
Penguin Books (N.Z.) Ltd, 182-190 Wairau Road,
Auckland 10, New Zealand

Penguin Books Ltd, Registered Offices:
Harmondsworth, Middlesex, England

First published by Signet, an imprint of New American Library,
a division of Penguin Books USA Inc.

First Printing, July, 1991
10 9 8 7 6 5 4 3 2 1

 REGISTERED TRADEMARK—MARCA REGISTRADA

Printed in the United States of America

BOOKS ARE AVAILABLE AT QUANTITY DISCOUNTS WHEN USED TO
PROMOTE PRODUCTS OR SERVICES. FOR INFORMATION PLEASE WRITE
TO PREMIUM MARKETING DIVISION, PENGUIN BOOKS USA INC.,
375 HUDSON STREET, NEW YORK, NEW YORK 10014.

To Jim

1

"If you value your safety," Sir Bartholomew told Miss Laura sternly, "do not leave the shelter of these walls, lest your life fall victim to such imprudence."

"She'll leave," muttered the reader, turning the page and continuing to read.

Laura nodded submissively. Sadly however, though appearing to be the mildest and softest of her sex, wholly devoted to Sir Bartholomew's will, and looking up to him as a superior being—here the reader made a sound periously akin to an unladylike snort—not half an hour had elapsed before the beguiling child descended into the castle garden and from thence through the outer gate into the mysterious forest beyond.

With a light step, she hastened toward the blackberry patch, but scarce had she picked a dozen of the luscious fruit before darkness descended all about her in the form of a voluminous cloak. Two iron-muscled arms clamped fast around her from behind, and she heard the dreaded but unmistakable sound of Count Rudolfo's evil laughter.

"So, sweet beauty, you are mine again!"

Carolyn Hardy glared up in disgust at the ornate ceiling of Bathwick Hill House library, "I knew it," she muttered. "What an idiotish female Laura Lovelace is!"

To be sure, Miss Hardy, with her glossy black curls, rosy cheeks, and sparkling aquamarine eyes, had felt an instant empathy with a heroine possessing "soft ringlets the color of a raven's wing and eyes of sapphire-blue," but Miss Laura's insistence upon behaving at every turn in the stupidest manner possible had soon put empathy to flight. It was all very well to be desired for one's beauty, Carolyn thought; nonetheless, it would have been gratifying had the author allotted Miss Laura at least a modicum of intelligence as well.

Miss Hardy had small opinion of comeliness in and of itself. After all, she was the acknowledged beauty of her own family but thought it no great distinction, since most of the other younger members of the Hardy family were male and since only two of them (and her godmama's son, who didn't count) might have given her any competition.

Indeed, since she lacked the height and willowy figure (not to mention the vast fortune) required to be considered a diamond of the first water, in most gatherings of highborn young females her appearance would have occasioned little remark. That she was generally popular despite these deficiencies could be attributed to her generous spirit and vivacious personality, although neither quality was particularly noticeable when, as was presently the case, Miss Hardy suffered from boredom.

She was curled up on a claw-footed sofa in the library's west-window embrasure, doing her best to forget the chilly gray October day outside by concentrating on this latest offering from the pen of the author who currently enjoyed her greatest favor, but it was slow going. She found herself constantly wondering why Sir Bartholomew Lancelot did not wring his beloved's graceful swanlike neck instead of worshiping the ground she trod upon.

When the heavy, carved door of the library swung open, Carolyn looked up from her book with a frown of annoyance occasioned more by her irritation with Miss Laura than with the interruption, but her grim look was enough to halt in her tracks the thin, mousy-looking lady who had opened the door.

"Oh, dear," Miss Judith Pucklington said, hitching more securely onto her shoulders the several shawls with which she had draped her meager body, "I don't wish to intrude, but Shields informed me that there was a fire in here, and I thought—"

"Come in, Puck, do," Carolyn said instantly. "You look half-frozen, which is not to be wondered at, I'm sure, since I believe this may well be the only warm room in the house, except for Sydney's snuff room, of course, but you will not wish to be sitting in there."

"Goodness me, no," Miss Pucklington replied, still poised on the threshold like a timid bird ready to take flight at the least hint of danger. "I should never go into that room without his leave. Indeed, I should not have entered this one had Shields not assured me that Cousin Sydney is still away from home."

Carolyn chuckled, setting her book aside and stretching her limbs, cramped after more than two hours of reading. " 'Tis the odious smell of snuff that keeps me from invading that particular sanctum of his, but nothing more. Surely you do not fear Sydney, Puck."

"Oh, no," Miss Pucklington protested, distressed, "for although Cousin Olympia has frequently insisted that he had a most violent temper as a child, one simply cannot credit it, for he is always most kind, although I cannot like his man—so odd looking, you know, and Ching Ho being such a queer name—but I should never presume, in any case." Her gaze drifted wistfully to the hearth. "What a very large fire that is, to be sure."

"Yes, isn't it?" Carolyn agreed, regarding the leaping blaze with satisfaction. "I found that I couldn't see to read if I sat near the fire, and I was freezing here by the window, so I commanded the youngest footman—Abel, I think his name is, although even after more than three weeks of living here, I cannot keep all the servants' names straight in my head—"

"Oh, dear me, no. There are ever so many."

"Yes, well, Sydney does like his comforts, and he can afford them, I daresay, thanks to his Uncle Henry Beauchamp's having left him this house and his entire fortune besides. At all events, I asked young Abel to pile the wood on. He filled the basket, too, to overflowing, so we can be as lavish as we like. But do come in and shut that door, Puck. There is the most chilling draft while you stand there."

"Oh, dear, how very sorry I am," exclaimed Miss Puckling-ton, pulling the door to with a snap and remaining pressed up against it, "but I am persuaded that I ought not to disturb you, my dear. To be sure, my own room is like an ice house, but after Cousin Olympia's saying so firmly that we ought not to waste Cousin Sydney's money on mere creature comforts—"

"Rubbish," Carolyn said. "Sydney would be the first to squander his fortune on creature comforts, for he doesn't believe them *mere* at all. As to disturbing me, you will be doing no such thing, for I am quite out of patience with the characters in this book, and I shall welcome your company. Indeed, I begin to wonder how such foolish books as this one ever amused me."

Miss Pucklington eyed the slim, gilt-edged blue volume curiously as she moved to take a seat in one of two matching wing chairs facing the fire, scooting it to an angle that allowed her to face Carolyn without craning her neck. "That cannot be the book Cousin Olympia gave you at breakfast," she said as she produced her knitting bag from beneath her myriad shawls and withdrew a tumble of brightly colored wool from its depths.

"Good gracious, no," Carolyn replied, wrinkling her nose. "Godmama cannot have read so much as the first page of that book, for even she could not be so daft as to believe I would read such fustian. I expect 'twas the title made her hope it would do me good to read it. 'Tis called *Modern Manners*, and you must know she was a trifle displeased with my behavior when we took tea with the dowager Viscountess Lyndhurst on Wednesday last."

Miss Pucklington smiled, bringing a twinkle to her pale-blue eyes. "As I recall the matter, Cousin Olympia's displeasure had less to do with the viscountess's tea than with the fact that you spent the afternoon chatting with the young viscount. A most unsuitable young man for you to know, Cousin Olympia told me. A reputation, you know," she murmured, blushing.

"According to Godmama and Sydney," Carolyn said with a grimace, "every gentleman in Bath under the age of a hundred and three is unsuitable for me to know. But *Modern Manners* won't help their cause, for it was written nigh onto a hundred fifty years ago and 'tis a treatise on the excellence of the Puritan way of life . . . Godmama cannot have known that, for the Saint-Denis family has always held by the Anglican faith. Well, since there has been an Anglican faith, at all events," she amended. "And there is nothing amiss with Viscount Lyndhurst, reputation or no. He is certainly no Count Rudolfo."

"Count Rudolfo? Whoever is Count Rudolfo?"

Carolyn indicated her book. "He is the villain of this lurid tale, and quite my favorite character."

"Oh, dear!"

Carolyn shrugged. "I know one is not supposed to like the villain, Puck, but at least Count Rudolfo is not stupid. He never misses an opportunity to do evil. Right from the very first, when he abducted Miss Laura Lovelace from the convent—"

"Convent!"

"From right under the noses of the nuns who raised her, for of course Laura is an orphan." She sighed. "All the best romantic heroines are orphans, you know, though personally I have never found the orphaned state to be a romantic one."

"Certainly not."

"No, for you are one, too, are you not?"

"I suppose I am," Miss Pucklington said with a small frown. "Mama died during my third Season and dear Papa went aloft nigh onto ten years ago, which is when I began to live with Cousin Olympia. But one does not think of a woman of my years in such terms, of course. Your own case is a far more melancholy one."

"Perhaps," Carolyn said, still thinking about her book. "One wonders what became of the parents of all those heroines. This author, who calls herself 'a Gentlewoman of Consequence, residing in Bath,' after the fashion of her ilk, writes that Miss Laura's parents died in each other's arms, which I thought romantic but odd, especially since I have been unable to discover *why* they died. It doesn't make any difference to the story, of course, and one doesn't really want to know the details." She grimaced, remembering with painful clarity the deaths of her own parents within days of each other, though definitely not in each other's arms. The gruesome sights, smells, and sounds of typhus could not be thought romantic by anyone.

Miss Pucklington clicked her tongue in distress. "You must not dwell upon such sorrowful memories, my dear."

"Not sorrowful ones," Carolyn said frankly, "just rather horrid ones." Then, seeing that her companion looked more distressed than ever, she added, "Truly, ma'am, though my parents' deaths were awful and I am most sincerely sorry for their suffering, it has been nearly seven years since their passing, and I do not grieve for them. In point of fact, I didn't like them very much."

Miss Pucklington's eyes widened and she looked anxiously around as though she feared someone else might have heard. "You must not say such things, Carolyn. 'Tis vastly unbecoming."

"Why? My parents were both distant, chilly persons who scarcely ever paid me any heed. That my mother always smelled delightfully of flowers is the most pleasant memory I have of either of them. No doubt she expected to notice me when the time came to present me at court, and Papa no doubt expected to have to frank me for a Season or two, but since they both died before either event came to pass, I did not receive even that much of their attention. Indeed, since they sent me here to Bath to school when I was nine, and since I generally spent my shorter holidays with Godmama and the others at Swainswick, it was only by the greatest mischance that I happened to be at home in Devon when the typhus struck. Even then, it was only because my old nurse insisted upon my staying away from them both that I chanced to witness the dreadful effects of the disease that killed them."

"Because she insisted you stay *away*?"

"Of course." But Carolyn had the grace to look ashamed of herself as she added, "I had then a lamentable habit of wishing most to do that which I have been commanded not to do, a habit I trust I've outgrown. I made a mistake that time, of course, and was most fortunate not to have become ill myself."

"I should think so." Miss Pucklington would have said more, but the library door opened again just then, startling them both.

It was only the footman Abel, who bowed awkwardly and said, "Yer pardon, miss, but I thought I'd stoke up the fire a bit if you was wantin' me ter, 'n' see if anything else were wanted."

"Thank you," Carolyn said. "You may put another log on, if you will, but that will be all." When he had gone, she grimaced comically at Miss Pucklington. "I was afraid it was Godmama."

"I, too," her companion confessed, "though, of course, Cousin Olympia is laid down upon her bed, just as she is every afternoon at this time, or else I should be with her and not here with you. But perhaps you ought to be getting on with reading your book, my dear, while you may still enjoy the luxury of this glorious fire. You needn't heed me, you know, for I have my knitting to occupy me, and I am very much accustomed to sitting quietly and entirely unnoticed."

"I know that must be true," Carolyn said, curling her legs under herself again and leaning back into the curve of the sofa. "You are forever at Godmama's beck and call, are you not, and must always be at her side to be ignored or bullied at her whim. How often you must long for solitude!"

"Solitude!" Miss Pucklington was shocked. "Goodness me, no," she said. "I count myself fortunate, most fortunate, indeed, for were it not for dear Cousin Olympia's generosity, I should very likely have been left to starve when Papa died, for he made no arrangement for me, none at all. I was most grateful when Cousin Olympia so generously took me under her wing."

Carolyn sighed. "I suppose I should be grateful to her, too, but 'tis exceedingly difficult on such a day as today, when the sky looks like coming on to storm and one can place no dependence upon Godmama to remember that she promised to take me to the assembly tonight at the Sydney Gardens Hotel. Truly, on such days, this house begins to feel like a moss-covered tomb in which I have been buried alive."

Miss Pucklington's gaze shifted significantly to the gilt-edged blue book. When she looked back at Carolyn, there was a glint of amusement in her eyes, but she made no comment.

None was necessary. Carolyn's cheeks grew pink as she said, "Perhaps I am talking a bit like Miss Laura Lovelace, but one does, from time to time, find life in the pages of one's books a good deal more interesting than reality. I am certainly not so foolish as Miss Laura is, however."

Miss Pucklington blinked. "Is she very foolish?"

A glance at her open countenance told Carolyn the question was an innocent one. "Not foolish so much as stupid," she said.

"She refuses to learn from her mistakes. Why, I am only halfway through the second of three volumes, and Count Rudolfo has just abducted the brainless wench for the fourth time. This time she went into the forest beyond Sir Bartholomew's manor house after he warned her to stay in his walled garden, and only because she wished to gather wild blackberries. And of course, Count Rudolfo was just waiting for her. Moreover," she added on a note of disgust, "the season is supposed to be early spring."

Miss Pucklington clicked her tongue. "I fear 'tis the way of most romantic heroines to be intrepid rather than wise, but Miss Laura can scarcely be blamed for her creator's not realizing that wild blackberries cannot be had so early in the year."

"Well, if I were Sir Bartholomew, I'd wring her silly neck or beat her till she screamed for mercy," Carolyn said flatly, "and the fact that heroes never do such things only goes to prove how unrealistic tales like this one really are, because any gentleman who accepted responsibility for her surely would lose his temper when she continues to behave as she does."

"True romantic heroes," Miss Pucklington said wistfully, "see no faults in their fair beloveds, or else they love them to distraction in spite of their faults."

"Goodness, ma'am, do you read such stuff as this?"

Miss Pucklington's guilt was written all over her face as she said, "Not often, I confess. 'Tis difficult to indulge in such common tastes in Cousin Olympia's presence."

"I should think so," Carolyn said, her imagination boggling at the thought of Miss Pucklington with her long thin nose buried in any gothic romance, let alone in the presence of the august Olympia, dowager Lady Skipton. But Carolyn's duty was clear nonetheless. "Look here, ma'am," she said, getting swiftly to her feet, "the first volume of this tale is on the shelf behind Sydney's desk—just here." She reached for the book and took it down. "I daresay he must subscribe for nearly everything that's printed, because I'm forever finding new ones, and he has said I may choose whatever I like. He would say the same to you, I know. Here, take it. 'Tis a most diverting tale, for all my criticism." She held out the book, and Miss Pucklington, pink with guilty pleasure, accepted it at once.

"I am sure I should not," she said, caressing the cover. "Oh, what will Cousin Olympia say?"

"Nothing at all if you do not show it to her," Carolyn said, her eyes dancing with mischief, "and you know perfectly well that Sydney will not care a whit."

"No, for he is most generous, is he not? And whatever Cousin Olympia may say about his childhood temper," she added on a more spirited note, "Cousin Sydney would never wring a young woman's neck. Nor would it ever enter his head to beat her, no matter what foolish thing she might have done."

"No," Carolyn agreed, laughing as she tried and failed to conjure up a vision of the elegant Sydney Saint-Denis ever exerting himself to such violent action. "He would fear to muss his clothes, would he not? Moreover, I doubt he has any temper, for I have certainly never seen the least hint of one."

"No," Miss Pucklington said gently, "and I am persuaded that in past years some of your pranks must have sorely tried the patience of a lesser gentleman. But no doubt, now that you are so near to coming of age—only a month, after all—you have outgrown your love for practical jokes."

"There was not much scope for such nonsense either at Swainswick when last we were there, or since we came to Bathwick Hill House," Carolyn told her with a grin, "but it does not do to allow oneself to become too sedentary, and 'tis rather a sore point with me that I have never managed really to stir Sydney up. One day I should like very much to astonish him with such a joke as he would find impossible to ignore."

"Oh, dear," Miss Pucklington said nervously, "I ought never to have mentioned the subject, but it is not wise to provoke him, my dear, for we are all dependent upon his hospitality. Cousin Olympia assures me that we would not like to live in the Dower House, and I cannot think she would willingly return to Lord and Lady Skipton at Swainswick."

"Nor would they willingly receive her," Carolyn said with a laugh. "Not after she left in such high dudgeon after that awful argument with Matilda just a month after we returned from London. Matilda has invited us to spend Christmas at Swainswick, however, so perhaps they are on speaking terms again.

In any event, I have no fear that Sydney will throw us out into the cold.''

"Our circumstances are scarcely similar, however," Miss Pucklington said. "I am merely the poor relation, while you are the beloved godchild."

"Not Sydney's godchild," Carolyn pointed out.

"No, but his mother's. And you have your fortune, as well, do you not? My father left me nothing when he died."

"These days," Carolyn said dryly, "five thousand invested in the funds is an independence, ma'am, but scarcely a fortune, certainly not to the *beau monde*. That fact I discovered the instant I made my come-out. I did have several eligible offers— indeed, I have been twice betrothed, have I not—but I am still unwed for the simple reason that I could not imagine myself married to any of them, and since Godmama has said she will hire herself out as a cook's maid before she will ever again stay at Skipton London House with Matilda, my second Season was no doubt my last. Godmama promised I would meet any number of eligible young men in Bath, but of course, the town being no longer the fashionable place it once was, I seem to meet only unsuitable ones, so although I did think it would be amusing to live in Sydney's house, he keeps flitting off hither and yon to auctions and whatnot, and it has not been amusing at all.''

"Nevertheless," Miss Pucklington said, "you will never be entirely dependent upon relations for your bread and board, as I am, nor so apprehensive of being left alone in the world."

"Well, I don't know about that," Carolyn said without thinking. "The funds could be wiped out, I suppose, and most women are dependent upon someone, are they not? Of course, if you mean that I shan't ever have to toady to some rich relative out of fear of being disowned if . . . Oh, forgive me," she exclaimed, stricken by the bitter look on Miss Pucklington's face. "I didn't mean that the way it sounded, Puck. I spoke heedlessly. Oh, you must forgive me!"

"You said nothing that is not true, so there is nothing to forgive," Miss Pucklington said, setting aside the book and picking up her knitting. "I shall just finish my shawl before I begin to read. You must pardon me if I do not speak any more just now. If I do so, I shall lose count of my stitches."

Carolyn knew that Miss Pucklington could knit blindfolded. She knew, too, that she had killed, for the moment at least, any desire in the older woman to read a romantic tale. Consequently, and not for the first time, she found herself wishing she had bitten her tongue before speaking her thoughts aloud.

She picked up her book, but it was some time before she was able to concentrate again on Miss Laura's adventures, because the steady clicking of knitting needles sounded a constant rebuke in her ears. At last, however, the fire's crackling warmth and the rhythmic soughing of the wind through the trees outside the window relaxed her and she was drawn again into the tale.

When the library door flew back on its hinges and the dowager Lady Skipton, her stout figure swathed in dark-blue silk edged with yards of ecru lace, sailed into the room with a fat liver-and-white spaniel huffing and puffing in her wake, Carolyn and Miss Pucklington both jumped. "So here you are, the pair of you," the dowager announced, raising her gold-rimmed lorgnette to her pale-gray eyes and glaring at them through it.

With rare presence of mind, Miss Pucklington slipped the blue volume from her lap into the knitting bag and dropped her knitting atop it as she scrambled to her feet. "Cousin Olympia, I thought you were resting. Why did you not send for me?"

Plumping her bulk down in the second wing chair with such force that Carolyn feared for its slender, delicately arched legs, Lady Skipton straightened her lace cap and said, "I should not have to send for you, Judith. Pray, hand me that red-velvet cushion. Heaven knows," she added as Miss Pucklington hurried to place the cushion at her back, "I do not expect much in return for my generosity, but I do think you might have the goodness to remember when it time for dear Hercules to have his little walk."

"Oh, dear," Miss Pucklington said, "how very remiss of me, to be sure. I had no idea the hour was so far advanced. I'll take him at once, shall I?"

"You'll have to fetch his lead, for I forgot to bring it down with me, and see he don't muddy his little paws as he did yesterday. Mama likes her little man to have tidy paws," she added in an entirely different tone as she reached to pat the spaniel, fawning at her ankles.

Carolyn, glancing at Miss Pucklington, said, "It is very cold out today, Godmama. Perhaps, just this once, one of the footmen could take Hercules out."

"Hercules does not like footmen," Lady Skipton said. "He bites them. And if Judith had not been stifling herself here in this hot room, she would take no notice of a slight chill. I thought," she added, turning a basilisk glare upon Miss Pucklington, "that I gave strict orders there were to be no fires lit before supper. 'Tis an unconscionable waste of Sydney's money, and though it was wrong in my brother Henry to have left it all to him as he did, I will not tolerate waste."

Before Miss Pucklington could gather her wits to reply, Carolyn said, "I ordered the fire, ma'am, for I chanced to remember that Sydney would dislike it if the damp air were to harm his books or prints."

"I am aware of that," the dowager retorted, looking down her nose and adding with the air of one determined to have the last word, "but the fire needn't have been such a large one."

Miss Pucklington said in a hearty tone, "Come along, Hercules, lad," whereupon the spaniel trotted obediently after her, leaving a distinct odor behind to inform Carolyn as plainly as words would have done that the dowager had been indulging her pet in too many of her own favorite bonbons again.

Lady Skipton, sniffing, looked accusingly at Carolyn, who flushed to the roots of her hair. But although she opened her mouth to deny responsibility, she shut it again when she could think of nothing even remotely acceptable to say.

"Stop gaping," commanded the dowager. "You look like a hooked fish, which is not at all becoming to any young woman. If you've got something to say, say it."

Pressed, Carolyn blurted, "Shall I send for one of the footmen to bank the fire, ma'am?"

"That will not be necessary," the dowager said, stretching her feet nearer to its warmth. "I shall sit here with you until they announce that supper has been served. 'Tis likely Sydney will honor us with his presence tonight, and I make no doubt that if he does, he will applaud the little economies I have instigated in his absence."

Since that topic was no more promising than the previous one,

Carolyn said, "He has been away a sennight this time, ma'am. Why do you believe he will return tonight?" As she spoke, she tried to slip her book behind her without drawing notice to it.

The dowager seemed not to notice as she said, "I am told that the Black Dog Trust held a meeting this afternoon at Westbury, and you know my son takes his duties as a turnpike trustee most seriously. I have told Mrs. Shields to set supper back an hour to accommodate him."

Carolyn sat up straighter. "But if you set supper back, ma'am, we shall be late leaving for the gardens."

"And what, pray, makes you think we are going out? I am certain I had no such intention."

"But you did! That is, you said we might attend the next assembly there, which is tonight. What is more, it is nearly the last one until spring. Oh, you must remember, surely."

"I remember no such thing. And why are you wriggling so? Proper young ladies sit up straight with their feet placed firmly upon the floor and their hands resting neatly in their laps. Do so at once, and . . . Good gracious, what is that?" she demanded as the book, freed by Carolyn's automatic obedience to the familiar command, fell between the sofa's back and seat and crashed to the floor. "Bring that to me at once. I cannot imagine what sort of book it must be that you attempt to conceal from me."

Feeling suddenly more like a child of ten than a young woman rapidly approaching the twenty-first anniversary of her birth, Carolyn fumbled beneath the sofa for the book, then got up and reluctantly approached her godmother. It was at times like this, infrequent though they were, that she valued Lady Skipton's general lack of concern with her conduct. As she put the volume in the dowager's outstretched hand, Carolyn mentally braced herself for reprimand.

"This is not the book I gave you to read this morning."

"No, ma'am."

"You would have had no need to conceal that book, I think."

"No, ma'am."

"I cannot imagine," the dowager went on, "where you can have come by such a book as this."

"She got it from me, I'm afraid." The words, spoken in a

gently apologetic, masculine voice, came from behind them, and both ladies turned their heads in surprise toward the tall, slender, fair-haired, elegantly attired gentleman who had entered the library so silently that neither had heard him do so. The owner of Bathwick Hill House had come home, thus gratifying his mother by fulfilling her prophecy and delighting Miss Hardy by his exquisite timing as much as by the simple fact of his return.

2

Mr. Saint-Denis, instantly noting Carolyn's delight and unmistakable relief at his arrival, wasted no time in self-congratulation on his timely arrival, for he knew he could not long depend upon his mother to remain silent. However, no sooner had he opened his mouth to continue his bland speech when Carolyn interrupted him without ceremony to demand to know where on earth he had come by his "hideous" waistcoat.

Amused, he opened his dark-blue coat to give them a better view of the pink-and-gold-silk confection beneath and drawled, " 'Tisn't hideous, my dear, but quite admirable in fact. Trust meetings are such sober occasions, you know, and one is expected to dress appropriately, but I do like a touch of color to brighten a dreary day. I had thought to wear it evenings with knee breeches and pink and gilt clocked stockings, but Weston prevailed upon me to order an emerald one for evening and to don pantaloons and Hessians with this. You must not fail to give me your opinion of the other rig when I wear it."

The dowager, rarely interested in anyone's clothing but her own, said sharply, "Never mind that, Sydney. This book is not suitable for a young girl to read, and so you must admit."

"I cannot agree, ma'am," he replied, moving nearer the warmth of the hearth. " 'Tis precisely the sort of foolishness that all young women delight in reading, though I do trust that Carolyn at least has the sense to enjoy such stuff without believing everything the idiotish author tells her to believe.''

Carolyn did not rise to his bait for once, but said sweetly, ''If you would like to show off your knee breeches, sir, there is to be an assembly tonight at the Sydney Gardens Hotel.''

''At my hotel?'' He smiled, wondering how it was that he had not noticed before how greatly time and two London Seasons had improved her looks. Though he usually visited the city only to replenish his wardrobe or attend an auction, he had heard enough about her activities there to believe she had not altered much from the mischievous girl who had plagued him so in his youth.

He was forcibly reminded of that imp when she wrinkled her nose at him just then and said with dignity, ''It's been years since I was childish enough to believe the gardens or hotel were named for you, sir, so pray don't tease me.''

''I shouldn't dare,'' he replied, gracefully taking snuff from an elaborately figured silver snuff box. ''I'd be terrified to find myself trying to sleep tonight in an apple-pie bed.''

She chuckled. ''I doubt you are ever terrified, Sydney, and I haven't turned up your sheets since before you visited China.''

''Can it be that long? That must be nearly five years ago.''

She nodded. ''Before we came to live here, I'd scarcely seen you since your Uncle Beauchamp died and left you this house. Only during your brief visits to Swainswick at Christmas.''

''Then the least I can do to renew our acquaintance properly is to escort you to the gardens tonight.''

Lady Skipton said austerely, ''I have not said I wish to go.''

Seeing Carolyn about to protest, Sydney said calmly, ''I do not doubt, ma'am, that if you find you cannot care for the outing, Cousin Judith will agree to chaperon Carolyn.''

''That will not be necessary,'' Lady Skipton replied. ''Since you desire it, there is no more to be said. We will all go.''

Winking at Carolyn, Sydney bowed and left the room, making his way up the stairs to his bedchamber, where he found his valet unpacking his cases.

''You'll have to stop that for now, Ching,'' he said. ''I have decided to go out this evening.''

''Indeed, my master,'' said the valet, whose proper English attire did little to disguise his Oriental heritage. Bowing low, he said in a lilting voice that retained but a trace of an accent, "You are not in general capricious, sir, but I believe you said not an hour since that you had formed the intention to remain within doors this evening. I trust nothing is amiss."

"One would think," Sydney said plaintively, "that considering how much I've learned from you in the four years you have been with me, you might at least have learned how unbecoming curiosity is in a gentleman's servant."

"Self-cultivation," said Ching Ho, moving with swift grace to help him out of his tight-fitting coat, "has no other method but to extract its essence from one's fellow man."

"Good Lord, what does that mean?"

"Only that if one would understand oneself, my master, one must first understand others. Will you wear knee breeches?"

"Yes, I am to escort my mother and Miss Carolyn to an assembly. I'll wear the new green waistcoat as well."

"Ah, Missy Carolyn," the valet said wisely. "I see."

"No, you don't see, you inscrutable rascal, if you think I mean to set up a flirtation with her. She is the merest child, for one thing, and a guest beneath my roof, for another."

"I do not understand western ways," Ching Ho said, stepping to the wardrobe. "In my country, a man may easily choose to fix his interest upon a woman living beneath his roof, for she must obey his will in all things."

"Well, take it from me, it won't answer here," Sydney said. "As it is, the chit will lead me a merrier dance than I like if she means to disport herself here as she did in London. While she lived beneath my brother's roof, I could leave it to him to look after her—not that he or Matilda did any such thing, or Mama, for that matter—but now it is up to me to see that she don't go betrothing herself to some other complete ass, thinking she can cry off later, as she did in town. That won't answer here in Bath, where the quizzes like nothing so much as a bit of scandal to nibble, but as there are few eligible young men here, one expects the worst. The black coat, Ching, the black coat. Put that blue thing away. And make haste, man, we've less than three hours, and my supper to eat in the meantime."

Rather more than three hours later, at the hotel's carriage entrance, Mr. Saint-Denis dismissed his coachman with orders to return for them at eleven—later than which no assembly in Bath ever persisted—and offered his arm to his mother, magnificently attired in rose satin and a silver-plumed turban. Ahead of them, visibly shivering in white muslin with sapphire-colored ribbons that matched her eyes, Carolyn walked up the steps with Miss Pucklington, swathed in shawls, at her side. They passed into the vestibule beneath the hotel's high, round portico and followed a number of other people along the wide corridor to the ballroom, where musicians in an arched gallery provided harmonious background for the hum of conversation.

To Carolyn's disappointment, the room seemed at first to be filled with elderly ladies and a few gentlemen who were of an age with them. There seemed to be no young men at all, unless one counted Sydney, who was nearer thirty than twenty. To be sure, there was a scattering of very young ladies whose mamas believed the late-autumn Bath assemblies provided a perfect introductory opportunity for daughters who would make their London come-outs in the spring, but Carolyn had no interest in them. She had nearly decided she had wasted her time, not to mention a very becoming gown, when, just as Lady Skipton and Miss Pucklington paused to speak to an acquaintance, the dowager Viscountess Lyndhurst approached, accompanied by her tall, handsome son.

Greeting them both warmly, Carolyn turned to Sydney as the viscountess moved on to talk to Lady Skipton. "Do you know Viscount Lyndhurst, sir?"

"We've met," Sydney said, nodding politely.

"Indeed, we have," the dark-haired younger man agreed with a brief, oblique glance at him, "though not above twice, I daresay. Don't seem to run in the same fields, do we, Saint-Denis?"

Sydney murmured a polite response, but the viscount had already returned his full attention to Carolyn.

"Do you suppose we'll be able to form a full set of competent dancers?" he asked her with a droll grimace as he gestured toward the assembled company. " 'Tis always the same with these late Season gatherings, I believe—more observers than participants. Still I see there are some young angelics being dangled before our appreciative masculine eyes."

Carolyn laughed but found herself wondering how it was that the viscount, with his dark good looks and fashionable attire, appeared somehow unfinished, even rather untidy, next to Sydney, who was, as usual, precise to a pin in his cream-colored knee breeches, dark coat, and snowy linen. Even the bright emerald waistcoat he sported seemed just right, while the more restrained embroidered one the viscount wore seemed somehow rather gaudy.

The viscount's behavior toward her seemed different, too. In his own house he had been flatteringly attentive, but now his attitude bordered on the possessive, and when the music at last grew louder and the master of ceremonies announced that the grand march was about to begin, she was not at all surprised when he held out his arm to her, although he had certainly not asked for the honor of escorting her. Nevertheless, she was anything but pleased when Sydney intervened.

"My privilege, I believe," he said quietly.

Lyndhurst bristled at first, but after casting a glance at the company and another at Sydney, he shrugged and smiled at Carolyn. "Reserve the first set of country dances for me then, Caro, my love. And don't dare to tell me you've already promised them elsewhere, for I'll not accept a second put-off."

She agreed, concealing her displeasure at his use of her nickname so that Sydney would not guess her feelings. She wondered if he would comment but wasn't surprised when he did not, and when he held out his arm in his customary polite way, she placed her fingers lightly upon it and allowed him to guide her to their place in the line, noting—also without surprise—that a stout figure topped by a silver-plumed turban and a thin one draped in shawls were just disappearing into the card room.

The grand march was followed, as always, by a stately minuet, and Carolyn was glad Sydney was unlikely to engage her in conversation, for she knew she would quickly betray the confusion she was feeling if he were to ask her about Lyndhurst. Though she was annoyed with Sydney for interfering, she was equally annoyed with the viscount for casually assuming she would allow him to partner her in the grand march without first having had the courtesy to ask her to do so.

Despite her annoyance, however, when the first set of country dances was called, she greeted Lyndhurst with pleasure, for she had observed him gazing at her more than once during the intervening time and could not help but be flattered by the fact that he seemed to have eyes for no one else, although many more people have arrived. While she danced with him, she saw several other young acquaintances among the company, including a fair-haired, handsome young man with twinkling hazel-green eyes, who stepped up to claim her hand the minute the country dances ended.

She greeted him with delight, persuaded that he, at least, would not be too much criticized by either her godmother or Mr. Saint-Denis. She had first met Brandon Manningford several years before, when he was a student home on holiday and she had been one of the young angelics allowed to attend her first grownup parties in Bath. Though his visits home were sporadic at best, since most of her Bath swains were of an age with her godmother, it was scarcely surprising to anyone that she formed a friendship with Mr. Manningford. They had many acquaintances in common, in London as well as in Bath, and since he was interested only in finding new ways to amuse himself, excluding matrimony, she had come to look upon him as a brother rather than as a potential flirt or suitor, and she was always glad to see him.

Turning now to Lyndhurst, who still hovered attentively at her side, she said, "You know Mr. Manningford, sir. His family have lived in Bath forever, I believe."

"Not really forever, Caro," Brandon retorted, laughing as he exchanged nods with the viscount, "and I know Lyndhurst quite well, of course. Dash it all, everyone is acquainted with everyone else in Bath. Moreover, I took a monkey off him less than a month past, when he wagered I couldn't slip old Nolly into the Pump Room without raisin' a dust."

"That awful bear!" Carolyn exclaimed. "I thought you got rid of him. Wasn't it enough that he once nearly tore your leg off? Now you've got to go frightening old ladies in the Pump Room!" But she was grinning. She knew she would have heard if there had been any dire consequences, and Brandon's penchant for the outrageous matched her own love of a good joke. Indeed, she had often envied his creative imagination, well aware that her own was not nearly so droll. "Tell me about it," she begged.

"Assure you, I didn't frighten anyone but one steward I met on the way out," Brandon insisted. "Took old Nolly in at the crack of dawn, you see, sat him in an armchair under the musician's gallery, and plied him with three or four quarts of good stout ale till he went off to sleep like a lamb. Slept the whole morning away, as I knew he would. A few customers looked at him oddly, to be sure, but when I asked if they didn't think he was an excellent example of the taxidermist's skill, they just wandered away again, muttering things to themselves."

Carolyn chuckled. "Then what?"

"Nothing much. At noon, a couple of m' friends marched through the place playing a fife and drum, and I got old Nolly out during the uproar. Poor fellow was still sufficiently muddled to go quietly. But look here," he added, glancing around, "the set's forming for our dance, Caro. You'll excuse us, Lyndhurst." He held out his arm to her, but when she moved to place her hand upon it, somehow she found the viscount's arm where Brandon's had been.

She stared at Lyndhurst in amazement when he said smoothly, " 'Fraid not, old man. Dashed hot, these country dances, and I told the little lady I'd take her outside for a breath of air. Daresay you'd prefer to be in the card room anyway, if the truth were known. Don't generally see you at such affairs as this."

"No, and you wouldn't see me tonight," Brandon said frankly, "if old Lady Lucretia Calverton hadn't dragooned me into dancing attendance on her. Dashed if she didn't want to bring along that white mop on legs she calls a dog. Tell you what," he added, shaking his head, "I'm dashed fond of dogs, even fat, overfed ones, which Henrietta ain't, but one does draw the line at bringing them to balls. Well, stands to reason, don't it? Don't dance, do they?"

Carolyn, wanting nothing so much as to nip the viscount's pretensions in the bud but not certain how best to do so, had been listening silently, but now she laughed and said, "God-mama's Hercules is overfed and fat, and has any number of rude habits besides, but she dotes on him as much as Lady Lucretia dotes on Henrietta, and I believe she *would* bring him to such affairs if the notion were ever to occur to her."

"Saint-Denis would never allow it," Brandon retorted.

"Sydney?" Carolyn laughed again. "I wish I may see him attempt to forbid her to do anything she pleases. She did not even consult him before moving us all, bag and baggage, into his house. He is simply not the forbidding sort."

Lyndhurst sneered. "Damned fop, that's what Saint-Denis is, all snuff boxes, China lacquer, and lace ruffles."

"Not entirely," Brandon said with a crooked grin.

Frowning, Carolyn said, "I don't think I've ever seen him wear lace."

"Lord, he don't have to wear the stuff to be a lacy sort," Lyndhurst informed her. "But come along, love. We're in the way of this set that's forming. You'll forgive us, Manningford."

"No," Brandon said, staying put and looking steadily from one to the other. He was not as large as the viscount, but he was solid enough to provide an effective barrier, and there was a moment's silence before he apparently realized that the single word was insufficient and added, "Thing is, don't think you ought to." He fixed his gaze on Carolyn. "Not the thing to be going outside with him, don't you know. Saint-Denis wouldn't like it."

At the sight of the viscount's darkening brow, Carolyn experienced a delicious thrill at the base of her spine. Not only was he as handsome as she had imagined the heroes of her favorite books to be, but he had the dangerous look that was *de rigueur* with them as well. Brandon, too, was looking dangerous, although she had never before thought him a heroic type. Reckless, perhaps, even irresponsibly madcap, but not heroic. Still, he had filled out a bit since she had last seen him in London, and he did not look at all reckless or foolish when he met Lyndhurst's glare with a steady, stubborn scowl.

The viscount growled, "You are in the way, Manningford."

"Don't be a clunch, Lyndhurst. We can scarcely initiate a brawl right here in the hotel."

"You can name your seconds, however," the viscount observed with a gentle malice that made Carolyn gasp.

"Daresay I could," Brandon agreed, "if I were such a nodcock as to consent to meet you. I'm not, though, so you needn't think to count me among your victims. Even if I were a veritable prince of Corinth, which I'm not," he added frankly, "I wouldn't be fool enough to meet you. I know your reputation too well."

"Coward."

The word, hissed between the viscount's teeth, set Carolyn's skin aprickle. She glanced around, but no one appeared to have noticed that the two men were nearly at daggers drawn. Knowing there would soon be a fight if no one moved to prevent it, she racked her brain for something to say to ease the tension.

Brandon's jaw had tightened when Lyndhurst spoke the single word, and for that long, anxious moment, he said nothing. But then, relaxing, he said without rancor, "Daresay I am a coward if bravery is measured by one's willingness to be murdered. But unless you're prepared to knock me down in front of all these chits and old folks, you might as well take yourself off like a gentleman and leave Caro to dance with me."

"Carolyn?" The viscount looked down his nose at her in clear and haughty expectation that she would snub Brandon.

Breathing more easily, she said, "Perhaps we can walk later, sir, but for me to go outside with you now would be to set all the tabbies talking, which is a thing I could not like."

Without another word to either of them, Lyndhurst bowed stiffly and turned on his heel, whereupon Brandon let out an audible sigh of relief.

"Don't mind telling you," he confided, "I'm dashed glad to see the back of that fellow. Really, Caro, you ought never to have agreed to go outside with him. Not a wise thing to do, m'dear, not wise at all, assure you."

She shook her head at him with a look of amused reproach. "I did no such thing, but even if I had, are you, who put a bear to bed with a stranger, and who purchased a full suit of livery for his kitchen cat, daring to preach propriety to me?"

"Dashed good notion, that livery," he said, chuckling. "If old Puss ever mislays himself, the neighbors will know precisely where to return him. M' father threw a fit when he discovered what I'd done, or so his man told me. Didn't see the old fellow m'self, of course."

"I think it is sad that your papa never leaves the Royal Crescent," Carolyn said, remembering the many tales she had heard about the eccentric Sir Mortimer Manningford.

"The Crescent! He never leaves the third floor of the house. Sits up there in his library behind his great desk, scribbling his memoirs or some such muck all day. Has done since m' mother passed on. Or so I'm told. Don't remember that far back, m'self, but I never see him. Leaves notes for the servants if he wants something. Sees m' brother, Charlie, once a year, of course, but Charlie's the heir. And even he has to make an appointment. Stays twenty minutes and goes away until the next year. M' sister Ramsbury was used to see him on the odd occasion, but now she's married and lives in London, of course."

"He sounds fascinating," Carolyn said wistfully. "I should like very much to meet him. Don't you sometimes just itch to peek in and see precisely what he's doing?"

"Lord, no," Brandon said. "Why would I? Dashed prickly sort of fellow, if you ask me. Don't do to rile him."

"But don't you sometimes get lonely and wish he would pay you more heed?"

"I should say not. One has one's friends, after all, and I'd as lief not have a parent always looking over m' shoulder, quizzing me about what I'm doing. M' sister Ramsbury used to do that frequently, and I can tell you, I prefer to do as I please without a lot of dashed interference."

Carolyn chuckled. "You sound just like Godmama."

"What?" He looked hastily around again. "Look here, m' girl, we've missed our set altogether, so we might just as well take a turn about the garden as stand here like a pair of dashed gateposts. You can explain that piece of nonsense to me outside where no one else is likely to overhear you."

She laughed. "In the garden? Brandon, really, 'tis just as improper for me to go outside with you as with Lyndhurst."

"Fustian, it can be no such thing," he insisted as he drew her toward the tall French doors leading into the garden. "I ain't a loose screw, for one thing—well, not with the ladies, at all events, so take that dashed impertinent grin off your face. I certainly ain't likely to seduce you behind the nearest bramble

bush. Unlikely to do that to anyone,'' he added with a comical
look. "Too dashed prickly, by half.''

"There are no brambles in these gardens,'' she retorted as
he reached to open the door, but as she spoke, another thought
occurred to her, halting her in her tracks. "Would he?''

"Would who do what?''

"Lyndhurst. Would he try to seduce me?''

"No doubt about it. Man's a blasted bounder. Surprised you
don't know that. He falls tail over top in love forever at least
once a fortnight and don't count the cost. Ruined more than
one reputation, I can tell you, so you don't want to encourage
him, Caro. Dashed dangerous, Lyndhurst is.'' He frowned.
"Shouldn't have said that. Fatal. Noticed before that you fool
women dote on dangerous men. Always thinking you can tame
them. Can't, you know, but it's probably why you got yourself
betrothed to those poor fellows in London and it's why you're
standing right there in front of me now, thinking you can tame
Lyndhurst. Forget him and tell me what the deuce you meant,
telling me I talk like old Lady Skipton. Dashed silly thing to
say, if you ask me.''

Carolyn didn't answer him at once. Instead, she glanced back
over her shoulder, looking for the viscount, wondering if he
was at all like either of the two gentlemen to whom she had
been so briefly betrothed. When she saw him and realized that
his dark gaze still rested intently upon her and that his eyes still
glittered with that delicious look of danger, another blazing thrill
shot up her spine. Deciding that he was indeed very like them,
she allowed her gaze to lock briefly with his.

"Caro!''

Startled as much by the unfamiliar snap in Brandon's voice
as by the impatient tug of his arm beneath her fingers, she looked
quickly back at him to see that he was holding the door open
with an exasperated grimace on his face. "Forget about him,''
he said, drawing her across the threshold. "Tell me.''

"Tell you what? Oh, about Godmama? It was only that I once
asked her if she missed Lord Skipton—her late husband, that
is, not Sydney's brother—and she said, 'Not a bit,' that she was
free now to do as she liked without having to answer to anyone

else. When you said what you did about doing as you please, you sounded just like her.''

"Oh, well, if that's all.'' He drew in a deep breath of the chilly night air as the door swung shut behind them, muffling the sounds of music and dancers, as well as the constant underlying hum of conversation. The torchlit garden before them was lovely, and she ignored the cold when Brandon drew her toward the widest of several gravel pathways that seemed to beckon to them. "I say, Caro, coming out here was a dashed good notion. One can scarcely breathe inside. And look,'' he added with increased enthusiasm a moment later as they approached a lighted open area. "Some of the lads are playing at bowls on that green yonder.''

When they drew nearer, Carolyn, shivering, saw that "the lads'' were a mixed lot of older and middle-aged gentlemen—with but one or two younger—who had escaped the festivities inside, and also that most were a good deal merrier than a simple game of bowls might warrant. "They're drunk,'' she said shrewdly as she hastily stepped back into the shadows cast by shrubs lining the gravel pathway, hoping they had not seen her.

"Only a bit well to live,'' Brandon said, watching them. "Someone must have slipped a jug or two past the master of ceremonies' long nose. Oh, that was a fine shot, that was,'' he added, absently drawing her nearer, oblivious to her reluctance.

"I'm freezing, Brandon. I think we ought to—''

"Oh, don't spoil sport. Look, Honeyford has the shot now. He's a particular friend of mine. Dash it, don't the fellow know how to do the thing? Here, Honeyford,'' he called out, releasing Carolyn and striding toward the group, "I'll show you how, man.''

His appearance in the midst of the gamesters was greeted by laughter and a number of ribald comments. A jug was promptly passed to him, and he drank thirstily before passing it on to another man. Reaching for the ball, he bowled it straight toward the pins, and when the shot was declared an excellent one, he shouted his pleasure and snatched up the jug again, tilting his head back and guzzling deeply.

Carolyn watched in dismay as the others laughingly urged him on. She knew they had not seen her, and she had no wish to emerge from her place in the shadows or to call out to Brandon, but she felt cold and vulnerable where she was. No other couples or any ladies at all had come out, for at this season few people wished to wander at night to visit the grottoes, labyrinths, groves, and waterfalls that made the gardens such a treat in warmer months. She had reached the point of wondering if there was any way at all by which she might recall her erstwhile escort without drawing the attention of the others when Lyndhurst's deep voice sounded close behind her, startling her so that only her own hand clapped across her mouth prevented her from shrieking.

"A man who would abandon beauty in this wilderness is no gentleman," he murmured low in his throat, and when she whirled about, she found him disturbingly close to her. There was enough light from nearby torches to see that he was smiling, gazing at her with the intensity that was so characteristic of him. For once, however, his attitude moved her only to sharp anger.

"You ought not to startle a person like that," she snapped, keeping her voice down with an effort.

His expression did not alter, nor did he look away, and the torchlight seemed to set hot sparks leaping in his eyes, filling them with a smoldering heat that, although it made her feel increasingly feminine and desirable, made her hope that Brandon had not forgotten her very existence, as indeed it seemed he had.

She shivered.

"You're cold."

"No, no, the night is not so very cold."

"Nor yet warm enough for that dress," he said. "Come, walk with me. 'Twill set your blood moving and warm you." There was meaning in his voice that sent more shivers through her.

She believed she had only to insist upon returning to the warmth inside for him to take her back, and so it was that her hand found itself tucked into the crook of his arm instead, and somehow she found herself, within minutes, whisked out of sight of the bowlers, whose laughing voices soon faded into the distance, making the garden seem strangely quiet.

It was daring, and very thrilling. She had never done such

a thing before in all her life. To be sure, there had been other stolen moments, even a few stolen kisses shared with other handsome young men. But never like this. The others had managed to lure her behind a curtain or perhaps even into a separate room, but she had never felt so alone with another man, so distant from her own party, so vulnerable.

When Lyndhurst guided her down a turning and into the shadow of a large overhanging willow tree, she felt momentary panic. There was no torchlight here, only the light from the slender crescent moon and blanket of stars overhead, and that heavily filtered through tree branches. Suppressing her fears, she told herself again that she could easily manage the viscount, that there was nothing to frighten her in his company. She reminded herself that his mama and her godmama were bosom bows, that he would therefore have to respect her wishes and behave himself or suffer dire consequences if he did not.

"Caro, you are so beautiful," he murmured as he came to a halt and turned to face her, placing his large hands upon her shoulders and letting his fingertips explore the warm flesh beneath the lace edging of her low-cut bodice.

Heady words, and his voice was so low and caressing, surely not the voice of a dangerous man. His very confidence and air of experience lulled her fears, and she smiled up at him. "Thank you, sir." Even in the dim light, she was aware of the intense look in his eyes.

His fingers tightened against her flesh as he said huskily, "I couldn't bear it when you came out here with that idiot, Manningford. You are too good for him, Caro. You need a man who knows how to treat you, who understands you need a firm hand on the rein. I'm going to kiss you, love. I can wait no longer."

Every nerve ending in her body came alive, and although she disliked hearing him call Brandon an idiot, the description was apt enough just then for her to ignore any immediate inclination to defend him. Thus it was that when Lyndhurst pulled her into his arms, she went willingly enough, albeit with more curiosity aroused than passion, since the scene had begun just as all her favorite authors were wont to describe such moments.

His muscular arms caught her and held her captive, and when

she looked up at him, his mouth captured hers in a burning kiss. But there all similarity to the tenderly written passages that had so often delighted her came to an abrupt end. There was no answering surge of rapture that swelled from her toes and coursed through her veins. Nor was there delight or joy or an instant awakening of true love. Instead, she felt a sharp sense of panic when she attempted to pull away and he would not let her go.

His arms tightened crushingly around her, and she felt his tongue pressing against her lips. There had been nothing about tongues in any of her books. Not one word. She struggled and tried to turn her head away. She even tried to hit him, but he was too strong. Indeed, she realized when she felt one of his hands push her bodice aside, he was holding her easily with only one hand and still she could not free herself. His hand was beneath her lace now, beneath even the silk, moving over the soft bare skin of her breast toward its tip.

She tried to kick him, but her thin slippers did no damage except in failing miserably to protect her toes.

Sydney Saint-Denis's familiar drawl startled them both. "Oh, here you are, Carolyn. I have been looking for you."

Carolyn went still, not wanting to look around, not wanting him to see her, hoping that he would think he had made a mistake, for even worse than being trapped by Lyndhurst was having Sydney find her in his arms.

3

Sydney took a long, steadying breath, mentally reciting the brief Chinese phrases that would help force his temper back under his normal, rigid control. It had been a very long time since he had felt this close to losing it. There had been many such times before his two years in China, of course, but none since till now. The feeling receded quickly enough, and he said in the same amiable tone he had employed before, "Sorry to take you away when I know you looked forward to this assembly, but Mother is feeling a trifle bilious and has expressed a desire to return home. Cousin Judith is attending to her, of course, and I daresay you could find someone else willing to look after you, but I felt certain you would want to accompany them."

"You intrude, Saint-Denis," Lyndhurst snapped, glaring. "Do I?"

The viscount had removed his hand from beneath Carolyn's bodice, but it still rested possessively on her shoulder, and Sydney felt his body relaxing and his mind clearing. In his head he could hear an echo of Ching Ho's lilting voice cautioning him to remember that "The supple willow does not contend against the storm, yet it survives." When Lyndhurst, without another word, suddenly released Carolyn, Sydney was not surprised, for he had seen such reactions before. It was simply a matter of will.

With Carolyn, however, it was a far different matter. She

was astonished when the viscount released her, for she had heard no change in Sydney's drawl when he spoke the two short words, and when she had peeped around at him, she could see nothing unusual in his manner. But Lyndhurst said nothing more, not even when Sydney held out his arm to her and she placed her fingers on it. The whole scene, she thought, was very strange, for no matter how one strained one's fertile imagination to do so, one simply could not imagine Sydney in the role of rescuer. Thus, it was all the more irritating to feel obliged to him.

She found it difficult to believe the episode had ended so simply, and as she walked with him back to the torchlit pathway and on toward the ballroom, she found that she was expecting more, expecting Lyndhurst to follow them, somehow to force the issue. If he was following them, however, she could not hear him, and she would not give him the satisfaction of looking back.

"Do you want to walk a little longer before we return, to recover your countenance?" Sydney asked politely as they drew near the broad stone steps leading into the ballroom.

His words, reminding her again of the circumstance in which he had found her, brought a surge of delayed mortification that nearly stopped her feet in their tracks and her breath in her throat. Taking herself in hand, however, she managed to reply with tolerable calm, "There is no reason to walk farther, sir. I am not distressed."

"I disagree," he said with a note in his voice that she could not decipher. "You cannot have expected Lyndhurst to behave in so ungentlemanly a fashion."

She did not wish to argue the point, particularly since she could not with any honesty refute it. "I was afraid he would be angry with you," she admitted.

Surprisingly, Sydney chuckled. "I believe you expected him to demand my blood and are disappointed that he did not."

"Don't be foolish," she retorted, nettled.

"He could not do so, of course. He knows you are a guest beneath my roof, so he must have realized what a solecism he would commit if he refused to relinquish you to my care. You were not wise to come out with him, however."

The words were matter-of-fact, spoken without the least note of censure, but Carolyn bristled nonetheless. "I can take care of myself, Sydney," she said tartly. "I was curious to learn how Lyndhurst would behave, but I could have managed him perfectly well on my own. And although I am living under your roof, that does not give you the right to tell me what to do."

"Dear me, did I do so?" He drew her with him away from the steps, back toward the central garden path.

"You said I was unwise!"

"Yes." Amusement gleamed in his eyes.

"You have no right to reproach my behavior, particularly when you are making me do the very thing you said I was wrong to do with Lyndhurst."

"Perhaps you are right," he said, "but you must still agree that I know more about his character, and my own, than you can know, so you'd be wise to heed my advice when I offer it to you."

"Well, I don't agree," she snapped. "It wasn't Lyndhurst who brought me outside but Brandon Manningford, and you can't say I was unwise to come out with him, for not only is he harmless but his family and yours have known one another forever."

The amusement in Sydney's eyes deepened. "Do you hear yourself? Certainly, I can say you were unwise to come out here, no matter who escorted you, for only observe the consequences. And to be pretending that I should approve of young Brandon, who is as loose a screw as can rattle, only because Mama has allowed you to run tame with him and because I call friends with his sister and her husband, is the height of foolishness."

When she would have responded, hotly, he silenced her by saying quietly, "You are in general a more worthy opponent, Caro. Either you are too cold to think properly, or Lyndhurst upset you more than I realized. You went so still in his arms when I spoke that I thought myself mistaken in believing you'd been struggling with him. But whether I was mistaken or not, you must agree that my years and experience, if not merely my masculinity, make me a better judge of the British male than you can hope to be."

She would admit to no such thing, but she did not argue with him, deciding that there was nothing to be said to any man who made so a daft a statement, and certain that the time would come when she would prove him wrong or know the reason why. Silence reigned between them until Sydney said, ''You were all over the shop, you know, which is not the way to go about it.''

''Whatever are you talking about?'' she demanded.

He reached for her hand. ''Look,'' he said, ''I'll show you. Bend your fingers so that your fingertips touch the top edge of your palm. Like that, yes,'' he said when she had obeyed him. ''Keep your thumb in. Now, if a fellow grabs you like Lyndhurst did, jab him in the throat or ribs with your knuckles.''

''Well, I never saw anyone make a fist like that, and I doubt he would ever notice it,'' she said, looking at her small hand.

''A featherweight like you can do more damage with knuckles braced like that than with a rounded fist,'' he said, ''especially if you keep hitting at the same place, rather than flailing away as you were doing. You'll divert his attention to the pain, and once you've done that, bring your knee up between his legs as hard as ever you can. He will notice that, I promise you.''

''Well, I suppose he might,'' she replied naïvely, ''but I doubt I could do it, even in this skirt, and skirts not meant for dancing are even more narrowly cut than this one, you know.'' She experimented, finding that although she could raise her knee a little, she could not, without pulling her skirt up a good distance, raise it high enough to do as he recommended.

He raised his quizzing glass to watch her and said, ''Daresay you're right. Well, if you find yourself in a rare-enough pickle, you'll just have to hike up your skirt, that's all. Or if you like, I'll teach you a few other tricks.''

She could not imagine any tricks he might know that would be of any more use to her than what he had just suggested, but she did not say so, for she had no wish to hurt his feelings and, even more to the purpose, she could no longer ignore the chill. When she shivered, he noticed at once and took her back inside, where she discovered that although Lady Skipton had not asked him to do so, he had indeed sent for his carriage.

Inside the carriage, he said no more about what had happened, and Carolyn was grateful to him, for she had no wish to hear

Lady Skipton's observations on the subject. After some consideration, however, she realized that she could trust Sydney not to betray one foolish lapse of judgment to his mother. Lyndhurst was not really dangerous, after all. It was only the dark garden and her own active imagination that had made him seem so. And while she had not been particularly wise to go with him, he would surely never really have dared to seduce her.

As for having gone out with Brandon, it was the outside of enough for Sydney to cavil at that. To be sure, Brandon had deserted her, but that had been through nothing more malicious than thoughtlessness, for which he would be most apologetic when next they met. So certain was she of this that it came as no small shock when they chanced to meet in Milsom Street the following afternoon to be greeted with Brandon's reproaches.

"Where did you disappear to last night?" he demanded after making his bow to her and to Miss Pucklington, who, wrapped in a myriad of her most colorful shawls as protection against the day's chill, had walked into town with her to exchange two books at the subscription library. "One instant you were beside me and the next you'd disappeared into thin air. Not at all the thing to do, m' girl, and so I should not need to tell you."

"Well, of all the cheek!" Carolyn retorted. "You no sooner saw those horrid men swilling blue ruin, or whatever was in that jug, than you left me to join them with never another thought for me or my safety. And now you dare to criticize me."

He grimaced at her. Then, clearly becoming aware that Miss Pucklington was watching them both with an expression of avid interest on her thin face, he said hastily, "Forgive us, ma'am. 'Tis nothing of consequence. Just a minor disagreement between friends, but we ought not to be sniping at each other in the street this way, putting you to the blush for our manners."

"Oh, don't bother about me," Miss Pucklington said kindly. "I need not remember or repeat what I hear, you know."

Carolyn, her attention on Brandon, had likewise forgotten her companion, but now she glanced at her with merriment in her eyes. "Dearest Puck," she said, "I doubt you have ever forgotten a single word spoken in your presence. But we needn't mind her, Brandon," she added. "Puck never gives one away."

"Thank you, my dear," Miss Pucklington said, turning pink as she moved to allow a gentleman to pass by, "but I daresay Mr. Manningford is right in saying that we ought not to stand here blocking the footpath, you know. Perhaps he would care to escort us back to Bathwick Hill House for a hot cup of tea."

But that did not suit Mr. Manningford. "Tell you what, Caro," he said, plainly accepting Miss Pucklington as an ally, "I still don't agree I was at fault. Well, dash it all, you ought to have stayed with me and not gone flitting off by yourself, oughtn't you? But I ain't one to contradict a lady," he added hastily, if inaccurately, when a steely glint instantly replaced the twinkle in Carolyn's eyes. "I'll make it up to you by riding with you tomorrow and you can say whatever you like to me then. Since I know you dislike riding on your own with only a groom to bear you company, I can't say fairer than that, can I?"

"You'll forget," she said flatly, unappeased.

"No, I won't," he retorted. "Might, in the usual way of things, but the fact is, I left m' gold watch as collateral for a horse I bought, and I want to get it back. Horse is worth more than the watch, but I might want to do business with this fellow in future, so there you are."

"But how will wanting to get your watch back make you remember you're to ride with me?" she demanded.

"The gypsy camp is on Saint-Denis's land," he said as though that simple statement explained everything.

"Gypsy camp? Goodness, are there gypsies on Bathwick Hill? Sydney cannot know that."

"Oh, I shouldn't think it would bother him. Gentle-enough folk if you keep your pockets sewn shut."

"Well, Godmama would not approve at all, but how exciting! Will you really take me to their camp?"

He looked for a moment as though he were having second thoughts, and she knew that he had not previously considered that it might not be quite the thing to do, so she said quickly, "I should like to visit one above all things, and I know I shall be perfectly safe with you."

"Safe? Of course you'll be safe with me. What a dashed silly thing to say!'' And he made no comment whatever after that about the proprieties, or lack thereof.

Miss Pucklington was not so reticent, however, once he had gone and they walked together along the broad expanse of Great Pulteney Street, toward Bathwick Hill. "Cousin Olympia will not approve of such an expedition," she said gently.

"No, but I don't intend to tell her," Carolyn said. "Sydney probably will not approve either, but I shall go with Brandon all the same, and I shall be perfectly safe, too, Puck. He won't dare to desert me a second time."

"He truly deserted you last night? I didn't know."

"Oh, that was nothing," Carolyn said airily. "We were only in the garden, after all, so it was no great thing. I mentioned it to him only because I wished to remind him that a gentleman does not walk off and forget the lady he is escorting. He would never do so at a gypsy camp. And, in any event, I have never heard of any gypsies hereabouts doing anyone any harm."

"They steal," Miss Pucklington said flatly.

"Well, of course they do," Carolyn agreed. "Gypsies always steal. 'Tis their nature, I suppose, through not having had the benefit of a Christian upbringing. Although," she added with a mischievous grin, "I have never heard of them actually stealing babies, despite the great number of romantic novels that are written about beautiful young girls who are stolen from their wealthy families at birth and raised by the gypsies."

"Surely, you don't believe you were stolen by gypsies?" Miss Pucklington inquired suspiciously.

"No, of course not," Carolyn said. "Nothing so interesting ever happened to me. I do not live in the pages of a book, you know." On the contrary, she thought, her life was perfectly ordinary and Lyndhurst the closest likeness to a hero she had ever met. Most depressing, for dangerous as he could look, he was really only annoying, not exciting at all. And no doubt, the gypsy camp, if Brandon did remember to take her there, would turn out to be just as depressing, and dull into the bargain.

Her outlook had improved, however, after a good night's sleep, and by the time Brandon presented himself at Bathwick Hill House the following morning, she was looking forward to the outing with pleasurable anticipation. Thus, she was not at all pleased to see Sydney approaching them from the direction of the stables just as Brandon was lifting her into her saddle.

"Say nothing about where we are going," she hissed, shooting an oblique glance at her nearby groom to assure herself that he was out of earshot.

"No fear of that," Brandon muttered, adding in a louder tone, "Good morning, Saint-Denis. A fine day, is it not? Been out riding already, I expect."

"Some time ago," Sydney said, holding out his hand.

His buckskin breeches and dark-blue coat, Carolyn noted, seemed to have been molded to his trim, well-muscled body, and had clearly been tailored by experts. His snowy neckcloth was tied in a less intricate style than he sported with his evening dress, but not a hair was out of place, and she decided that if he had been riding, he had maintained an extremely sedate pace. That would not do for her. Her impatience communicated itself to her mount, and the black gelding fidgeted beneath her.

"Where are you off to?" Sydney inquired, glancing at her but making no move to steady the gelding.

"Oh, just hereabouts," she said airily, "if Brandon can manage to bestir himself to mount within the next hour or so."

"Patience, madam," Brandon said. Stepping toward his long-legged roan and taking his reins from the groom, he swung into the saddle with the easy grace of a man who spent a great deal of his spare time on horseback, then glanced at her with teasing laughter in his eyes. "Sure you want to do this, m' dear? Not too dangerous for you?"

Startled, she glared at him, then glanced quiltily at Sydney, who regarded them both with an air of polite inquiry. "Dangerous?" he said.

Carolyn held her breath, but Brandon only laughed again. "She challenged me to a run through the woods north of here. Know them like the back of my hand, of course, but she'll have to think about what she's doing. Gives me an edge, don't you agree? Care to lay odds?"

Carolyn shut her eyes, waiting for Sydney to announce that he would accompany them, but once again he surprised her. "You're taking Cleves, I trust." He was smiling, but she was glad she had not ordered her groom to remain behind.

Affecting an offered attitude, Brandon murmured that certain people seemed to have no faith in him, and both men laughed. Annoyed with them, Carolyn waited only until she and Brandon had ridden out of the gates, with Cleves a discreet distance behind them, before expressing her displeasure.

"You ought never to have said such a thing!"

"What would you have had me say?" he demanded. "Unless you wanted me to tell him a real bouncer, that was the best thing I could think of to put him off. He knows you, don't he? Knows that's precisely the sort of nonsense you'd like better than a new gown. What's more, we are riding in the woods, and you will have to think about what you're doing, or you're likely to have that pretty blue riding habit of yours stolen right off your back by the Romanies. I'm only hoping that fellow will give me back my watch and not just nip off with the money I've brought him. Still, he can't think I'd send him more custom if he played me false, can he?"

"No, I don't suppose he can." A moment later she said, "What is it like, the gypsy camp?"

"Like any gypsy camp, I imagine."

"Don't be maddening, Brandon."

He glanced at her. "Sorry, but I've seen more than one, you know, and they all look the same."

"I have never seen one," she said with forced patience.

"Oh, well, then, let me see." He frowned, evidently collecting an image of the place in his mind. Finally, just as she was about to demand that he get on with it, he said, "Mostly caravans and animal pens and people. Surely, you've seen their caravans. A fellow can't drive on a highroad anywhere in England without being delayed by one somewhere along the way."

"I've seen them," she agreed. "Very colorful, but the people always seem a trifle . . . well, a trifle unwashed."

"Lord, of course they are. You don't think they bathe along the way, do you? Dashed uncivilized that would be, and no doubt complaints would be lodged against them first time they tried it on. Dash it, complain m'self if water was sloshin' out the back of the caravan onto the road. M' horses would slip."

She laughed. "Are you never serious?"

"Never." He grinned at her. "Fact is, it will be better if you see the place for yourself. I'm no hand at describing things." He was silent for several moments after that. Then he glanced at her again before saying ruefully, "Look here, Caro, I've been thinking about last night, and the fact is I didn't behave well. You were right about that. Never should have walked off without making sure you were right behind me. Not that you ought to have been, of course. No place for a lady, that bowling green. Not then, at all events."

She smiled at him. "I'll accept your apology and thank you for it. I didn't think you would offer me one."

He shrugged. "I can be civil when I want to be. Hope nothing awkward occurred. Notice you didn't say anything about where you went after I abandoned you."

"No." She felt warmth flooding her face at the memory of Lyndhurst's aggression and the embarrassment of being discovered in such a fix by Sydney.

"What happened?" When she looked away, he said more sharply, "What? Good Lord, Caro, you weren't—"

"No, no," she said before he could say aloud what he was so clearly thinking. "Nothing like that. Only Lyndhurst found me where you left me and made rather a nuisance of himself."

"Oh, did he?" Brandon's brows snapped together, and for once he looked as dangerous as any romantic young lady might wish. "I shall have a word with his lordship," he said grimly.

Instead of pleasing her, however, his look and tone of voice dismayed her, and she said hastily, "There is no need for that, truly. Nothing happened except that Sydney came along and saw us standing there together. I'd have preferred anything else, believe me, which was why I was so annoyed with you for leaving me. Only try to imagine how mortified I was."

But to her consternation, Brandon seemed not to comprehend her feelings. At the mention of Sydney's name, he relaxed in his saddle and smiled at her, saying, "Oh, Saint-Denis was there, was he? That's all right, then, except I daresay he'll have a few things to say to me about the impropriety of leaving ladies alone in gardens. Deserve to hear them, of course, but perhaps if I steer clear of him for a few days, he'll forget. Want to let the fidgets out of that nag of yours?"

Believing any further attempt to make him understand must prove futile, she agreed, and they put their mounts to a canter. The path they were on led through a shady wood and was hard-packed and well-tended. The air was crisp with a suggestion of approaching winter, and the leaves were bright with color. In no time at all, Carolyn was so taken up with the sights, sounds, and smells of the wood and the pounding of hooves on the dirt path that all other thoughts faded from her mind.

Brandon was ahead of her, and when the path widened sufficiently, she urged her mount to a faster pace to catch him. He let her draw abreast, then leaned lower across his horse's neck and eased his hold on his rein, giving the animal its head. The pace was a reckless one, but Carolyn didn't mind in the least, and when it appeared that she might fall behind, she touched the black on the flank with the tip of her whip.

It was enough. The gelding sprang forward, closing the distance again. Seeing Brandon duck down, hugging the roan's back to avoid a low-hanging branch, she did the same, and while the movement stopped her from seeing the tree root that rose several inches above the path ahead, it saved her from flying headlong out of the saddle when the gelding stumbled and nearly fell with her. Its pace dropped to a halting walk in the space of a breath or two, and as she sat up again, her hat askew, she realized immediately that her horse was injured.

Brandon, looking back over his shoulder, saw what had happened and jerked his mount sharply about, reaching her at nearly the same time Cleves did.

"Miss Carolyn," the wiry, middle-aged groom exclaimed, drawing up beside her, "I thought you was a goner. What the master will say, I can't think."

"Then don't think," Brandon snapped, bringing the roan to a plunging halt and leaping from the saddle. "Better yet, don't tell him. You hurt?" He flung the words over his shoulder at Carolyn as he bent to examine the black's leg.

"Are you talking to me or to the horse?" she demanded as she straightened her hat and shoved an errant strand of hair back into place.

"Don't be nonsensical," he said sharply. "You'll have to dismount. He's strained a fetlock. Here, Cleves," he added, taking her reins and handing them up to the groom, "make your-self useful and lead him. I'll take Miss Carolyn up behind me."

"Why don't you just order poor Cleves to give me his horse," Carolyn asked as Brandon helped her down. "Surely, you won't want that poor nag of yours to carry a double burden."

"No, I don't, but it don't signify, for we've only a short distance to go now." Then he looked at her as though he had just become aware of the irony in her voice. "You miffed? I didn't let him stumble. You did. Ought to be ashamed, riding neck or nothing like that. I can't think what Lady Skipton will say."

"Well, don't think to cozen me into thinking you'll tell her," Carolyn retorted, "for I know you won't, and if I was riding neck or nothing, 'twas only because you challenged me to do so. And after telling Sydney you'd take care of me, too."

"Well, if he don't know how difficult that is, no one does," Brandon replied, returning his attention to the fetlock.

"Want me to have a look at that, sir?" Cleves asked.

"No, what for? Know as much as any groom does, m'self, don't I? Going to need compresses, and the sooner the better, but I daresay they'll have what we want at the camp."

"Camp, sir?"

Brandon looked at him. "Gypsy camp, and don't go giving me any lip, man. 'Tain't your place to be saying where we should or shouldn't go."

Cleves looked shocked. "No, sir, and like as not them gypsies know a sight more than both of us together about strained fetlocks. Some of 'em 'ave got magic in their fingers."

Satisfied, Brandon lifted Carolyn to his saddle and swung up behind her. A quarter-hour later they entered the camp.

Seven caravans nestled beneath the trees surrounding a clearing, and steam curled from pots bubbling over campfires near all but one, where a girl with long black hair tied back from her face with a red scarf, and golden hoops dangling from her ears, turned a small roasting animal on a spit. Other plump, dark-haired children played all-hide among the trees, shrieking and laughing, ignored by the several adults who could be seen nearby.

The whole scene fascinated Carolyn, but she was particularly captivated by the women, whose tight bodices and full skirts looked as though they had been made up of odd bits of bright fabric and contrasting braid. Despite the unmistakable curiosity flashing in their black eyes as they watched the visitors, not one moved to greet them.

"You seek help for your *gree*?" a gruff voice demanded.

Carolyn's view of the man's approach had been blocked by Brandon's left shoulder, so it seemed almost as though he had appeared out of thin air. He was of middle age, large and brawny, and he carried himself like a lord.

Brandon said casually, "I am looking for the Rom called Salas. I owe him money."

"You owe my son *roop* or *suhakie*?" the man demanded. "Silver or gold?" Then he shook his head, realizing that Brandon still did not understand him. "Little or much, and for what?"

"For a horse, a *gree*," Brandon said. He grinned. "Much to him, I think. He has my watch. I want it back."

The big man smiled back, showing yellowing, crooked teeth, one blackened in front, before his gaze flicked briefly over Carolyn and back to Brandon. "You wish to sell your *raiena*, your lady? My son needs wife, and she is much pretty."

"Well, as to that," Brandon murmured, as though he were giving thought to the matter, "I should have to—"

"Brandon!" Carolyn dug him in the ribs with her elbow.

He grinned again. "Fact is, sir, she ain't mine to sell. You'd have to talk to her . . . Ouch, Carolyn, quit that!"

But she didn't answer him for the simple reason that her attention had been diverted by the sight of one of the most handsome young men she had ever laid eyes on. He walked up behind the older Romany, his dark eyes gleaming with interest as he looked her over, his teeth flashing white in a huge smile when he caught her gaze. Flushing, she looked away.

Brandon, too, had seen the younger man. "Ah, there you are Salas, old man. I've come to redeem my watch and to pay what I owe you for this nag."

"A fine *gree*," the young man said. "He goes well for you?"

"Very well," Brandon said, shifting Carolyn a bit in order

to extract his purse from his waistcoat. "Here's your money. Where's my watch?"

The young man's eyes sparkled with humor as he reached into the pocket of his coat and extracted a gold watch. "Salas has a better one than this. You may have it back."

"Thank you." Brandon grinned at him. "Think you could take a look at the lady's nag there. Strained a fetlock on the trail. Daresay it needs a compress applied to it, soonest."

The gypsy nodded and knelt to examine the injury. Carolyn saw that his hands were large but gentle as they moved swiftly over the leg. Now that he was not looking at her, she found it difficult to take her eyes from him. Muscles rippled beneath his coat, and his manner was as lordly as his father's, his profile positively princely. Except for such trifling distinctions as the contrasting colors of their hair, skin, and eyes, he looked just as she had imagined Sir Bartholomew Lancelot must look.

When Salas turned toward them as he arose again, she noted the natural grace with which he moved, and a daring notion shot into her mind. She tried to suppress it, calling herself a fool, but it remained to tantalize her with possibilities. She had wanted to teach Sydney a much-needed lesson. Was it possible that the opportunity had come to do just that?

4

Salas's voice interrupted Carolyn's reverie. "The *gree* should not walk farther today, lady," he said. "We will keep him here, and you may return for him tomorrow."

Brandon said, "I don't know if—"

"Leave him," Carolyn said, adding when the two gypsies looked at her in astonishment, "Shadow is mine, you see, and I should take it kindly if you would tend to him. My groom said your people have got magic in their fingers."

"Magic in many limbs, pretty one," Salas said, flashing her a wide, teasing smile. "I would be pleased to show you."

"Thank you," she said crisply, "but I should be grateful if you will confine your attention to my horse, and perhaps be so kind as to lend me another to ride home."

"As you wish," he responded, unoffended. "You will then, all of you, return tomorrow?"

"We shall," she said firmly. "Thank you."

"Are you daft, Caro?" Brandon demanded when she was mounted again and they had ridden some distance from the camp. "You don't want to have anything more to do with those fellows."

"Oh, but I do," she said, grinning at him. "I have the most delightful plan for that beautiful man."

"Look here, my girl, if you think for one minute that I'll

let you make a cake of yourself over some damned gypsy—''

"Don't be nonsensical," she said, laughing. Then, glancing over her shoulder, she added, "Fall back a bit, Cleves. Mr. Manningford and I wish to speak privately."

"Very well, miss, but beggin' yer pardon, am I to tell anyone you've gone and left that black with them gypsies?"

"Good gracious, I never thought about that. And we've this horse to explain at well," she added, patting the bay she rode. "What can we tell them, Brandon? It won't do for Sydney to discover we've been to the gypsy camp."

"What, running scared?" he said. "Serves you right. It's his nag, after all, not yours as you told those fellows. And since Shadow's better bred than that slug you're riding now, Saint-Denis might not have any more confidence in their returning him than I have. I think you'll come a cropper this time."

"No, I won't. They won't wish to offend him, after all, if they are camped on his land, so I doubt that they will steal Shadow. Salas looked much too gentle to do such a thing."

"Well, I wouldn't count on that. Just what do you think you can tell Saint-Denis, or his stable man, for that matter?"

"Beggin' yer pardon," Cleves said, "but I could say as I'd left 'im at one o' the tenant farms 'n borried that nag in 'is place, 'n that I'll trade 'em round again, come mornin'."

"Good enough," Brandon said. "You do that. But you," he added to Carolyn when the groom had fallen behind, "will leave well enough alone. Cleves can fetch the nag without us."

"Oh, no, he cannot," Carolyn said. "That would not suit me at all, Brandon, and I'll need you there to help me."

He looked suspiciously at her. "Help you with what?"

"Salas is a perfect foreign count," she declared, twinkling.

Brandon's eyes widened. "You're daft."

"No, I'm not. Sydney will never guess Salas is a gypsy if we dress him suitably and tell him not to talk very much. Can't you just imagine what he will look like in evening breeches and a snugly fitting coat?"

"And where," Brandon demanded grimly, "does your fruitful imagination suggest he's going to get such stuff, if you please? No, don't tell me. I am to manufacture it out of whole cloth."

"I don't think you will have to do that," she said. "Surely you must know someone of his size who would lend you a coat and a decent pair of breeches."

"Well, I don't," he said flatly.

"Brandon, don't be difficult. I am doing this on your account as well as my own." Faced with his blatant disbelief, she flushed and said, "Well, nearly, anyway. It was when I said I had no reason not to trust you to take me into the gardens that Sydney said I was a poor judge of men and must trust his judgment above my own. Now, I ask you, was that fair of him? All I want to do," she added hastily when he did not at once reply, "is to give him back a bit of his own, to prove to him that he doesn't know as much as he thinks he does."

"I don't know," Brandon said. "A canny fellow, Saint-Denis. I doubt you can fool him so easily as that."

"Well, I can. You wait. I saw how Salas moves and how he carries himself. In his way, he's as puffed up with his own esteem as Sydney's brother, Skipton, is. I mean to get Godmama to invite Salas to dinner, thinking he's a foreign count, you know, and then just watch. Sydney will be as polite as can be to him and will never suspect he's entertaining a gypsy."

"You'd better hope he doesn't," Brandon said, but his eyes were alight now with mischief. "I say, Caro, it will be a fine hoax if we can carry it off. M' sister Ramsbury's husband is of a size with that fellow. Daresay there are a few of his rags about the house somewhere that I can filch."

"Even if Sydney isn't fooled," she said, relaxing now that he had entered into the plan, "he won't be angry. For one thing, he never is, and for another, he is accustomed to my pranks. Indeed, I mean for him to know," she added with a chuckle, "just not until after we have succeeded in hoodwinking him."

Brandon shook his head at her, but now that he had agreed to help, he entered into the plan with wholehearted enthusiasm, and when he called the following day to escort her back to the gypsy camp, he had an unwieldy bundle of clothing tied to his saddle.

"A full rig, complete to the shoes," he announced with satisfaction as they rode out through the gates, followed at a distance by Cleves, leading the gypsy horse.

"Won't everything be dreadfully wrinkled?" she asked, doubtfully eyeing the bundle and hoping they would not have the misfortune to meet Sydney.

"Lord, I won't leave it with him. We'd never see it again. Best thing is if he comes to my house and dresses there, so my man can see that all is done right and proper. Then I'll bring Salas here with me. Just brought the things today so I can see if they fit. Salas still has to agree to the plan, you know. You're taking a deal for granted, thinking he will."

"Oh, he will," she said confidently.

"And just how do you know that?"

She grinned at him. "Well, I don't, actually, but I fancy he will if we offer him recompense for his participation."

Brandon frowned. "Hope he don't want too much. I'm not precisely plump in the pockets just at the moment. Are you?"

"Well, not precisely, but I've a bit by me and I thought we could pay him more later if he will only agree to the plan."

Brandon looked doubtful but said only, "Have you spoken to Lady Skipton?"

"Not yet. I want to be certain Salas will do as we ask before I mention him to her. Then, all I'll have to do is tell her you know a foreign count who wishes to visit Bath without making a noise, and she will hasten to invite you and your guest to dine if only so that she might puff it off later to all her bosom bows. Puck will love it, too. The difficulty will be to assure Sydney's presence that evening, but I think I can manage that by affecting an interest of my own in the count."

"No doubt," Brandon said dryly. "I see no way now of avoiding a lecture from Saint-Denis. First I disgrace myself by abandoning you to the mercies of a villain like Lyndhurst, and now I introduce you to a foreign count about whom Saint-Denis knows nothing. I perceive dangerous shoals ahead."

She laughed. "Poor Brandon. And you will not know in the least how to avoid them, will you? Not having had any experience in such matters."

He grinned at her. "Very well, think what you will, but before you can cook up this rabbit stew of yours, my dear, you must first catch your rabbit. Then we can discuss the difficulties involved in serving him up to Saint-Denis."

They fell silent after that, but Carolyn was not concerned that her plan might fail. Something in the way the young gypsy had looked at her the previous day gave her to know that his sense of mischief was as well developed as their own, and she was certain he would agree to do as they asked.

Salas was the first to greet them when they entered the camp, expressing his pleasure in seeing them again and assuring them that the black's leg was altogether mended. While Cleves examined the fetlock for himself, Brandon began to explain their plan to Salas. The gypsy's first reaction was to stare in disbelief, whereupon Carolyn added her voice to the discussion.

"It will be amusing for you," she said. "You have only to call upon Mr. Manningford at his house in Bath when the time comes, and he will instruct you in precisely what you must do. You have only to be rather dark and mysterious, and silent. 'Tis for a wager, you see. All you need to do is satisfy them for one evening. You will get a very fine dinner out of it, and perhaps we can pay you a little something afterward for your trouble," she added, hoping he would not demand too much.

Salas smiled at her, causing her to remember again, and with an inward sigh, Sir Bartholomew Lancelot. "Lady," the gypsy said softly, "a man would be much of a fool to deny you, but what is to happen to Salas if your plan fails. Your master will be much displeased, I think, and then there will be no gold for Salas."

"He is not my master," Carolyn said sharply, adding on a more reasonable note, "he is, of course, the master of Bathwick Hill; nevertheless, I can assure you that if he should discover our hoax, he will know perfectly well that it was no idea of yours. In any case, Mr. Saint-Denis will never guess that you are not precisely what we say you are."

"Then Salas will do as you ask. You need pay him nothing."

Carolyn, despite what she had told Brandon, was as surprised as he was that the young man agreed so readily. She had been prepared to argue as long as necessary to convince him, and felt a little as though the wind had gone out of her sails. When Brandon went off with Salas a moment later to let him try on the clothes, she soon realized she was drawing a considerable amount of interest from the other occupants of the camp. She smiled at one woman who stood nearer than the rest, but the woman moved no closer. Nor did anyone else, and since they all continued to stare silently at her, she was glad when Brandon returned.

"I felt like a freak at a fair," she told him as he retied the bundle of clothing to his saddle. "Did the things fit him?"

"All but the shoes," he said, turning to help her mount. "Jacket don't fit as snug as it ought, but I daresay anyone thinking about it will put that down to his being foreign. I thought we'd be at a standstill over the shoes, though, for after all, even a foreign count wouldn't be likely to dine barefoot, but Salas said he knows where can come by a pair."

"Legally, I hope."

He grinned at her. "As to that, I didn't want to ask. Told him to come to town tomorrow so I can rehearse him. I'll let him know the exact date of his performance when we know ourselves."

She nodded. "I'll speak to Godmama today. I think we can arrange it for Thursday evening. Will that suit you?"

He agreed, adding that the sooner it was done, the better.

"You won't forget?"

"Certainly not," he retorted, offended.

Carolyn apologized, twinkling, and they parted amiably at Bathwick Hill House a half-hour later, with Brandon agreeing that she should send word to him at Royal Crescent just as soon as she had spoken to Lady Skipton.

She did so at once, and the dowager, despite making a number of disparaging remarks about foreigners in general, was as pleased as Carolyn had thought she would be at the notion of entertaining a count who would not make himself available to her rival members of Bath society to entertain. When Lady Skipton began at once to discuss her menu with Miss Puckling-ton, Carolyn ventured to say, "I hope Sydney will dine with us, ma'am. 'Twould be a shame for him to miss meeting the count."

"He will not neglect to do full honor to a visitor to this house," the dowager said firmly.

Carolyn was on tenterhooks for the next three days, and the arrival of Thursday evening did little to calm her. Despite several messages from Brandon, assuring her that everything was in train and that she would have nothing to blush for in her guest, she could not help being afraid that Sydney would take one look at Salas and know him for a gypsy. Thus, she was gratified to see, when the butler announced their guests, that Mr. Saint-Denis, precise to a pin as always, greeted them both with his customary politeness and showed not the slightest sign of believing Salas to be anything but what he professed to be.

"Like you to meet m' friend, Count Salas von Drava," Brandon said glibly to the company at large as he drew Salas forward.

Carolyn had all she could do not to stare. Never for one moment would she have believed that the handsome, well-dressed man who clicked his heels together and bowed to Lady Skipton and Miss Pucklington, then turned to nod with aristocratic arrogance at Sydney, was the same man she had met at the camp. If he had seemed lordly then, he was regal now as he looked down his nose at Sydney much, she thought, as if he beheld a toad.

"Welcome to Bathwick Hill House, von Drava," Sydney said.

"Not *von Drava*," Salas said, his smile indicating that he had elected to treat Sydney as an equal. "Am Salas to friends. And this beautiful lady," he added, turning toward the dowager, "she is your mother? But she is too young!"

He was talking far more than Carolyn had intended him to talk, and she glanced anxiously at Brandon. Receiving no more than a shrug in response, she turned back to see that the dowager, beaming with pleasure, had held out her hand for Salas to kiss. Carolyn was startled to see the gypsy bend without hesitation and with singular grace to do so, and even more startled when she caught him peeping up at her through his thick lashes, his eyes alight with mischief.

Miss Pucklington came in for her share of attention, too, and seemed to look upon their visitor with benevolence. As the evening progressed, Carolyn relaxed more and more, certain that their prank would go undiscovered. There was one bad moment, however, when Sydney asked where Salas's home was located.

Carolyn glanced quickly at Brandon to see that he looked as disconcerted as she felt.

Salas was unperturbed. "Dravos," he said, frowning. "How to tell you, who know nothing of my country? It is *dromo*— how you say—wild, not like here. Has few farms, no hedgerows, only many high mountains. Far away—many days' travel."

"Near Hanover, I expect," Lady Skipton said. " 'Tis a pity our royal family has not the benefit of a true English heritage, do you not agree, Count?"

Salas blinked at her, but Brandon, seizing the opportunity, said hastily, "Even an English heritage ain't been of much use to those members of the royal family who've got one, ma'am. Only look at that wicked devil Cumberland, accused of murder and even worse, if we but knew it. Won't let poor Prinny alone. Follows him everywhere, frightening him into thinking he wishes him ill. And Prinny, born and bred here but treated like a dashed outsider by Parliament whenever he wants his allowance raised. Feel for him, I do. In my experience, a man's allowance ain't never sufficient to his needs."

This diversion was successful, and Carolyn gladly assisted him in encouraging the dowager to criticize the royal family in general and the Prince Regent in particular. Catching Sydney's gaze resting upon her for a long moment, she was conscious of a wish that he would look elsewhere, but in spite of that brief interlude, the conversation continued without anyone's attempting to return to the dangerous topic of Salas's antecedents.

Custom notwithstanding, Lady Skipton was not about to allow her son to monopolize their guest and informed the gentlemen that she was certain they would prefer to have their port served in the drawing room rather than to remain in the dining room, and no one attempted to gainsay her. Brandon, however, believing it unwise to tarry, soon invented another engagement for his companion and bore him off. When they had gone, Sydney gave Carolyn another long look, but although his expression gave her pause, she relaxed when, saying that he had matters to attend to in his library, he bade the ladies good night and left the room.

Alone with the dowager and Miss Pucklington, Carolyn sat torn between wanting to run straight to the library to reveal what she had done and wanting to stay right where she was to savor her victory. Lady Skipton, with Hercules curled in her lap, began to recount each detail of the evening to her companion, as though Miss Pucklington had not been there, and Miss Pucklington, knitting placidly, responded with only the added color in her cheeks and the glint of excitement in her eyes to reveal her pleasure at having dined with a foreign nobleman.

Watching and listening, Carolyn felt a sudden need to remind them that their guest did not want his presence in Bath talked about.

"Gracious, no," the dowager agreed, stroking the spaniel. "I daresay he may even be in England on a secret mission for his government, and one would in no way wish to jeopardize such an undertaking. I shall not even write to tell Skipton about the honor afforded us until Count Salas is safely away again."

"To think," Miss Pucklington said with a gentle sigh, "that the count trusted us with such knowledge. It quite puffs one up in one's pride, does it not?"

Carolyn's heart sank. Before that moment she had thought only of fooling Sydney. The dowager and Miss Pucklington had meant no more to her than extraneous characters in a play. But now she saw difficulties ahead and wondered if she would be at all wise to tell Sydney what she had done.

The dowager, having diverted herself by mentioning her elder son, said, "Did I tell you I had a letter from Swainswick today?"

Miss Pucklington nodded, but she might as well not have responded at all for the heed that was paid her, and Carolyn, knowing the gist of the letter if not the content, fixed an expression of interest on her countenance, certain that no more than that would be required of her.

"Poor little Harriet has got a sore throat again, and still

Matilda fails to reprove the children's governess for keeping her out so long in inclement weather. I shall have to write to Skipton, and I daresay it is not too early to be putting a flea in his ear about the danger of allowing so sickly a child as young Stephen to go off to Eton. What do you think, Judith?'' However, she did not pause long enough for her companion to answer, nor did Miss Pucklington seem anxious to do so.

Not, Carolyn thought, that it would have been prudent for Miss Pucklington or anyone else to suggest that the informant might be biased, since most information about the household at Swainswick came from the nurse, who had served the dowager Lady Skipton since his present lordship was six weeks old and who now served his lordship's household in the same capacity. It was no secret that Nurse Helmer held the children's governess in great aversion, although Miss Rumsey's only fault, as nearly as Carolyn could discern it, was that she had had the misfortune to have been selected for her post by the children's mother, rather than by their grandmother or their nurse.

While Lady Skipton continued verbally to dissect her elder son's household into its many objectionable parts for the edification of her companion, Carolyn was able to consider what might be the best way to inform Sydney that despite his self-proclaimed ability to read male character, he had been well and truly fooled by a spurious count. She still had not decided what to do by the time the dowager announced it was time to retire, but she no longer had any urge to burst in upon him to gloat over her victory. A more subtle approach was required.

She wracked her brain while her abigail prepared her for bed and for nearly half an hour after the girl had gone. No idea came to her then or in her dreams, which were full of foreign counts and swashbuckling heroes, the last of whom chose to lock her, for unspecified reasons, in the highest turret of his great stone castle. When the crash awakened her, at first she had the odd notion that the castle walls were tumbling down and that she was falling with the turret stones, to certain death.

She sat bolt upright, trembling, telling herself instantly that she was a fool to allow a nightmare to frighten her. But when a second crash came, followed by more bumping and banging noises, she realized that the noise came from below, either from the drawing room or from the library beneath it, on the ground floor. Jumping out of bed and snatching up a robe to fling over her nightdress, she flew barefoot out of her bedchamber and down the stairs and, when the drawing room proved to be empty, down the grand stair to the hall.

The library door stood open, and the lamp on the desk cast an orange glow over a scene that astonished her. Salas, no longer in his finery but in the shirt and breeches he had worn the first time she laid eyes upon him, was lying on the carpet beside the desk, trussed up like a Christmas goose, with Sydney's man leaning over him, tying a knot in the rope. The only other person in the room was Sydney, wearing an elaborate green brocade dressing gown and observing Ching Ho's captive through his quizzing glass. The only sign that he was at all perturbed was that he neglected to lower the glass when he looked at Carolyn, and she was suddenly reminded of the time she had rubbed stove blacking around its gold rim so that after he pressed it to his eye, he had looked as though someone had hit him. That prank had been one of her more successful efforts.

She wondered where the others who had helped Ching Ho subdue the powerful gypsy had got to; then, glancing at the ormolu clock on the mantel and seeing that it was past three o'clock, she decided Sydney must have already sent them back to bed. "What happened?" she asked, glaring at Salas and dreading the reply.

Ching Ho looked at his master, whereupon Sydney lowered his quizzing glass, glanced casually at the gypsy, then back at Carolyn and said, "You will catch a chill."

"That doesn't matter," she said, looking at Salas again, surprised to see a twinkle in his eyes. "What is he doing here, and why have you got him all tied up?"

"I should think the answers to both questions would be painfully evident," Sydney said, looking again at the gypsy. "Your Count Salas von Drava here decided to help himself to those valuables upon which he could most immediately lay his thieving hands. Not the most acceptable way to repay one's hospitality, I should have thought, but then I believe Romanies possess a uniquely original notion of property rights."

"You know he's—" She broke off, looking sharply at Ching Ho. "That is . . ." Flushing, she bit her lower lip, then looked back at Sydney, unable to continue.

"Caro," he said in a tone of gentle reproof, "this fellow peppered his conversation tonight with Romany words. Or did you think I was unaware of the camp, which is on my own land and not precisely concealed? I couldn't think what you and Manningford were about with your foreign counts, but although I saw no necessity for raising a dust over the matter at dinner, I do draw the line at allowing my possessions to be misappropriated." He gestured toward a collection of articles on his desk that had clearly been removed from the cloth bag lying beside them. Then, looking directly at her, he said, "Shall I ring for a servant to escort you back to your bedchamber?"

She hesitated, wondering why it should disturb her to have him look at her so, but Salas moved just then, drawing her attention. "What are you going to do with him?"

"You and I will discuss the matter further in the morning," he said. "In the meantime, I would prefer that you say nothing to my mother about her erstwhile guest's attempted burglary. Or to Cousin Judith, if you please."

She nodded, able to discern no threat in his voice, only calm, but she knew he must be vexed, and while she told herself firmly that she did not fear his anger, she could not pretend that she looked forward to hearing what he would say to her in the morning. Glancing again at the gypsy, she saw that he was relaxed despite what must be an uncomfortable position, and she felt a surge of irritation. A common thief ought at least to fear the consequences of being caught in the act, but the gypsy clearly feared Sydney's wrath no more than she did. Perhaps less. Salas's manner was not precisely insolent, but he was clearly amused by something she did not understand.

"You will forgive me," Sydney drawled, "if I suggest that your attire is not appropriate to the company. Ching Ho has, of course, inured himself to the oddities of western culture— chiefly to those habits of western women that would be forbidden to Chinese ladies—and no doubt your friend Salas won't object to your nightdress, but if you mean to remain here, you ought at least to fetch your slippers."

Looking down in dismay, she thought she understood the gypsy's amusement, though the realization did nothing to ease her irritation with him. Glaring at him, she snapped, "You ought to be flogged for this."

Salas smiled. "A female has greatest beauty when her eyes flash sparks, missy. Salas likes very much."

"Go back to bed, Caro, now," Sydney said, but if there was a snap in his voice on the last word, she didn't hear it, for with her face burning with fury at the gypsy's words, she spun on her heel and strode angrily from the library. Not until she was back in her bedchamber, lying stiffly under her quilt, did she remember Sydney's promise that they would talk in the morning.

She did not sleep well. It was not the first time that one of her jokes had gone amiss, but it was the worst. The fact that she had so wildly misjudged the gypsy was bad enough, but that Sydney had known him for what he was all along was singularly deflating. She had been so certain he had been deceived. Not for the first time she cursed the way his polished manners concealed his thoughts. She squirmed at the thought that she had not considered the likelihood of his knowing the gypsies were camped on his property. Then she squirmed more, remembering that Ching Ho knew what she had done, that she had so foolishly put the house and its occupants at risk.

Unlike Miss Pucklington, she stood in no awe of Sydney's Chinese manservant, but she did have respect for him. Although he possessed none of the stately hauteur of the other upper servants, his dignity was flawless and his manners, in their own way, as polished as his master's. Though he was of slight stature and medium height, he possessed the confidence of a man of size, and she had often wondered what his position had been in China before he had agreed to accompany Sydney to England. To imagine him a prince or king of some sort had been easy, but when she had repeated this fantasy to Sydney, he had laughed.

"Not even upper class," he had said. "Only a man with certain talents who needed me as much as I needed him, and who can live better here than in China."

The manservant had betrayed neither awareness of her state of undress nor knowledge of her prank, and had stood by with little expression on his face during her conversation with Sydney. Still, she knew he would have had to be both blind and deaf not to know precisely what had transpired, since his English was excellent, better even than the gypsy's.

She did not want to think about Salas, but no matter how many sheep she counted, they kept looking like him or like Sydney, for the only thing she could find that would banish Salas's image from her mind was the unwelcome anticipation of what Sydney would have to say to her on the morrow.

5

After Carolyn stormed from the library, Sydney signed to Ching Ho to close the door, then looked down at the gypsy. "I think you are going to be a nuisance, my friend," he said.

Salas, his smile as bright as ever, said, "It is true that gentlemen do not like their affairs spoken of to others, and a magistrate's court is a most public place, sir. And, too," he added with a smirk, "the lady is most beautiful."

Sydney tapped his glass against his open hand. "Almost you tempt me," he murmured.

The smirk vanished, and Ching Ho said swiftly, "If you have sympathy for others, my master, they will have sympathy for you."

"Will they, Ching? I wonder." But after a brief silence, he shrugged. "Let him go, I suppose. See him off the premises and make it clear to him that he and his tribe are no longer welcome at Bathwick Hill. That will annoy your father, I believe," he added gently, looking back at Salas.

The gypsy grimaced and said no more. Ching Ho stooped to untie his knots, and satisfied that his man might be trusted to see the gypsy camp vacated by morning, Sydney left and went up to his bedchamber. The gypsies were the least of his worries. More important was how he was going to deal with Carolyn, for there was at least one complication resulting from the evening's events that he had decided she would have to rectify by herself.

When he thought of her eruption onto the scene in the library, he suddenly wanted to laugh. She had looked so dismayed and so childlike with her bare feet and her hair in a tangle that he had even felt a brief urge to comfort her, although he could not remember ever having a similar urge when she had spent her school holidays with his family at Swainswick. Then, he had quite frequently wanted nothing more than to strangle her.

Realizing that these thoughts did nothing to assist him in deciding what to say to her, he removed his dressing gown and got into bed to consider the matter at length. Instead, he found himself remembering what she had looked like after her mad dash down the stairs, with her dressing gown half-open, her blue eyes wide with dismay, and her bosom heaving. The memory was a pleasant one, and he allowed it to linger until he fell asleep.

When he awoke in the morning, he still had little idea of what he intended to say to her, but he realized it would be best for them to have their discussion where they would not be overheard. That much decided, he rang for Ching Ho, dressed with his usual care in buckskins and top boots, and made his way to the breakfast parlor. It was still too early for his mother or Miss Pucklington to put in an appearance, but he doubted that Carolyn would keep him waiting long.

When she entered a half-hour later, he was still there, seated at his ease, his attention on the newspaper he was reading. A rack of toast at his elbow, three pots of jam, and a cup of coffee were all that remained of his breakfast. He glanced up. "Good morning," he said. "I trust you slept well."

Carolyn had not slept well, and was in no good humor as a result, but she murmured a polite response and moved to examine the dishes on the sideboard. When a footman appeared in the doorway to ask if she wanted anything from the kitchen, she did not reply, being aware only of Sydney, sitting behind her, no doubt watching her and waiting to say whatever it was that he meant to say. She had lifted three lids without seeing what was beneath them before she could stand the suspense no longer and turned sharply to face him. To her surprise, he had laid down his paper and was inspecting the contents of one of the pots of jam through his quizzing glass.

"Sydney, I—"

"Do you think this jam is blackberry, or something else?" he inquired, looking up at her.

"How should I know? Look here, Sydney, I know . . ." She broke off, flushing when he looked pointedly at the footman.

"Will you hazard a guess, Fredericks?" he asked.

The footman grinned at him. "Don't know what it is, sir. To my mind, jam is jam."

"Then I daresay we won't need you any longer, unless—" He glanced at Carolyn. "Do you want tea, Caro?"

"No, thank you." She turned away and began to scoop food onto a plate, paying no heed to her selections, filling time only until the door had shut behind the footman. When she turned again, Sydney had ventured to put jam on his toast and was looking at it as though it would now reveal more of its nature to him. "Sydney, I never meant . . . that is," she added in confusion when he looked up at her with the same expression with which he had been regarding the jam. "You must think I was a fool to—"

"Not a fool precisely," he said, setting the toast down and picking up his paper as he got to his feet and moved to hold her chair for her. "We will not discuss it now, however. Perhaps you would care to ride with me later. At eleven, shall we say?"

Since it was clear that despite his toast he had no intention of staying to chat, there was nothing to do but accept his invitation; however, once he had gone, she had no appetite left for her breakfast. Though she was not looking forward to the interview, she had wanted to have it over and done. Her emotions were no less mixed when she found him waiting for her on the front drive an hour later.

Cleves and Sydney's own groom were with him, holding the horses, and Sydney stepped forward to meet her. "I thought we would ride toward Bathford," he said. "I have not ridden that way for some time, and I thought you would enjoy seeing a bit of the old Roman road to Cirencester."

Something told her she would enjoy little about it, but she

agreed, watching him closely while he helped her mount to see if she could detect any sign of anger. There was none. Still, she could not doubt he was vexed with her, for she knew how much he valued his treasures, many of which he had acquired during his two years in China. In any case, what man could possibly accept with fortitude a thief introduced to his household?

Sydney said nothing to the purpose until they were well away from Bathwick Hill House and the grooms had fallen a considerable distance behind. By that time, Carolyn was fidgeting in her saddle, casting covert glances at him, trying to imagine what he would say. When he casually complimented her riding habit, she could stand it no longer.

"Please, get on with it, Sydney," she said sharply. "You must have a number of things that you wish to say to me, and I cannot deny that I deserve to hear most of them, but you can't think for a moment that I knew Salas would steal from you."

"He didn't steal from me," Sydney said calmly.

"No, but only because your servants discovered him in time and were able to subdue him. Don't quibble."

"Very well, I shan't. I don't think you knew for certain that he was a thief before you introduced him to my household, Caro, so I will acquit you of malicious intent."

"Thank you." But her conscience pricked her just then with an echo of her own declaration to Brandon that all gypsies were thieves, and her cheeks burned at the memory.

Shooting her an oblique glance, Sydney said, "You have nothing for which to thank me, I'm afraid, for although I acquit you of malice, I cannot acquit you of spite unless you can tell me you had reason for what you did beyond a misguided wish to prove me wrong when I said I know more than you do about men like Manningford and Lyndhurst."

He looked directly at her then. His expression was as amiable as ever, and she would have given anything to be able to assure him that she had any number of other reasons. She could not do so, however, and the shrewdness of his insight made her uncomfortable. She wished he would smile.

A note of resentment crept into her voice when she said at last, "You ought never to have said such a thing to me, Sydney.

You made me angry, and when I get angry with you, I . . .''
She glanced at him ruefully. "Well, you know what I do."

"I do," he said dryly. "I expected, at the very least, to find grated red pepper in my snuff pots."

Grimacing, she said reminiscently, "That was one time I did get a reaction from you. Usually, in those days, you ignored my pranks, deeming them unworthy of notice, but that time you were vexed and told me not ever to do it again."

"That time," he said with a small, reminiscent smile, "I discovered your prank only after I had taken the tainted jar to Oatlands, where, having refilled my box, I offered the first pinch to none other than the Prince of Wales."

"Goodness," she said, awed, "you never told me that."

"I didn't think it good for you to know how much you had embarrassed me," he said. "His highness has had the kindness to respect my expertise in certain matters, including snuff, which is a hobby we share, but at that time I was a callow youth and feared his sneezing would be the death of him. Such a prank today, when his regency has reminded him of his mortality, would make him think me in league with his enemies to kill him."

"Well, I wouldn't do such a thing now," Carolyn said, diverted, "but he cannot truly believe anyone wishes him dead. Even Godmama does not wish such a thing, though she has small opinion of the royal family."

" 'Tis only a few months," Sydney said, "before his regency becomes unconditional. Prinny knows he stands in the way of those who are tempted by such power. But I do not wish to talk about him. You ought to have recognized the danger of your joke, Carolyn. Gypsies are scarcely noted for their integrity."

"I know, but Salas seemed different."

"Only in that he is tall, dark, and handsome."

She glanced at him suspiciously. "What do you mean?"

"Your judgment of him was no better than your judgment of Lyndhurst, or of Manningford."

"You think I trusted Salas only because he is handsome?"

"Your reasoning doesn't signify in the least," Sydney said, "since it was clearly as faulty as your judgment. In any case, I am more concerned with another aspect of the matter, which is your willingness to allow others, innocent of offense to you, to be taken in by this man. I hadn't thought you capable of such insensitivity, Caro. You disappointed me.''

Sudden tears sprang to her eyes, startling her as much as the unexpected ache in her throat did, and she found she could not speak for several moments. Dashing a hand across her eyes, she fought for control and was grateful when she looked at him to see that Sydney was apparently interested only in the road ahead.

When she was able finally to speak, she said brusquely, ''I realized last night that I ought not to have involved Godmama or Puck, but there is no need for them to know what I did. I told them Salas wanted no one else to know he was in B— Oh, dear! The servants. Surely one of them will tell your mama what happened in the night.''

''No servant will tell her,'' he said quietly.

''Are you certain?'' When he nodded, she said on a note of relief, ''Then there is no reason to disabuse either Godmama or Puck of the notion that they have met a foreign count.'' After a pause, she muttered, ''I am very sorry for what I did, Sydney, but at least they will not know what a dreadful hoax it was.''

''I'm afraid you will have to tell them,'' he said quietly.

''Oh, no, I won't. Why should I? Godmama would never understand, and Puck likes thinking she has met a foreign count. What harm can it do?''

''You are not still thinking clearly, Carolyn,'' he said, ''or you would not need to ask about the harm.''

She stared at him, seeing an inflexibility in his expression that she had never seen before. Wanting very much to understand him, she mused aloud, saying slowly, ''The magistrate will hear the whole tale, of course, and then others will hear, and Godmama will—'' She broke off as her thoughts whirled into an enticing tangent, then exclaimed, ''You need not charge him, Sydney. Set him free. He did not actually steal anything, after all, and I am certain he will not try to do so again.''

''He is free,'' Sydney said. ''The entire camp moved out this morning, no doubt heading south to a warmer climate. I had no wish for Mama to learn about the burglary, nor did I wish to see the whole sorry tale made a gift to the Bath quizzes.''

"Then why do you not leave well enough alone?" she demanded, angry at the thought that he wished only to avoid being made to look foolish and seemed to have no concern for how she would look. "Why tell Godmama or Puck anything about it?"

"Do you honestly think they will not find out if we don't tell them?" he asked, unruffled by her display of temper.

"Barring the servants—and you say they will not tell—no one else knows anything about it."

"Manningford knows."

"Well, he won't talk." But even as she said the words, she wondered if they were true. There had been no reason before to swear Brandon to secrecy, and while he did not know yet about the burglary, she would have to tell him. Since he never minded making himself the butt of his own tales and rarely concerned himself with the feelings of others, she knew she could put little faith in his remembering any promise she might winkle out of him now about keeping such a good tale to himself.

Sydney was watching the changing expressions on her face, and he said now, "Just so. Even if he does not speak, do you think Mama will not soon be telling everyone she knows about her mysterious count? Bad enough if her bosom bows only wonder why none of them has ever heard of him. Much worse if they find out the truth and Mama is made to look the fool."

Carolyn paled at the thought. "That would be dreadful. Oh, Sydney, I never meant any of this. I wanted only . . ." But she could not finish, comprehending as she did now that she had acted out of pure impulse and ought to have thought her plan through more carefully before doing something that might have hurt them all. "I'm sorry," she said, swallowing tears and hoping he would not see how distressed she was.

"No need to tell me that," he said quietly, "and if you talk to Mama today, no real harm will have been done, for I doubt she has had time yet to post any letters or talk to her friends. This road we are turning onto now is more than a thousand years old. Come on, and we'll give these nags some exercise."

Following willingly when he spurred his sleek bay hack to a canter, she was grateful for the cooling effect of the crisp air, and astonished that so ancient a road was still in good repair.

When he drew his horse up again a quarter of an hour later, she saw with rueful amusement that scarcely a single fair hair was out of place beneath his hat. He was not breathing hard, and she could not imagine how he did it. Tendrils of dark hair curled about her face, and her hat tilted drunkenly over her brow.

He smiled at her as she righted it, and her spirits lifted. "Ready to go back?" he asked.

She agreed, quailing at the thought of facing the dowager and Miss Pucklington but determined to have the confrontation over and done quickly. Leaving Sydney in the hall when they returned, she went at once to the morning room, where she found the two ladies alone except for Hercules, who was happily engaged in worrying a cushion under the sofa.

"Here is Carolyn, Judith," Lady Skipton said in an irritated tone that nearly destroyed Carolyn's fortitude at the outset. The dowager sat near the window overlooking the hedged garden on the east side of the house, and her russet bombazine skirts rustled as she shifted her position to face Carolyn. "I cannot think why you must come to us in your riding habit, my dear, but it is of no consequence now, for Matilda has put me out of temper. Only listen to this," she added, holding up a letter. "As I have just been telling Judith, Matilda has now quite passed beyond the bounds of what I will tolerate."

"Good gracious, ma'am, what has she done now?" Carolyn asked as she stooped to rescue the cushion. This was not done without spirited objection from Hercules, but she succeeded at last and returned it to the sofa as she took her seat there.

The moment she had done so, the dowager, having watched her with a jaundiced eye and an air of extreme patience, said Matilda had now gone her limit. "Laboring under a mistaken belief that my Louis-Fifteen console table belongs at Swainswick, she desires that I shall return it to her, if you please. The nerve of that woman, choosing to believe that my belongings are hers. I had thought to leave that table to Skipton in my will, but now I shall have it to Sydney, for I never heard the like."

Surprisingly, in view of the uncountable number of furnishings that the dowager had brought with her from Swainswick to Bathwick Hill, Carolyn knew the table to which she referred, an elegant piece with gracefully curved legs and a classically decked frieze. She had no wish to attempt to convey to her godmother the fact that the console table, like most of the furniture she had carried away, did indeed belong to the estate and not to her, but was spared the necessity by the dowager's habit of talking without expecting a reply from her audience.

"Not one line about poor Harriet's health, of course, or dear little Stephen," she said, "but she dares to take exception to the gift I sent Reginald for his eleventh birthday and seems to believe I have encouraged his misbehavior at school. I do not understand the woman."

"What did you send him, ma'am?" Carolyn asked, being in no rush, now that she had a chance to speak, to change the subject to the previous evening's activities.

"A perfectly splendid archery set. Very dear it was, too."

"I collect," Carolyn said dryly, "that it somehow contributed to the mischief."

"Reginald," said the dowager loyally, "did nothing very terrible, whatever Matilda may say."

Miss Pucklington said in a reasonable tone, "It cannot be thought unwarranted, Cousin Olympia, for a master at Eton to object to being made the target of a steel-tipped arrow."

"Reginald did not shoot a master, Judith. He made a guy to resemble him out of a few of the man's clothes stuffed with straw. A perfectly understandable act, I'm sure."

Carolyn chuckled. "Not to the master, perhaps."

"Nonsense," declared the dowager. "He would have liked it a deal less had he been *in* those clothes. He made a great piece of work out of a mere game, and he ought to be ashamed. Matilda insists that Reginald was lucky not to have been expelled, but that is absurd. 'Twas only a boy's prank, after all."

Carolyn, seeing an opening not to be missed, drew a quick breath and said, "I hope you will be as understanding about something just as childish that I have done, ma'am, although I fear that you will not."

The dowager, whose mouth had been open to continue her diatribe against her daughter-in-law and the minions at Eton, snapped it shut for a brief moment to level a gimlet eye at her goddaughter. "What's that you say? What childishness? You are not eleven years old, you know."

"I know I am not, ma'am, but that did not prevent me from being childishly thoughtless in this matter, a fact that Sydney has made abundantly clear to me."

"My son is displeased with you?"

Carolyn realized that she had said the wrong thing. Remembering the economies enforced upon the household during its master's absence, as well as her godmother's uncharacteristic tolerance of Sydney's wishes, she began to see matters in a new light and hastened to put the dowager's apprehension to rest.

"To be sure, he was vexed, ma'am, but on your account and Puck's, not his own. You see, he knows I deceived you both when I attempted to play a practical joke on him. I simply didn't think, and so I must apologize to you both and hope you will not be incensed with me, though you have every reason to be."

"What practical joke?" Lady Skipton demanded. "I thought you must have outgrown such foolishness."

Making no attempt to insist that it had been a very long time since she had last done such a thing, Carolyn said earnestly, "You of all people must know how it is with me when someone says I must or I must not, and when Sydney insisted that his judgment of people was greater than my own and that I must always trust him to know best . . . Well, you can imagine how I reacted. 'Twas no more than a challenge to be met."

"I daresay," the dowager said grimly.

Miss Pucklington said, "We know how it is, my dear, but what is it that you did?"

"The most dreadful thing, Puck. I'm afraid Count Salas is no foreigner. That is, he is, but he is not a count. Oh, dear," she added ruefully, "I am making a mull of this. The plain fact is that he is an impostor. I introduced him to Sydney merely to prove that he would accept a man for what he appeared to be as easily as anyone else would. I had no intention of . . ."

"Of fooling us as easily?" Miss Pucklington suggested. When Carolyn nodded apologetically, she said, "I am sorry to hear that the count was not what he appeared to be, for I quite enjoyed his conversation, you know, but I daresay Cousin Sydney was not deceived at all if the man was not genuine, so no doubt you have learned a valuable lesson, my dear.''

This was not precisely the way Carolyn wished to view the matter, but she kept a still tongue in her head and glanced back at her godmother to see how that lady was taking the news that she had been duped. The signs were not good.

The dowager was frowning heavily. ''If Sydney was not deceived, why did he not say so at once?'' she demanded.

''I believe he did not wish to create a scene at your dinner table, ma'am. He hoped that Salas would do nothing to disgrace you, and he preferred that you discover the deception in a more private manner. I assure you, he thought only of your comfort.''

''Very kind of him, I'm sure. 'Tis a pity you and your accomplices did not think of my comfort before you decided to amuse yourselves in such a fashion. Must I now expect to receive the condolences of my friends for falling victim to this deceit?''

''Oh, no, ma'am. Neither Salas nor Brandon will tell anyone else, for Salas has gone away, and once Brandon knows you are in possession of the facts, he will say nothing to anyone. I will see to it that he understands he must not.''

''I see. Who is this Salas, if you please?''

Carolyn swallowed. ''He . . . I'm afraid he is a gypsy.''

The explosion she anticipated did not materialize. To her surprise, the dowager nodded grimly as though she had expected no less. ''Bad enough that he was foreign,'' she said. ''Of course, I knew him for a rogue the instant I laid eyes on him, but I did not like to say anything, not wishing to embarrass you or Mr. Manningford when you had said the man was his friend, but I did keep my eye upon the silver. Sydney can be very glad of that, and so I shall tell him if he mentions the matter to me.''

Carolyn could think of nothing whatever to say to that, but as usual, there was no need since the dowager continued in this vein for some time, talking herself into a good humor by the time she was done simply by congratulating herself on what she viewed as her own shrewd perception, and since Miss Pucklington contributed only such comments as might be guaranteed to please, there was no one to contradict her. Carolyn made her escape twenty minutes later with a feeling of quite undeserved relief.

Though she feared that word of what she had done would somehow leak out, her apprehension was eased by the news several days later that Mr. Manningford had gone to out of town and then eased even more when she learned from Cleves the next day after that the gypsies had moved well to the south.

"Near Uphill they be now, making their way into Cornwall for the winter," he said as he tightened her saddle girth before their morning ride. "Can't think why it should be warmer near the coast there than what it be here, but so it is. One would think all that air from over the water would be a sight colder."

"There is a warm ocean current that flows near the west coast," Carolyn told him, greatly relieved by his news. "You are certain they are gone, Cleves?"

"Aye, miss, and the folk in Cornwall be right welcome to them. Magic with horses, they be, but even more magic with making the belongings of others disappear, when all's said."

She stared, wondering for a brief moment if he might have been one of the servants called to the library to subdue the gypsy. Then she realized that the notion was an absurd one, that there would have been no need to send to the stables for help with more than enough menservants at hand within the house. Odd, though, she thought, that she had not seen so much as an oblique look from one servant to another to indicate secret knowledge. Not Ching Ho, of course, but one would expect at least one of the others to boast of having caught a burglar in the act, yet not so much as a wink had she seen.

6

November was upon them at last, with Carolyn's twenty-first birthday fast approaching, and the numerous festivities of the Christmas season to follow. Of primary importance to Miss Hardy, of course, was the anniversary of her birth, for on that auspicious day, she would at long last come of age.

"Not that it means a great deal, really," she complained to Sydney when he mentioned the upcoming date as they indulged themselves one rainy afternoon in a game of chess in his library. "It is not as though I shall come into control of my fortune, after all, or even be able to set up my own household."

His eyebrows lifted in gentle inquiry. "I had no idea that you wished to leave us, Caro. Have you been unhappy?"

"No, of course not." She smiled at him. "No one could be unhappy under this roof. You are very kind to have us here."

"I see what it is," he said, moving his queen's bishop. "Not unhappy, merely addled of mind. You are generally more likely to reproach me than to call me kind, Caro. What's amiss?"

She laughed, thinking how comfortable a companion he was. "You may roast me all you like, but I shan't allow you to provoke me only because I choose to thank you."

"There is no need to do so, however," he said more seriously. "You are welcome here."

"I am glad of that, of course. Not that you had much to say in the matter when your mama decided to remove us here."

He raised his eyebrows again.

"No," she said, "don't try to cozen me into believing you might have stayed Godmama from her purpose. I should not believe you. She was determined, you know, which means she would not have listened to your excuses or to any suggestion that she go elsewhere. Certainly, not to the Dower House."

"No, I suppose not. She might have accepted the lease of an elegantly furnished house in town, however." His tone was musing, as though the notion had only just occurred to him.

Carolyn laughed again. "Are you wishing you had thought of it at the time, sir? I assure you, such a scheme would not have answered even if such houses existed, which they do not. The only elegantly furnished ones are occupied by their owners, who are all so firmly entrenched that they have no notion of selling. The ones available to lease are shabby genteel remnants of the days when Bath enjoyed an influx of the *beau monde* each year, and those were not precisely elegant even then."

"I suppose not, but you have not explained why you should wish to set up your own household. It would not answer, you know. You are still too young."

"I am determined not to argue with you today, sir, and so I shall not tell you what I think of that statement, particularly in view of the fact that I have not the least desire to set up my own household, now or in the future."

"Then, what on earth—"

" 'Tis the fact that I could not do so if I wanted to," she said, moving her king's rook. "Your queen is in check."

"So it is," he said amiably without glancing at the board. His gaze was fixed upon her face. "Explain yourself, Caro. I am fascinated. You do not wish to set up housekeeping, yet you are vexed that you cannot do so. What else do you not wish to do that distresses you by its impossibility?"

She sighed and leaned back in her chair. "I suppose you mean to make me laugh at your absurdities, but 'tis truly no laughing matter. People make much of a young man's coming of age, but much less of a young woman's. Indeed, they are more likely to commiserate with her than to congratulate her. Do you know that I am nearly upon the shelf, Sydney? I have been twice betrothed, of course, but since I cried off both times, I have dwindled into spinsterhood, a fact that more than one kind soul will no doubt point out to me at my birthday celebration.''

"Then we are still to celebrate the day?" There was amusement in his eyes, but there was also understanding, and it warmed her heart to see it. It was like him not to dwell on the fact that it was her own fault she was not married. He was kind and gentle, and she had come to cherish such quiet times as this with him and to wish they were more frequent. He listened to her as no one else did, and seemed to think her opinions and thoughts worth hearing. Even his teasing was a comfort to her.

"Perhaps you think I should prefer not to celebrate," she retorted, "but the fact is that it has been weeks now since the hotel assembly, and the weather has been so bad these past few days that no one calls and Godmama does not go out. I should resist strenuously should anyone suggest canceling my birthday rout party. Still, it would be pleasant if the date were really a milestone and meant that I should now have control over my own destiny. Do you think me foolish for wishing such things?''

He shook his head. "No, indeed. I have often thought it unfair that women have not more freedom to do as they wish. To be sure, it is worse in China, where ladies have no freedom at all and are wholly subject to their menfolk. Englishwomen are fortunate by comparison, but it is absurd when men in this country pretend that the women are not as capable as they are, for I've known any number of my own sex who are perfect cod's heads at managing their estates, or their day-to-day affairs, for all that, and many women who could do better.''

"Of course they could," Carolyn agreed. "History shows any number of females taking the reins for one reason or another and doing very well. Only look at our queens! I'm glad you agree that it's unfair, Sydney.''

"Oh," he said with a twinkle as he moved his queen at last, "it does no harm to agree. Agreeing changes nothing, after all.''

"You!" Glaring at him, she would have given anything to have been able to move just one single piece and checkmate him, but she could do no such thing, and the fact that half an hour later he was forced to agree to a draw was small comfort.

As her birthday drew nearer, activity in Bathwick Hill House increased accordingly, for there were preparations to be made and Lady Skipton desired nothing so much as to augment her younger son's status with the *beau monde* by the excellence of the food and entertainment. Although she received little encouragement from Sydney in this endeavor, neither did he attempt to dissuade her, even agreeing with his customary serenity to the information that she had accepted, on his behalf, an invitation for the week following Carolyn's birthday celebration, for them all to attend a house party at the Duke of York's estate at Oatlands.

"The duchess is a friend of mine, you know," Lady Skipton said complacently after informing him of the treat. "I was present at her wedding—the one at Queen's House, not the first one in Berlin—and we have been friends ever since. I don't approve of York—as selfish a man as his brothers—but I should not wish to be remiss in my duty toward Frederica. You like Oatlands, Sydney, and we can take dear Hercules with us." She patted the little spaniel, curled up on the settee beside her. "You will like that, will you not, my little man?"

The dog, being engaged in the important and rather noisy task of cleaning one forepaw, did not respond, but Sydney's attention was well and truly caught. "Take your dog, ma'am?" he exclaimed. "Surely not! The duchess cannot—"

"The duchess," his mother informed him firmly, "dotes on dogs. She has a great number of them herself, as you must know, and they are allowed the run of the house. No one minds them."

Carolyn, biting back a laugh, dared to look at Sydney. That he was actually struggling with his emotions for once was perfectly evident, but when he spoke, his tone was carefully even. "You have said that the house party is to be a large one, ma'am, that the regent himself will attend."

Lady Skipton was unperturbed. "Certainly he will," she said, "since Frederica means to give a ball in his daughter's honor. Even a man so consistently inattentive as he is to his only offspring would not wish to court the disapproval of the *beau monde* by ignoring his duty toward her upon such an occasion, particularly when it is Frederica who gives the ball. I believe several of York's brothers mean to attend, but they will not disturb her peace. She never allows them to do so."

"But you cannot take your dog," Sydney said patiently.

Amanda Scott

Carolyn, seeing that the dowager was entirely prepared to explain at length why Hercules ought to go, said gently, "You know, ma'am, it is not altogether unreasonable to fear that the duchess might mistakenly believe you intend Hercules to be a gift. Do not people frequently bestow pets upon her?"

The dowager looked shocked, and although she said she thought she could explain the truth of the matter very well, thank you, Carolyn saw that the point had gone home and did not think she need say any more. Discovering that Sydney had relaxed and was regarding her with lazy approval brought a blush to her cheeks, and she looked away, taking the first opportunity to change the subject to the preparations for her rout party.

In the few days remaining before that event, the weather proved particularly inclement, making some occupants of Bathwick Hill House wonder if any of the invited guests would come. Only the dowager was unconcerned.

"No one," she declared at the dinner table two days before the rout party, after Miss Pucklington had expressed anxiety on Carolyn's behalf, "will wish to miss the opportunity of being entertained in this house. Everyone is well aware of what a superior house this is, and will welcome the opportunity to see the foreign oddities that Sydney has collected in his travels. 'Tis a pity, I think, that Matilda and Skipton have chosen this of all times to visit her mother, for they might have brought the children, you know, and now I shall not see them until we visit them at Swainswick for Christmas. I have been thinking, Sydney," she added before anyone had thought of a suitable reply to her last, daunting statement, "that you will wish to arrange a few tables of display in the library."

Sydney said calmly, "I don't think I will, ma'am. Bathwick Hill House is no museum and I do not intend that it shall become known as one. I don't mind showing my treasures to those who appreciate their value or who wish to seek my advice regarding some intended purchase of their own, but I have no wish to flaunt my things before all and sundry."

The dowager stiffened, and Carolyn, expecting to draw her fire and not knowing precisely why she should wish to do so, said hastily, "Might not persons who do not understand your generosity of spirit describe such a display as vulgar, ma'am?"

"Nonsense," the dowager said haughtily. "Why, the regent himself seeks Sydney's advice when he wishes to add a new trifle to his collection. If he considers him to be an authority on such matters, sure your guests will be more than delighted to be granted an opportunity to view Sydney's own little collection."

Carolyn blinked at hearing the vast assortment of articles Sydney had acquired during his sojourn in China described in such a way, but Sydney, taking snuff with a delicate twist of his wrist, said with amusement, "One fears the display you intend would suggest instead that we have prepared a sale of goods. No, no," he added, smiling at the outraged expression on his mother's face, "I was only funning. Nonetheless, and though I have no wish to distress you, my belongings are not for public view."

Carolyn held her breath, but she was not so astonished as she might have been several weeks before, when the dowager nodded regally and said, "It shall be as you wish, of course, though I am sorry you should have disliked the notion, for many of our friends, I am convinced, will be very much disappointed not to have the opportunity to view your treasures."

"My friends have seen what they wished to see, ma'am."

"Oh, your intimates, of course, but I shall not quibble, my dear. It shall be as you wish."

"Thank you."

Nodding, she returned her attention to her dinner, and Sydney turned to Carolyn. "Have you any special request for your birthday, Caro? You have not expressed a wish for any particular gift that I know about."

"I can think of nothing that I need, sir."

"Oh, but on such an occasion, need is not important. Surely, it is the right of any young woman who reaches her majority to ask for a special gift, perhaps even one she believes to be unattainable or outrageous."

"Is it?" She grinned at him. "And how do you know so much about it, sir? Do you think I will demand the moon or a few stars? I shall not, for I don't know what I should do with them if I got them. I should infinitely prefer a bouquet of spring flowers, but when one's birthday comes in late autumn, one cannot wish for such things. In books, of course, one can," she added with a teasing look at Miss Pucklington. "If one can gather blackberries in springtime, no doubt one can also collect spring blossoms in autumn, but not, unfortunately, in real life."

When Miss Pucklington blushed and glanced guiltily at the dowager, Carolyn, realizing that she must not yet have finished reading about the adventures of Laura Lovelace and Sir Bartholomew Lancelot (although she herself had long since done so), quickly changed the subject. Lady Skipton did not appear to notice anything out of the way, but although Sydney accepted the change of subject, he gave Carolyn such a quizzical look that she decided some sort of explanation was due him.

She waited until they had gathered in the drawing room after dinner. Then, while Lady Skipton and Miss Pucklington, sitting comfortably near the blazing fire, put their heads together over the invitation list to determine which guests had accepted or declined, Carolyn accepted Sydney's challenge to a game of picquet and joined him at a table by the window.

"Poor Puck," she said in an undertone when they had begun their second hand and she was certain the others were too involved in their task to pay her any heed. "I nearly gave her away, and I would not do so for the world. I declare four."

"No good," he replied. "Gave her away?"

She explained as they scored the rest of their points and began to play the hand out, and when he chuckled, she said, "You may laugh, but I daresay she would rather be reading that book right now than counting guests for my party. Your discard."

Sydney studied his hand. Then, throwing a card, he glanced toward the fire and said, "She appears content enough."

"I should hate being so dependent. It must be dreadful." Taking the trick, she hesitated over her lead, trying to remember what points he had declared earlier and what he had played.

"It could be worse," Sydney pointed out, "but in a better world, I daresay Cousin Judith would be happier keeping a shop."

Carolyn stared. "A shop! Puck? You must be joking."

"Can you not imagine her as a stylish modiste? I can. Even Mama does not despise her suggestions when choosing a wardrobe."

"True." Carolyn frowned at the card she had selected. "It is too bad, isn't it? Puck does exquisite plain sewing and fancy-work, and her knitted creations are beautiful. Yet if she suggested selling one of them for extra pin money, people—the right people—would be very much shocked, so she is condemned to a lifetime of walking that dreadful Hercules and attending to your mother's whims."

"I do not believe she is unhappy, however. Is that your lead? If it is, I wish you would play it."

"I daresay you do," Carolyn said, putting down the ten of spades. "No doubt it is the very one you hoped I would throw. Oh, what a beast you are," she exclaimed when he took the trick. "I had forgotten you declared three knaves, and now I shall be lurched. But I'll be revenged, sir, before the night is done."

"I've no doubt of that," he said, smiling at her. There was a look in his eyes just then that she had not seen before, that made her pulse beat faster and made it somehow impossible to look away. But then he blinked, and the expression disappeared before she could decipher it. As she watched him deal out the next hand, she dismissed the moment from her mind.

They chatted amiably while they played until the tea tray was brought in and it was time to put the cards away, but Carolyn remembered that conversation again the night of her party when Miss Pucklington, attired in a puce evening gown and draped with an assortment of her best shawls, entered her bedchamber half an hour before it was time to go down to greet the first guests.

"Oh, Puck, thank goodness! I cannot get this bodice to drape properly, and poor Maggie is at her wits' end. But should you not be helping Godmama?" she added as Miss Pucklington moved swiftly to examine the rose-pink muslin drapery at her bosom.

"Cousin Olympia is in the dining room, my dear. Although the chef assured her he had everything he required, she wanted to see for herself that there will be nothing to criticize, and so she finished her toilette in good time for me to come to you. I believe a tuck just here and here will sort things out."

Five minutes later she stood back, regarded Carolyn's bosom critically, then nodded.

Carolyn sighed in relief when she turned to look at the result in the looking glass. "Oh, yes," she said, "that is perfect. I can't think why we didn't see the problem before."

"No doubt 'twas because you did not wear your pearls with it before," Miss Pucklington said, smiling. " 'Tis a lovely dress, my dear, and for once there are fires in all the rooms, you know, so you need not be chilled despite the fact that you are not at all well covered. Perhaps just one light shawl—"

"No, no," Carolyn told her with a laugh. "With everyone commiserating with me for having reached the ripe old age of one-and-twenty, I must not look a dowdy, as well. Oh, dear, Puck! My wretched tongue again. I didn't mean that you—"

"No, dear, I know perfectly well that you meant nothing by it. I like my shawls, you know, and would not be without them. One can add or subtract one or two and always be comfortable. Do not forget your gloves," she added, handing those articles to Carolyn, who kissed her cheek as she took them.

"I shouldn't dream of forgetting them. They are by far my favorite gift, for I know that you embroidered them yourself to match my gown." She pulled the first one on and smoothed it into place, admiring the exquisitely embroidered pink and lavender flowers on delicate green stems. Remembering Sydney's words, she said, "Do you sometimes wish you might set yourself up in an elegant shop, Puck, selling your wonderful creations, so that you need not be so dependent upon God-mama?"

For a brief moment there was an arrested look in Miss Pucklington's eyes, but she mastered herself quickly and said, "Whatever can have put such a notion into your head? A shop! Why, my mother was a Beauchamp, just as Cousin Olympia is, and a Beauchamp does not keep shop. Only imagine the scandal."

"Well, I think it's a pity that so few of us should be aware of your talents, ma'am."

Coloring, Miss Pucklington said, "I know you are funning, my dear, but I pray you will say nothing of the sort to anyone else. Goodness me, I should not wish to distress Cousin Olympia by letting her think for one moment that I thought—and I don't, truly I don't, but—"

Carolyn, wishing she had held her tongue, interrupted gently. "I won't say a word to anyone, Puck. I am persuaded that we ought to go down now. Our guests will soon be arriving."

Miss Pucklington glanced at the little clock on the dressing table and exclaimed, "Oh, yes, why, it seems only a moment ago that I left Cousin Olympia. How can half an hour have passed by so quickly?" Twittering as she went, she bustled beside Carolyn to the grand stairway, from the top of which they could see that several guests had already arrived.

Carolyn paused as the depressing thought struck her that despite the number of people invited to the ball, there was no single person she was truly looking forward to seeing. Reminding herself firmly that a number of young men had been invited who would no doubt prove entertaining, she lifted her chin and went down the stairs to take her place beside her godmother and Sydney to greet those guests who had been invited early to dine.

Lady Skipton said in an undertone, "I sent Judith to fetch you more than half an hour ago."

"Yes, ma'am," Carolyn said, turning to greet a majestic dame and the young girl following in her wake. By the time they had passed on, others had arrived and Lady Skipton was too taken up in the process of greeting them to quiz Carolyn any further.

From time to time before the last of the dinner guests had been greeted, she was aware of Sydney's glances, and she thought he must realize she was a trifle out of sorts, but when he finally ordered his porter to see to any latecomers and offered her his arm, he said only, "Shall I take you in, my ancient one?"

Relaxing, she smiled at him. "Not if you intend to spend the evening throwing my advanced years in my face."

The dowager, who had been gathering up her fan and her satin reticule, which had been placed upon the table behind her, turned and said, " 'Tis Sydney's place to escort you, Carolyn, and it is not at all becoming in a young lady of one-and-twenty to be childishly difficult."

"No, ma'am," Carolyn said, bowing her head for the simple

reason that it was safer than taking the chance of looking at Sydney. She did not do so again until the dowager and her escort had passed before them into the dining room, and when she did, she saw the laughter in his eyes that she had expected to see.

"May I help your decrepit self to a chair, ma'am?" he murmured wickedly.

She chuckled and said, "If you mean to keep this up, sir, I shall not be responsible for my actions. I am not so old that I cannot remember how best to be revenged upon you."

"Not that!" He held up his free hand in the gesture used by fencers to declare a hit. "I prefer to know that my snuff and my bed are safe tonight. And I should prefer not to discover salt in my sugar basin in the morning, if it is all the same to you."

"I never did anything so common as that," she protested.

"No, you were always creative. Let me see, there was the time you pasted my slippers to my bedchamber floor. I arose from my bed in the middle of the night in order to attend to some very important business—"

"Important business?"

He wagged his finger at her as the footman moved to hold her chair. "A lady does not inquire into a gentleman's business."

She grinned at him saucily. "Particularly not the business he attends to in the middle of the night."

"Just so," he retorted, bending nearer and adding under cover of the commotion caused by the ceremony of seating everyone. "On that occasion, I arose from my bed, placed both feet in my slippers, attempted to take the first step, and promptly fell on my nose. I was sorely tempted to visit you in your bedchamber to describe my displeasure to you, but since I could scarcely leave my room in my bare feet—"

"You ought to be grateful you had resources at hand and did not have to go down the corridor to the commode closet," she said, only to blush and sit down rather quickly when she caught the eye of the elderly gentleman being seated to her right and realized he might have heard her. "G-good evening, sir."

"That'll teach you," Sydney murmured in her ear before moving to take his own seat.

As the guest of honor, Carolyn sat at Sydney's right hand, but his attention throughout the meal was claimed largely by the stout, gray-haired lady on his left, a particular friend of his mother's who talked incessantly about her family and her husband's estate. Carolyn was thus left to the mercies of the gentleman on her right, who, whether he had overheard her unfortunate comment or not, displayed more interest in his dinner than in conversation. As she watched the others, she sipped her wine, pushed her food around on her plate, sipped a little more wine, and felt generally rather dull.

Most of the dinner guests were of another generation, for although both Viscount Lyndhurst and Mr. Manningford had been invited to dine, neither had yet appeared. She did not miss the viscount, nor would she have cared had his name been missing altogether from the invitation list, but she did miss Brandon, since he at least would have amused her. Deciding that he had either never received his invitation or had forgotten the engagement, she attempted to revive her sinking spirits by reminding herself yet again that other, no doubt interesting young men had been invited to join the party later for dancing.

After dinner, there was no thought of leaving the gentlemen to their port, and when Sydney escorted Carolyn from the dining room, they discovered that the other guests were already arriving. "Hello, Lyndhurst," Sydney said when that gentleman approached them. "Began to think we'd have to forgo the pleasure of your company this evening."

The viscount bowed to Carolyn. "Sorry to be late. Many happy returns, my dear."

"Thank you," she said, coloring as she remembered their last meeting. Despite that memory, however, she was more pleased to see him than she had expected to be. He was young, he was handsome, and he would be no threat to her here at Bathwick Hill House. He was a rake, of course, and reputedly a dangerous man, but that only made him more interesting. Her smile broadened as she held out her hand to him.

Taking it and giving it a squeeze, he looked deep into her eyes and said, "Will you walk with me? I should like some private conversation with you."

Sydney said swiftly, "Dashed sorry, old fellow, but I see my mother looking this way. Daresay she wants to make Carolyn known to one of her cronies. Come along, Caro.'' And before Lyndhurst could gather his wits, he had whisked her away.

"What are you doing?'' she demanded as he guided her, not toward the dowager at all but into the small anteroom leading from the rear of the hall into a little-used garden parlor.

At the moment both anteroom and parlor were empty, and without a word, Sydney shut the door behind them and leaned against it, reaching into his waistcoat pocket as Carolyn turned and repeated her question. Still without speaking, he withdrew a long, slim, green-velvet-covered box and handed it to her.

"What is this?''

'' 'Tis customary to open the box,'' he said, folding his arms across his chest.

She paused, looking at him. "This morning when Puck gave me my gloves and Godmama my lace reticule, you gave me that pretty Chinese lacquer box with the inlaid brass woodland scene, so what can this be?''

"Open it, Caro.'' He unfobbed his snuffbox, flicked it open without taking his gaze from her, then flicked it shut again and put it away. Had she not known he was never nervous, she would have thought him nervous now.

More curious than ever she opened the box. Inside, lying on black satin, were four delicate jewel flowers attached to a fine gold chain. She caught her breath, touching the first, a bugle flower made of amethysts. The others were a ruby rose with a diamond center, a sapphire cornflower, and something else of pink rubies that she could not identify. All had emerald leaves and finally wrought gold stems.

"They are beautiful,'' she said softly, gazing at them for a long moment before pointing to the last. "What is this one?''

"Lousewort,'' he said, grinning.

"Sydney!'' She looked up, laughing. "It is not!''

"It is, I assure you, and I'm glad it made you laugh. I've thought more than once tonight that you were a trifle out of sorts and hoped this little bauble might cheer you up. You said you wanted spring flowers. It is not a full bouquet, of course, but 'tis the best I could do on short notice. If you like, I daresay we can find more to add to the chain.''

"No, I like it as it is," she said, putting her hand on his shoulder and rising on tiptoes to kiss his cheek. "Thank you, Sydney. I shall always treasure my bouquet. Will you put it on me, please? I'll put my pearls in a drawer or somewhere."

"I'll look after them for you," he said, moving behind her and deftly unfastening the clasp. He slipped the pearls into his coat pocket and fastened the gold chain around her neck in their place. The flowers rested two inches above the edge of her bodice. "Very nice," he said, turning her. "Their delicacy suits you. Daresay we ought to go back to the others now."

"Indeed, we should. I want to show my necklace off."

When they returned to the large saloon where the dancing was to take place, they discovered that the musicians had been waiting only for their arrival to begin. After the first set, Sydney's attention was soon claimed by someone else, and Carolyn thought her next two partners rather dull. Moreover, the room was hot, so when Lyndhurst asked her a second time to walk with him, she accepted at once.

"Is there a punch bowl somewhere?" he asked, drawing her a little away from the crowd.

"Oh, yes, in the next room, and I should be grateful for some punch. Parties are always so noisy, aren't they, and the musicians seem to play louder and louder in an attempt to overcome the chatter, but everyone just talks louder. I am beginning to have the headache."

"My poor Caro."

"I am not yours, Lyndhurst," she said severely.

"Perhaps not yet," he said, smiling down at her in a way that made her want to slap him. The adjoining room was quieter but nearly as hot, thanks to the fire burning on the hearth, and when Lyndhurst handed her a glass of champagne punch, she drank it quickly. Another guest stepped up to speak to her, and a few moments later, when the viscount handed her a second glass of punch, she realized she had not even been aware that he had left her. She sipped as she continued to talk, and began to feel strangely relaxed and more cheerful.

When they returned to the larger room, Lyndhurst said, "I claim the privilege of leading you out for the next dance, my dear, and I'll not be denied."

She didn't care by then who led her out, so she placed her hand obediently in his, thinking her rout party had become a great deal more fun than she had expected it to be. When their set was over and Brandon suddenly appeared before them, apparently out of nowhere, she turned away from Lyndhurst without a second thought to greet him with delight and a scolding.

"Scoundrel, where have you been?"

"Oh, out and about," he replied airily as he took her hand and led her into the next set. "Went to Leicester and won a pony on a horse race, so I went on to Newmarket. Invitation never came my way, but most fortunately, I met someone or other who chanced to mention your party. Came straightaway back to Bath. Many happy returns, by the bye." He glanced around. "Look here, you don't really want to dance in this crush? Want some punch?"

Agreeing that the floor was too crowded, she went with him, and by the time her guests began to depart, she knew she had allowed her various escorts to ply her with too much wine. She had enjoyed the attention, however, and was feeling particularly pleased with herself for having managed to deflect every attempt to take her aside into a private room. Lyndhurst, visibly fuming at having been left so ignominiously when Brandon arrived, had made more than one attempt. Sydney had intervened the last time, but that hadn't distressed her at all, and she didn't much care about anything now. As she looked at the sweeping stairway, she wondered how it had got so high in just a few short hours.

"Going up?"

She turned to find Sydney behind her and remembered vaguely having observed him only a moment or two before, speaking to a few of the last departing guests. The dowager and Miss Pucklington had gone upstairs sometime earlier.

"What are you doing there?" she demanded. "You ought to be overseeing the culmination of this wondrous carouse." The words came out precisely, just as she had intended them to do, and she congratulated herself. She was not tipsy. Had she been the least bit inebriated, she could not have spoken so clearly. Nonetheless, perhaps it would be a good idea, instead of going up to her bedchamber at once, just to step outside for a moment to clear her head in case she chanced to run into Lady Skipton upstairs. She turned on the thought and moved toward the door, passing Sydney without a word, giving no consideration whatever to the fact that he had not replied to her question.

Sydney regarded her thoughtfully, watching as she made her way across the hall to the front door and gestured grandly to the porter, who was waiting to snuff the lights, to open it for her.

"Now, miss?" the man asked, glancing at his master. Smiling broadly, Sydney nodded at him, and the porter pulled the door wide, allowing Carolyn to sail through it without pause.

7

The night was cold but crystal-clear, and the stars blazed above her like scattered diamonds on the black-satin lining of her jewel box. Though the wide marble steps leading down to the drive seemed a trifle unsteady beneath her feet and the gravel of the drive felt sharp through the thin soles of her silk dancing slippers, she ignored everything except the sense of freedom and solitude that washed over her with the crisp night air. And if her shoulders were a mass of gooseflesh, the headache that had plagued her most of the evening was gone. All in all, she felt wonderful. She would stroll in the hedge garden.

The feeling of exhilaration lasted until she had passed through what seemed somehow to be a much-narrower-than-usual opening in the tall hedges bordering the east garden. The area beyond was dark, for there was no moon above, and despite the starlight, she could identify nothing ahead at first but deep, dense shadows. She paused unsteadily, seeking, listening. Was that a rustle? Was someone there? Peering ahead, she saw no movement and took courage from the fact, determined to have her walk. The narrow gravel pathway between lower, bordering hedges was visible now. She strolled bravely on.

Soon she noticed that her feet were hurting and that she was very cold. And she heard more noises—a crunch of gravel. Someone or something was prowling behind her. Whirling to look, she stumbled, and when she had regained her balance, she could see only more shadows. Taking a side path that glimmered gray beneath the stars, she hurried a little, then glanced again over her shoulder, experiencing a wave of dizziness and a sudden wish that she had remained indoors. Was that someone? She could see only the path, and only a few feet of that. Another wave of dizziness hit her, making her stagger when she began moving forward. She shut her eyes, but that only made her more giddy, so she opened them again in time to see a small shadow flit across the path just in front of her.

Startled, she cried out, realizing it was a cat only seconds before another sound behind made her whirl again. A much larger shape loomed out of the darkness toward her, and with a shriek, she spun on her heel to run, but her legs would not cooperate. Tripping over the nearest boxwood, she fell ignominiously flat on her face in the barren flower bed beyond it. As she scrabbled frantically on hands and knees to escape, there came a footstep beside her, and a strong hand grasped her arm. Hearing Sydney's voice say her name, she expelled a gusty sob of relief.

"Are you hurt?" he asked calmly.

"Just my dignity." She stared up at him, glad it was only he but furious that he had made her fall. "You frightened me witless. What were you thinking, to creep up on me like that?"

"You appeared to desire solitude," he said reasonably as he helped her up, "but after watching how unsteadily you walked, I decided to follow to be sure you found your way back again, and when you let out that almighty screech . . ." He let his voice trail into silence, evidently thinking he had said enough.

She brushed off her skirt and hands and felt quickly to be certain her necklace had not been lost. Finding it safe, she said with forced calm and careful enunciation, "I am perfectly all right. You may go back to the house now."

"May I, indeed?" There was amusement in his voice. "I think you had better come inside with me, Caro. You are in no state to be out here alone, as I should think this little incident would prove to you if you were thinking straight."

"I can think perfectly straight," she said, affronted. "Goodness me, Sydney, do you think me inebriated?"

"I do."

"Well, I am no such thing," she said, squaring her shoulders and ignoring a new wave of lightheadedness. Drawing a breath, she said carefully, "A lady never becomes inebriated."

He was silent.

Putting her hands on her hips, she glared at him. "Well?"

"I shan't be so rude as to contradict you," he said gently. "Are you ready to go back?"

"I wish to be alone, if you please."

"I don't think so. Your teeth are chattering."

"They are my teeth!"

When without further ado, he scooped her up into his arms and turned back toward the house, she shrieked, "No, Sydney! Don't you dare. Put me down at once!"

"No."

"Damn you, Sydney, I command you!"

"Command away," he said, making no attempt to conceal his amusement now, "but if you mean to swear at me, my dear Caro, I suggest that you lower your voice. It would not do for Mama or Cousin Judith, or indeed any of the servants, to hear you."

Opening her mouth to tell him she did not care what anyone thought, she hiccupped instead. Horrified, she clapped her hand over her mouth, only to find herself giggling a moment later. "I never giggle," she informed him in a confidential tone.

He was silent, and she listened carefully to see if he was breathing heavily from his exertion, but all she heard was the crunch of his feet on the gravel. They were on the drive. A moment later, the crunching stopped when he reached the steps.

"I daresay I am too heavy for you," she murmured, leaning her head against his shoulder and thinking how very comfortable it was there.

"Don't be foolish," he said.

"I can walk, you know."

"No doubt you can, in your own fashion, but I have no wish to follow you up the stairs, leaping at every stagger and lurch to try to catch you before you tumble down them again. 'Twould affront my dignity to be dancing about so."

"What about mine?" But she chuckled sleepily. "I had not

thought you strong enough to carry me, sir—certainly not up two whole flights of stairs—but I daresay it would affront your dignity even more to drop me, would it not?''

''I won't drop you.'' His voice was gentle, and deciding he was disinclined to tease her further, she allowed her eyelids to droop and her body to relax.

She stirred briefly when he laid her down upon her bed and again when she felt a hand at her bodice, but it was only Maggie. Sydney had gone. Strangely disappointed, she did little to help Maggie undress her and sank back against her pillows with a sigh of relief when the maid had gone.

She knew nothing more until she awoke the following morning to the painful realization that she had grossly deceived herself by imagining for so much as a moment that she had not had too much to drink. Her headache had returned with a vengeance, throbbing, pounding, bludgeoning her skull from the inside, and the clinking of the rings when Maggie opened the curtains was as the clanging of metal bars all around her. She groaned and buried her head beneath her pillow.

''Miss, are you ill?'' Maggie tugged gently at the pillow.

''Go away and leave me alone.'' Her own voice, muffled by the pillow, thundered in her head with blinding pain.

''I'll fetch Miss Pucklington,'' Maggie exclaimed, dismayed.

''I don't want her.'' Pushing the pillow aside and groaning when the light hit her eyes, Carolyn saw that the maid already had the door open. ''No, Maggie,' she cried, trying to sit up, ''come back!'' Her stomach heaved, and falling back, she clapped a hand to her mouth and pulled the pillow over her face again.

Maggie hesitated. ''But, Miss Carolyn—''

Another voice interrupted her. ''Run along, Maggie. I'll see to your mistress.''

''But, sir—'' There was a brief silence before Maggie said, ''Yes, sir. You've only to ring, sir, if you want me.''

''I know,'' Sydney said. ''Now, off with you.'' There was another silent moment while Carolyn lay rigid, appalled not so much at the fact that Sydney had entered her bedchamber but that Maggie had allowed him to do so. Then he said cheerfully,

"Good morning, Caro. I've brought you something to make you feel much more the thing, but you cannot drink it through that pillow, I'm afraid. You must sit up."

"Go away, Sydney. I detest you. You've no business to be in my bedchamber, and well you know it."

"I don't know it. You are in my charge, my dear."

"I am of age now," she muttered through gritted teeth, wincing at every word. "I am in no one's charge."

"As you pointed out to me not long since, your coming of age changes little," he said in a different tone. "This is my house, Caro, and I've every right to do as I please in it. Now, stop being foolish and sit up. Ching Ho's recipe is better drunk while it is still warm, as I know from my own sad experience."

Unaccustomed as she was to hear such firmness from him and curious despite her ills to see what he had brought her, she obeyed without more fuss, pushing the pillow to the floor and struggling to raise herself without making her head ache more than it already did. Sydney stood beside the bed, precise to a pin as always, in biscuit-colored pantaloons and a perfectly fitting dark-blue coat. To her astonishment, he carried a bouquet of violets in one hand and a steaming mug in the other.

Setting the mug down on the bed table, he recovered the pillow and shoved it behind her, then straightened again, letting her arrange her blankets herself. Yanking them high, though her nightdress was modest by any standard, she said carefully, "I must tell you, sir, that in view of the way I presently feel, those flowers of yours might soon grace my funeral wreath."

He chuckled. "Bad, Caro?"

She groaned. "Don't you dare to make me laugh, Sydney."

"Drink this," he said, his eyes alight with amusement as he reached for the mug. "It will make you feel much better."

She took it from him and eyed the contents suspiciously. "What is it?"

"Lord, I don't know. Ching Ho has any number of Oriental secrets to which I am not privy. That mixture is only one of them, but I can vouch for its excellence. Drink it down, and don't sip it either. Best if you hold your nose, in fact."

She sipped and made a face. "This is awful. I am persuaded that you mean to murder me with some Oriental poison."

"Nonsense. Drink it. You may trust me, Caro."

She looked at him for a long moment, then pinched her nostrils shut with one hand while she tilted the contents down her throat with the other. When she had finished, she handed him the mug and sat very still while she waited for the room to stop spinning. Thirty seconds later, when her head still pounded and her stomach seemed about to disgrace her, she glared at Sydney.

"Patience," he said. "It takes a few minutes, even for a brew of Ching Ho's manufacture. Smell your violets." He handed her the bouquet. "Here, I'll fill your tooth mug with water, and you may use it for a vase until Maggie brings you something better. These aren't really spring flowers, but I thought you would like them. I found them while I was riding through the wood this morning. Didn't think there would be a thing left after all the weather we've had, but these were nestled in the hollow of a tree root, just waiting for me to find them."

He continued to talk about his ride, speaking in his customary quiet way, and she closed her eyes, knowing he would not take offense. She felt herself relaxing, felt the pounding ease at last and finally disappear, whereupon she slept.

When she awoke more than an hour later, she felt greatly refreshed. Her headache was gone and her energy had returned. Rising, she rang for Maggie, then walked to the window to look out at the distant, sunlit view of the city of Bath while she contemplated the results of Oriental magic.

The city, appearing magical itself with the sun glittering on the golden Bath stone of which most of its buildings were constructed, looked peaceful and serene, tucked as it was in the bowl formed by the steep hills surrounding it. Compared to London, where activity hummed twenty-four hours a day, Bath was a sleepy village, and it was hard to believe that it had been much as it was now since the days of the Romans, but so it was, for Sydney had told her so. Indeed, she had learned as much at school, but she had never had quite the same faith in her mistresses at school as she had in Sydney.

Turning from the window, she smiled as her gaze came to rest on the little bouquet in her tooth mug. She had not thanked him. She would do so as soon as she dressed.

Once Maggie arrived, it was but a few moments' work to

don a simple blue morning frock and arrange her hair, but when she had dressed, she realized she was famished and wanted her breakfast. On the thought, she hurried down to the breakfast parlor, and finding it empty and devoid of food, she yanked the bell cord.

Abel entered seconds later, informing her that he had been awaiting her summons. "Master said ye would be right peckish when ye woke, miss. What shall I fetch ye?"

Ordering a full breakfast and a pot of tea, and telling him to hurry, she seated herself and waited impatiently, grateful when he returned a few minutes later with a rack of buttered toast, two pots of jam, and her tea.

"Cook be boiling an egg, miss. The rest be ready and waiting, so it'll not be long. I'll just go ter fetch it."

Munching toast and jam, she grinned at him but didn't attempt to express her gratitude until he returned with the rest of her breakfast. When she had finished, she left the sunny little parlor and went in search of Sydney, finding him at last in his snuff room.

Wrinkling her nose at the acrid smell, she quickly closed the door behind her, well aware that he insisted upon keeping the temperature in the room as constant as possible. A fire burned low in the grate, and the room was delightfully warm.

Sydney, with Ching Ho at his side, was bent over a counter on one side of the room, and only glanced up briefly at the sound of the door. "One moment," he said. "I want to finish this mix before I forget what I've added and what I haven't. I mean to give it to Prinny at Oatlands, so it won't do to make a mistake. He'll probably hesitate to accept it in any event, after the last time in that house that he dared try a mixture of mine."

"Surely, he ought to have forgotten that occasion by now," Carolyn said, refusing to be drawn.

"Very likely," he agreed. "But although he usually only pretends to take snuff these days, managing to lose his pinch somewhere between his snuffbox and his nose, he is still a connoisseur and will instantly recognize a poor mix."

"Well, this one, lacking any helpful addition from me, will be no such thing," Carolyn retorted, gazing at the many shelves containing neatly labeled jars of snuff. Moving closer to the counter, she saw that Sydney was carefully adding to the contents of an elegantly painted jar what looked like powder from several squares of paper carefully arranged before him. A twist of hard tobacco lay beside a wooden grater, and a small hammer and hand rake lay beside these. "What is that?" she asked when he drew a paper with a small amount of pinkish powder on it toward him.

"Crushed Chinese camphor," he said without taking his eyes from his work. "Prinny likes his snuff slightly scented. I'll also add a bit of Australian eucalyptus to intrigue him."

"He is said to have a whole cellar of snuff," Carolyn said.

"Yes, but nowadays he prefers a blend put up for him by Fribourg and Treyer. He still enjoys trying new mixes, however, and I flatter myself that he will like this one. Look at the snuffbox I found for him."

He nodded toward a silver box sitting by itself a little to one side, and Carolyn picked it up, laughing when she recognized the cameo framed in diamonds on the lid. "His pavilion at Brighton! He will adore it, Sydney. Where did you find it?"

"Had it from Jeffreys of Bath," he told her, "so he won't have seen it. He generally purchases his from Rundle and Bridge in London. Now, hush, and let me concentrate. Hold that paper, Ching Ho. It wants to move when I touch the powder."

Carolyn sat in a chair near the window and waited patiently until he had finished, whereupon Ching Ho swept the paraphernalia onto a tray and carried it out of the room to clean.

"How does he get the tobacco out of all those little holes in the grater?" she asked when the door had shut behind him.

"With a silver pin," Sydney told her, taking the chair beside hers. "Sorry you had to wait, but mixing is a process that won't tolerate a stop-and-start sort of attention."

She chuckled. "All that work just so someone can cock up his nose and compose his features into an expression of pompous dignity as he performs the solemn rite. Most men look as if they scorn the whole world when they take snuff."

"Not only men, my dear," he said, smiling at her. "Members of the fair sex also indulge."

"To be sure, but not nearly so many anymore, and women never make such a nonsensical ritual out of it."

"Not so. There once was a woman so devoted to snuff as to direct in her will that her coffin be filled with enough Scotch snuff to cover her body. Furthermore, the six greatest snuff-takers in her parish were to act as her pallbearers, wearing snuff-colored beaver hats instead of the usual funereal black."

"I don't believe you. You made that up."

He looked wounded. "I did not. Was there something in particular you wanted of me? I trust you are feeling better."

She blushed. "Much better. I came both to thank you and to apologize. It occurs to me now that I ought to have thanked Ching Ho, too, only I seem never to speak to him or he to me."

"Silent sort, is Ching," he said, "unless he has something he wishes to say. Generally, I find him restful."

"Meaning I talk too much, I suppose."

"I didn't say that. Is that the only reason you wished to talk to me? You did nothing for which you need apologize, you know, and I can think of no good reason for you to thank me."

"Well, I did have too much to drink last night. I hope I did not make a spectacle of myself."

"You did not. You were in high spirits, to be sure, but no more than anyone might expect on the anniversary of your birth."

"I haven't seen Godmama or Puck yet this morning."

"I promise you," he said with an understanding smile, "they will have noticed nothing amiss. And since Mama received one letter from Matilda and another from Nurse Helmer in the morning post, she will not have been thinking about you at all."

Carolyn grinned. "Did she, really? You know, Sydney, I don't recall that there was nearly so much skirmishing between them before we came here. Of course, when Godmama and I were in London for the Season, with Skipton and Matilda, the children were not with us, but before that, whenever I would visit, and even for the short period that I spent at Skipton Manor before we left for London, everyone was always very polite. It was only after we returned from London that your mama and Nurse Helmer seemed to form a coalition against Matlida and Miss Rumsey."

"The antagonism was just more subtly expressed before,"

Sydney said. "In case you haven't chanced to notice, my mama likes to rule the roast, and Matilda is rather a strong woman herself. I daresay Nurse and that governess . . . What did you call her, Rumsey?" When she nodded, he said, "Well, I think they are skirmishing for position. Nurse will lose, of course, because Matilda will make Skipton pension her off as soon as Stephen goes off to Eton—which explains why Nurse insists he is too sickly to go—and the governess will be kept on for young Harriet."

"Goodness, I believe you are right," Carolyn said, having not seen matters from this viewpoint before. "Did Nurse go on again about Stephen's ill health in today's letter?"

"I haven't a clue," he said, grinning. "When Mama's letter came, I was trapped in the room long enough to learn that Matilda, confirming that we are to go to them for Christmas, had suggested that would be the perfect opportunity for Mama to return what she calls the Louis-Fifteen table. For some reason, Mama did not choose to explain the matter in greater detail to me, and I refused to pursue it because I wanted to escape before hearing Nurse's latest grievances on behalf of the children. That woman used to terrify me. Still does, in fact. Treats me as though I'd never grown up. I'll wager she treats Skipton the same. If I were in his shoes, I'd have pensioned her off years ago."

"I daresay he is accustomed to her, you know," Carolyn said. "Furthermore, he pays no more heed to nursery matters than most gentlemen do. And in fairness to Matilda, though she must be fully aware that it is Nurse who keeps Godmama so well informed about the household, she also knows that it would be unthinkable to dismiss one who has served the family so long and well."

"Would it now?" he asked, smiling at her.

"You know it would. And say what you will, sir, I know you would not have dismissed her either."

"You know that for a fact, do you? Oh, Ching," he added when his manservant returned just then with the tray of articles he had taken away to clean, "I believe I forgot to mention that I shall have to attend a meeting of the turnpike trust this afternoon. I'll want to go to the stable shortly after one."

Ching Ho bowed. "At one, my master. I will see to the preparations."

"Yes, thank you. That will be all for now. You can put those things away later."

When the man had gone, Carolyn said with a chuckle, "He makes it sound as if he will have a great deal to do to see to the preparations, as he calls it, but I daresay it takes you a while to dress, does it not? Still, he could just as well have put those things away now. There is nearly an hour before you leave, and I should not have minded his presence. Indeed, I forgot, once again, to thank him for his remedy."

"He will not regard that," Sydney said, "and in point of fact, there is a small matter I wish to discuss privately with you. Since this is the one room that neither my mother nor Cousin Judith ever enter, it seems an excellent opportunity."

"What is it?"

He hesitated long enough for her to repeat her question before he said reluctantly, "It is about Lyndhurst."

"Lyndhurst?"

He gave her a rueful but teasing look and drawled, "You know the fellow. Large man, muscles, devilish leer in his—"

"Sydney, for goodness' sake, don't be absurd. You know perfectly well—"

"Sorry," he said. "The fact is, I don't like the fellow. He is not a . . . well, not a suita—"

"If I hear one more time," Carolyn cut in, gritting her teeth, "that he is not suitable for me to know or that he has a dangerous reputation—"

"Damn," Sydney swore, exasperated.

Carolyn said frostily, "I beg your pardon."

"That boot's on the other foot," he said with a sigh. "I should beg yours for making such a song about this, but the plain fact is that I think you are going to be displeased with me and I seem to be quaking as much as I did when Nurse used to say she rather thought my father would wish to know that I had been up to mischief. The truth is that I warned Lyndhurst off last night— told him he wasn't to keep pressing his attentions on you."

Carolyn was silent.

"I suppose you are vexed," he said, watching her as though

he would see into her mind. ''I know you dislike it when I—''

''I am not angry, Sydney,'' she said. ''I can't think why I'm not, but I'm not.''

''I thought you liked him,'' he said gently. ''You looked so merry when you danced with him, and when you put him off, I thought you were only flirting. But it won't do, Caro. It—''

''It was the wine, Sydney.'' She looked at him from under her lashes. ''It is the most lamentable thing,'' she said, ''but I cannot seem to care enough about any man to make a push to attract his interest. Oh, Lyndhurst is a romantic figure, I suppose—all those dark looks and his lordly manner. Indeed, I doubt that you have got rid of him at all, you know, but I find I don't much mind it if you have.''

''I'm glad of that.''

''Yes, but it is a depressing state of affairs, nonetheless. Do you not see? Here am I, already one-and-twenty years of age, and I have never truly been in love. Indeed, I doubt I shall ever fall in love, for I cannot imagine ever feeling such a deep passion for any man. I know what love ought to be, you see, for I have read any number of books that describe it in detail. Twice I even thought I might have found it, but I discovered my error on both occasions with the most amazing speed. I know I would have been miserable had I married either of those two wretched gentlemen, and I can tell you, I am very glad I have no stern papa to order me to marry where I cannot love.''

''You must never do that,'' he said firmly.

''You are such a good friend to me, Sydney,'' she said, reaching out to pat his hand. When he placed his other hand on hers, she looked at him for a long moment, aware of a rush of warmth through her body. But she rallied quickly and said, ''Now that you have routed my most promising suitor, sir, I hope you realize it is your duty to advise me what I must do next.''

He released her hand and glanced out the window before he said rather gruffly, ''You will come about, Caro. Do not let your imagined advancing years panic you into doing something you will regret. I cannot doubt that you will meet someone for whom you can develop the sort of tenderness you seek, and if you do not, you are always welcome at Bathwick Hill House.''

"Well, I believe I shall become a permanent pensioner then," she said. "I have looked over all the gentlemen in Bath, you know, and I doubt Godmama will take me to London again. However, I shall not repine. Perhaps I shall meet someone at Oatlands. Indeed," she added with an air of pensiveness not wholly belied by the sudden glint of mischief in her eyes, "perhaps I have not set my sights high enough. I do not approve of divorce, so the regent is out, but certainly a royal duke might do."

"My dear girl," Sydney said with an ominous frown, "if I thought for one moment that you were not jesting, I swear I would refuse to take you to Oatlands at all. A royal duke indeed! The most likely one to be there, besides York, is Cumberland, since he seems to have been chasing Prinny all over the map of late, and you would be most unwise to attract his notice."

"Is it true that he murdered his valet?" she asked with a look of polite interest.

"He says the boot was on the other foot," Sydney retorted, "that his French valet tried to kill him and the English one, an unctuous sort called Cornelius Neall, saved him, whereupon the Frenchman killed himself. Cumberland was hurt, because he is known to have recovered at Carlton House, but I don't know any more than that. In any event, Cumberland is not a suita—"

"Sydney," Carolyn said sweetly, "isn't it time you prepared for your meeting? I daresay it is already so late that you will never be dressed and away by one."

"Very true," he said, giving her a long look. "Ching will be waiting for me. And I suppose you want a nuncheon."

"Good Lord, no, I just ate," she said. "Moreover, since I wish to hear nothing about the disputed Louis table or about sickly Stephen, I mean to ride out or to walk in the garden."

"If you ride," he said with a smile, "beware of gypsies."

She made a face at him, and they walked upstairs together, completely in charity with each other again. When he left her at the door to her bedchamber, she went inside, thinking to ring for Maggie to help her change into her habit, but a moment's reflection convinced her that with only Cleves for company, such an outing would be a dull one. Moreover, the hat she customarily wore with her favorite habit needed mending, and although Maggie had said she would find glue to repair it, she had not yet done so. A walk in the garden, where there would be small chance of encountering the dowager to regale her with Matilda's latest offenses, would, she decided, do her just as much good.

As she made her way toward the east side of the house, she caught sight of Sydney and Ching Ho across the way, walking toward the stables. Since she had not thought Sydney could be ready to leave so soon, she was surprised to see them. She waved, but they did not see her, so she walked on to the garden, where by daylight, dressed warmly and with the sun shining on the hedged borders and gravel paths, she found it hard to believe she had been frightened the night before. She walked for a time along paths between mostly barren beds, then found a rustic seat near the end opposite the entrance and sat down.

A bird pecking at the brown earth drew her attention for a few moments, but then she allowed her thoughts to wander, barely aware of the songs of other birds in the trees and shrubbery, or the chattering of neighboring squirrels. Her thoughts moved first to the night before, then drifted idly and came to dwell at last upon Sydney.

Wondering why she had not reacted more to his warning off Lyndhurst, she remembered the night he had found her with the viscount in the hotel garden. She had not been vexed with him then either. Not until he had insisted that she trust his judgment over her own. The fact was that in most things she did trust him, and knew he would not willingly hurt her. But that did not mean his judgment of people was always better than hers. If she had misjudged one or two men, from time to time, or had let her flirtations sometimes go beyond what was wise, she had learned from her mistakes. For that was all they had been. And if now she sometimes had more confidence in herself just knowing Sydney was close at hand, that fact certainly had nothing to do with his judgment, only with the fact that he was a very good friend who took excellent care of her.

Sitting there on the bench, idly dreaming, she imagined herself the heroine of one of her favorite books, with a strong protector,

like Sydney, to look after her. Not as the hero, of course, for
Sydney was no hero, although he was a singularly attractive
man. She liked his slow smile, even his drawl, for his foppish
affectations delighted her despite the fact that she generally held
fops in contempt. It was the outside of enough, however, for
him to carry his protective instincts to such lengths as he did,
to have believed even for one minute that she had been serious
about flirting with the regent or Cumberland.

It might be fun, however, she mused lazily, to see if she could
stir him up a bit by doing that very thing. Since she could not
imagine any of the royal brothers taking her actions seriously,
she thought it might be the safest way to see if an exhibition
of her feminine wiles had the power to stir Sydney as childish
pranks never had. Indeed, she mused, perhaps she would even
flirt with Sydney himself, to try to make him see her as a woman
instead of a child who needed protection. The thought was a
tempting one, and she began to think the forthcoming visit to
Oatlands might be more interesting even than she had imagined.

When she left the garden at last, she saw Ching Ho coming
toward her from the stables and quickened her step, wanting
to thank him for his morning remedy, but she was diverted by
the sound of a carriage on the drive, and turned in time to see
Sydney in his curricle, disappearing out the gate toward the main
road. Knowing she had been in the garden for nearly an hour,
Carolyn stood for a long minute, wondering what on earth had
kept him so long in the stable. By the time she turned back
toward the house, Ching Ho had disappeared indoors.

8

The party from Bathwick Hill House arrived at Oatlands Park soon after midday the following Tuesday, having spent Monday night at Reading. They had their first view of the park from Sydney's luxurious traveling carriage when it reached the top of a hill from which they could also see Hampton Court Palace across the Thames. They could see only the rooftops of Oatlands, nestled in a thick growth of trees, until the carriage had passed the gate house and emerged from woodland onto the front drive. But compared with the magnificent structure seen just minutes before, the unpretentious blocklike house seemed to Carolyn to be very plain indeed, and she did not hesitate to say so.

"I have no great opinion of the Duke of York," Lady Skipton said unnecessarily, "but I give credit where it is due. When that elegant old Palladian manor house they first moved into burned down—fifteen years ago, that must be now—he might have let the whole place go, but knowing how Frederica loved it, he built her a new house at once. And, as you will soon see, my dear, though the facade is plain, the interior is perfectly splendid. Indeed, I believe Frederica might be altogether content if York could but try to behave himself. But he never will learn. The regent ought never to have reinstated him as commander of the army. 'Tis that sort of misguided forbearance that encourages York to misbehave."

Sydney, who had been dozing beside Miss Pucklington in the forward seat until Carolyn had spoken, regarded his parent sleepily from beneath drooping eyelids. "Really, Mama, one can scarcely blame Prinny for his brothers' misdeeds, and you must admit that of the lot, York is the best. Only contrast him with the wicked Cumberland, if you will. Moreover, York and his duchess were not on speaking terms for months before the Clarke scandal. At least now they appear to be friendly."

"I don't know that York is the best of them," Carolyn said provocatively. "The Duke of Cambridge must surely be thought unexceptionable. And while Clarence's language is a trifle unbecoming and Kent is thought to be rather severe, I have heard that both Cambridge and Sussex are pleasant gentlemen."

"One must be extremely tolerant, however," Sydney said, "to dismiss a score of mistresses—and in Sussex's case even wives—"

"Not a score of wives, surely," she murmured.

He was given no chance to reply, for the dowager, intent as always upon her own train of thought, declared positively, "I believe Frederica must have always been willing to speak to York, you know. That she remained at his side throughout that awful business—in London, too, when she don't like the place—is a conspicuous manifestation of her strong sense of duty to him. As for the scandal itself, I do not pretend to understand how Mrs. Clarke was able to sell army commissions, but she is a scandal in herself and has been so these many years past. However, here we are, and so we will say no more about it."

The carriage drew to a halt, the door was opened, the steps let down, and when no one emerged from the house to greet them, the dowager accepted Sydney's assistance to descend to the drive. Carolyn followed, glad to escape the confines of the carriage at last, and drew a long breath of the crisp, damp air while she waited for the others to emerge. The second carriage, containing the dowager's lofty dresser as well as Ching Ho, Maggie, and most of the baggage, drew up behind them, but still no servant appeared from the house to attend to them.

Leaving their minions to deal with the baggage, they passed up the wide stone steps, beneath a high semicircular portico supported on marble columns, through wide open double oak doors, into the lofty hall, where the royal porter condescended to greet them and beckon forth a footman to escort them to their rooms.

Carolyn found herself at last in a spacious pink-and-gray bed-chamber overlooking extensive gardens north of the house. The room was lavishly decorated with satin hangings, a massive crystal-and-gilt chandelier, and heavily carved cherry furniture resting on a thick Axminster carpet. The only detail of which she disapproved was the large, dirty gray mongrel curled up on the counterpane.

The dog lifted its head to regard her curiously when she entered the room, then laid it to rest again upon its forepaws without making any more overt attempt to greet her. She turned in dismay to the footman who had escorted her.

He grinned, looking at once younger and much less stately. "I'll take him away, miss. Like as not he won't be the last to visit you, howsomever, being as her highness's pets have no manners and go where they please. Just you ring for a maid if you find any more where it don't suit you to find them, and I'll have that counterpane changed at once. You won't want to be smelling that fellow all through the night."

"Thank you," Carolyn said faintly, watching as he strode across the carpet and snapped his fingers at the dog. Without so much as lifting its head, it looked up at him with indifference.

"Come along now," the footman said sternly. "You ain't wanted here, lad."

When the dog continued to ignore him, the young man finally lifted him bodily and turned to carry him out. The dog made no protest, but Carolyn exclaimed, "It is too bad to make you do this! You will have dog hairs all over your livery."

The footman, shifting the dog's weight, grinned at her again and said, "Lord love you, miss, but we all of us have dog hairs all over us, as does most of the furniture and all of the rugs in the place. 'Tis more than the maids can do to keep the carpets brushed from day to day, but if they did not keep a-trying, we'd soon be buried in the stuff."

"Goodness," Carolyn said, awed.

From what she had seen, she doubted any other servant would come, but the footman proved as good as his word, and the cover was changed before Maggie arrived with her baggage. A short time later, having changed her traveling dress for an afternoon frock of jonquil silk, Carolyn was trying to decide whether she should go in search of the dowager or simply remain where she was until someone sent for her, when Sydney rapped at her door, offering to accompany her downstairs to meet their hostess. Delighted to see him, she told him instantly about her canine visitor.

Sydney leveled his quizzing glass at her, looking her up and down before affecting his foppish drawl to say, "That dress becomes you, my dear. Makes me glad I chose this waistcoat instead of the first one Ching had out. Bustled with crimson songbirds, don't you know, and wouldn't have looked near as well with your gown as this white-and-gold thing does."

"Sydney, did you hear what I said to you? There was a dog—and one that would be hard-pressed to name his ancestors, I can tell you—sleeping on my bed. It was utterly filthy."

"It's gone now, isn't it? You oughtn't to let such stuff distress you if you mean to enjoy yourself here, Caro, for the duchess's dogs are bound to be all over the place. I daresay you'll find more than one underfoot even when we dine. I don't mind telling you, it makes me damned glad you managed to convince Mama to leave her wretched Hercules behind."

"But doesn't she ever wash them?"

"Mama? Certainly not. The servants—"

"You know I meant the duchess, Sydney," she retorted, her voice taking on a dangerous edge.

"Can't imagine her highness washing a dog, either."

Choking back a sudden, irrepressible gurgle of laughter, Carolyn shook her head at him. "You are altogether abominable, sir, and I shan't talk to you anymore. It must be the effect of this house. No doubt the inhabitants are all as crazy as loons and the affliction is a contagious one."

He gave her a direct look then and said without the drawl, "Don't offer that suggestion to anyone else, Caro. It makes no odds what you say to me, but there are men hereabouts who would take offense at such words, and some of them are dangerous.''

"Goodness, you sound grim," she said, "but you needn't fret, you know. I should certainly never say any such thing to the duke or the duchess.''

His expression relaxed. "I doubt if either one would take offense. York is too amiable and the duchess holds by that old Scottish proverb, 'Live and let live.' But others, whom it would no doubt behoove you to avoid altogether, are not so tolerant. If you cannot avoid them, Caro, at least set a guard on that impertinent tongue of yours.''

She had forgotten her determination to use her wiles to teach him a lesson, but she remembered it just in time to avoid telling him sharply that she would thank him to keep his advice to himself. Instead, lowering her lashes and looking up at him from beneath them, she said, "I shall certainly try to keep that in mind, sir, for I have no wish to displease you.''

Sydney gave her a long, suspicious look, and when she met it limpidly, he said at last in a sardonic tone, "I mentioned the matter only because I should not like you to displease anyone else, Caro—Cumberland, for example.''

"I have never actually met the Duke of Cumberland," she observed demurely, smoothing an imaginary wrinkle from her skirt.

"Now, that's precisely the sort of thing I mean," he informed her sharply. "Don't go making a cake of yourself. You'd do much better to play least in sight with him.''

"But you told me that most of what is said about him is only rumors," she said, fluttering her lashes. "I am persuaded that he cannot have done the half of what he has been accused of doing.''

"Less than half would be enough," Sydney retorted as they turned a corner and found themselves in an elegantly appointed anteroom. She thought he sounded a bit exasperated, but before she could press the matter further, a footman got up from an armchair near the opposite door and Sydney told him their names.

Nodding, the man said, "Follow me, sir. Her highness is receiving in the drawing room.''

There was time for no more private conversation after that, since they were taken directly to the duchess, whom they found in an enormous, high-ceilinged room, surrounded by laughing and chattering members of the *beau monde*, as well as a number of dogs with noticeably less-distinguished pedigrees. Frederica, Duchess of York, was seated in an armchair, receiving her guests with a tiny, bright-eyed, red-capped monkey in her lap.

When the footman announced their names, the duchess greeted Sydney as an old acquaintance and demanded at once to know where his mother was, thus giving Carolyn a brief moment after she arose from her curtsy, while Sydney explained that Lady Skipton was indulging in her usual afternoon nap and would no doubt be down soon, to collect herself and observe her hostess.

It was often said of the Duchess of York that not only was she the most popular member of the royal family but the only one among them who knew how to hold court. Indeed, Oatlands was called "the little court" by many, and nearly everyone who knew its mistress had only good things to say about her. Frederica was known for her dignity, her charm, her humor, and her charity. She was not, however, noted for her beauty.

Even shorter than Carolyn, she was particularly tiny next to her husband, who stood chatting with a guest beside her chair. She wore an expertly cut gown of china blue to match her eyes, and with her flaxen hair modestly arranged, she made a passable showing, but Carolyn thought it a pity that Frederica's teeth were so poor, and unfortunate that she had been marked by the smallpox in her youth. The duchess had had no beauty to spare.

Sydney begged leave to present Carolyn, and when Frederica nodded regally one moment, only to chuckle and shoo him away the next, saying she wished to get to know Miss Hardy without him hovering over them, Carolyn responded instantly to the warmth and sincerity of the welcome and promptly forgot the duchess's looks.

With an accent and manner more French than German, which gave her words a pleasing, musical quality and her gestures a bubbling vitality, Frederica said, "We are very pleased that you come to us, child, and hope you will enjoy your visit. Sit still, you."

Although the rider was clearly addressed to the monkey, which had suddenly evinced a desire to peer down the duchess's décolletage, Carolyn had all she could do to maintain her gravity as she replied, "Indeed, your royal highness, I should be very odd if I did not like it here, for I have heard much about the wealth of hospitality to be enjoyed at Oatlands."

"You must see my grotto," the duchess said in a confiding tone, her eyes atwinkle, "for it is of all places my favorite. You may bathe there, if you like," she added, feeding the monkey a nut from a little dish on the table beside her, "although I must warn you that the water—particularly at this season—is like ice. Only the bravest dare make the plunge."

Carolyn smiled as the monkey shoved the treat into its mouth and reached greedily for another. "I am not so brave, ma'am, but if the weather does not grow much colder, I shall certainly like to explore your gardens, and I am persuaded that I will find all manner of other things to do as well."

"Indeed, you will, child. And all manner of handsome gentlemen will beg leave to accompany you, I make no doubt."

A snort of laughter from her spouse showed her he had overheard her words. He exclaimed, "Well said, my dear, well said! Daresay the chit'll have the lads all atwitter. Pretty little thing, ain't she? Do I know you?" he demanded of Carolyn. "Daresay I ought to remember you, but I don't."

Carolyn curtsied. "We have not been introduced, your royal highness. Though I was presented to her majesty and to the regent on two occasions, I have never had the pleasure of making your acquaintance."

"Very pretty," observed the duke, but since she was uncertain whether he meant her words or her appearance, she had not the least notion of what to reply to him. Fortunately, he shared with Lady Skipton that trait of being able to converse at length without benefit of response from his audience. "You shall walk with me when you are done exchanging witticisms with my dear Frederica," he said, adding as he turned back to the guest he had been speaking to before, "Mark me, you'll not outwit her."

The duchess smiled at Carolyn's startled expression. "Do not heed him. 'Tis only his way of funning. I am well educated but not nearly intelligent enough to be called clever. Therefore do I invite to Oatlands persons like Mr. Brummell and Lord Alvanley, who are deservedly noted for their wit and who amuse me. Mr. Brummell does not honor us on this occasion, but Alvanley . . . Oh," she said in a different, less animated tone, looking beyond Carolyn, "you did say you had been presented to the regent, did you not?" Then, politely, she added, "Sir, perhaps you will condescend to remember Miss Carolyn Hardy."

Carolyn turned to find that the Prince Regent had come up directly behind her. Sinking into another deep curtsy, she was conscious of a fleeting hope that her narrow skirts, not to mention her knees, would survive the visit. If several royal dukes joined the company, plus the Princess Charlotte, she might well spend the greater part of her time bobbing up and down.

Allowing his gaze to drift over her person as she arose, the portly regent smiled and said affably, "Damme, but I could never forget so lovely a lady, and here is Alvanley to talk with you, ma'am, so you'll not miss her if I steal her away. We met in London, Miss Hardy, as I am persuaded you will remember," he added as the plump, round-faced Alvanley stepped forward to make his bow to the duchess.

"I remember, your royal highness," Carolyn said, returning the regent's smile as he drew her away from the duchess and hoping as she had hoped on earlier occasions that she would not somehow betray the mild contempt in which, like so many others, she had come to hold him. "I am flattered to think you would remember me among so many ladies of much greater beauty."

He responded gallantly, flirting with her, reminding her by his attitude that he was known as the First Gentleman of Europe. A few moments later, when he observed Sydney some distance away and announced that he had one or two matters to discuss with him, she curtsied again and watched him walk away, thinking that he was growing fatter than ever but that his increasing bulk didn't seem to distress him in the least. His manner was as elegant and polished as it could be.

Indeed, she thought, so polished were the royal manners that it had been impossible to tell by their behavior that the regent and the royal duchess were anything but friends, despite the fact that, as everyone knew, he rarely spoke to her, having taken offense at her refusal to associate with his mistress, Lady Hertford. For her part, the duchess was said to care little for any of the royal family, including her own spouse, who visited her only when he brought a party of friends to Oatlands to hunt or to play whist into the small hours of the morning.

Carolyn, watching idly now to see if Sydney would offer the regent his snuffbox at once, was alone for only a moment before the Duke of York approached and said in his bluff voice, "You mustn't think I had forgotten you, my pretty one."

She smiled at him. "I am not so conceited as to believe you ought to have remembered me, sir, particularly when your house is filled with so many other visitors."

He looked around as though he saw the large company for the first time. "Begad, so it is," he said, "but pay them no heed. I shall not, nor shall my Freddie when she tires of their conversation. Both of us a bit queer in our attics, I daresay, though not so queer as Ernest there." He indicated a man with bristling gray side-whiskers, wearing green regimentals, and a patch over one eye, who was watching them intently. "My brother Cumberland, you know. Can't think why he's even looking this way, since he ain't generally one for the ladies, but perhaps he saw you talking to Georgie—the regent, you know. He always wants what Georgie wants. Been like that from a child, poor fellow. But never mind him. I thought perhaps you might like to walk about with me a bit, perhaps see something of this place."

She didn't wish to do any such thing. Although his bluff manner and easy habits made it easy to talk to him, and the one pleasant advantage of having come of age lay in being able to move about freely without feeling guilty if Miss Pucklington or the dowager were not near at hand, she would not have minded the presence just now of a proper chaperon, for when York offered his arm, she could not imagine telling him to his face that she did not want to leave the room with him. However, they had walked for only a few moments before Sydney approached them.

"There you are, my dear Carolyn," he said languidly, nodding to the duke. "You'll forgive us, highness, but my mother has come downstairs and desires me to fetch Miss Hardy to her."

"Very well," the duke said, smiling at Carolyn. "We must have our walk another time, pretty one. Saint-Denis, Brummell gave me a new bit of lacquerware last week. Like you to have a look at it while you're here."

"I daresay if he gave it to you, sir, it is a fine piece and one that I should be most pleased to see. Allow me to deliver Miss Hardy to my mother before you indulge me, however."

The duke dismissed them with a nod, and Carolyn waited only until they were out of royal earshot before saying tartly, "Deliver me? You make me sound like a parcel, Sydney, and you are behaving yet again in a perfectly gothic manner. I doubt that Godmama expressed any sort of a wish for my presence, for she will have Puck with her and will be wishing to speak with the duchess, so she cannot even want me."

"I don't know if she does, but I didn't know any better way to get you out of York's clutches," Sydney said. "In any event, she has come downstairs and the duchess has gone somewhere, so you'd best stay with Mama for a bit. Keep you out of mischief."

"Good gracious," she said, "I am perfectly capable of managing my own affairs. Am I to understand that you winkled me away from the Duke of York because you think he cannot be trusted to keep the line? I never heard of such a thing."

"Just so," he said, nodding as though she had said something wise. "I knew you couldn't have heard much about York beyond common gossip. Stands to reason you wouldn't heed what Mama told you, knowing she don't like him, and in any event, I believe she does not keep the sort of eye out that she should."

"On me, do you mean?" Carolyn inquired gently.

"That is precisely what I mean."

"Well, you are talking nonsense. I don't need to be looked after like a child, and I will thank you to remember that."

"The thing is," Sydney said in a musing tone as though she

had not spoken, "one cannot expect you to know when the royal lads are amusing themselves, and you might think one or another means more by his behavior than he does. That happens, I'm told, to the most sensible of females. Each thinks that despite the infamous Marriage Act, which clearly prevents their marrying where they choose, she will somehow end up a royal duchess."

"One cannot indulge such hopes with regard to the regent or York," Carolyn reminded him. "They are already married."

"But as you yourself pointed out, Cumberland isn't, nor Clarence, nor Cambridge, nor Susssex, nor Kent."

"But all of them except Cumberland, *you* said, have wives or mistresses, so therefore Cumberland is the only—"

Sydney's air of indolence vanished. "See here, Carolyn," he said abruptly, "don't be such a little fool! I daresay," he added more calmly, having visibly taken control of himself, "that your fortune isn't large enough to tempt them beyond flirtation, but I wouldn't trust even York, with his duchess on the premises, to keep the line. As to Prinny or Cumberland . . ."

When he paused, clearly at a loss for what to say that would convince her, Carolyn, feeling truly mischievous now and wanting to see how far she could press him, widened her eyes and said encouragingly, "Yes, Sydney? What about them?"

"Dash it all," he said, "I don't trust you any farther than I trust them. If I'm such a cod's head as to tell you again to keep away from them, I know you well enough to guess you'll bid them 'come hither' if only to vex me. On the other hand, if I don't warn you and you fall afoul of one of them, I'll wish I'd spoken up. I'll tell you this, though. If I had any real authority over you, you'd soon learn to pay heed to me."

She was surprised by such vehemence, but not enough to let him preach restraint to her. "I shall attempt to remember your advice," she said politely.

Although she could see that he was not deceived, he said no more, delivering her in silence to the dowager's side. Then, offering as his excuse that York had said he had something to show him, he turned away again at once and left them.

"Dear me, Carolyn," Lady Skipton said, "what a sad crush this is, to be sure." One can scarcely blame Frederica for absenting herself, though one trusts she will recall our presence in time to join us for dinner."

Miss Pucklington said, "One wonders how many more persons even this great house can hold, does one not? But I believe it will be bursting at the seams by the time the princess's ball begins tomorrow night. Do you not agree, Cousin Olympia?"

But the dowager's attention had wandered. "I see that Frederica has not extended to Lord Yarmouth her disapproval of his mama's connection with the regent," she said with a sniff. "There he is now with his lady beside him—a flighty piece, I believe, but one could expect no less from a woman whom no less than three men have claimed to father and whose mother was an Italian ballet dancer!" She went on in this vein for several moments, pointing out others among the company whom she deigned to recognize and comment upon.

Carolyn, listening with but half an ear, looked about for friends of her own until it occurred to her that in such a collection of the *beau monde* she might see one or another of the gentlemen to whom she had so briefly been betrothed. She was startled enough by this unwelcome thought, and so intent upon her scrutiny thereafter that she ceased to hear her god-mother's voice and did not notice when she became separated from the other two ladies until, stepping back to make way for a couple to pass her, she bumped into the Duke of York.

"My dear Miss Hardy," he exclaimed, "how comes it about that I find you alone again?"

"Hardly alone, sir, merely unaccompanied." She smiled. "I had two companions but a moment ago, who appear to have been swallowed up by this crowd."

"More fools, they," he said, "to have left such a little beauty behind."

She grinned at him. "I am no different from all the other ladies who enjoy your pretty compliments, sir, so I hesitate to confess that those who left me are female, lest you should regret your kind words to me."

He laughed heartily. "Impossible! But do folks truly say that of me? Fancy your telling me that. Quite puffs me up in my own esteem to hear that, don't you know? Here, Ernest, do you hear what Miss Hardy has said? I am the man to come to for compliments. Not a mistake anyone would make about you, eh?"

Despite his unmistakable uniform, Carolyn had not seen the Duke of Cumberland following in York's wake, and she curtsied quickly when he stepped forward and said in his harsh way, "I do not know Miss Hardy."

"Well, it won't do you any good if I present you," York said, laughing again and winking at Carolyn. "Already said I pay the handsomest compliments, didn't she, and even if that weren't the case, our Georgie has his eye upon her. You don't want to distress him, I daresay."

"That point has never weighed heavily with me," Cumberland said, his gaze resting intently enough upon Carolyn to put her forcibly in mind of Viscount Lyndhurst and to send a delicious thrill of danger racing up her spine.

York said, "Did you ever see such a fellow, Miss Hardy?" Only fancy his continuing to wear the Hanoverian uniform, as he does, when poor Hanover has been in Boney's clutches these six years and more. And there's no good to be got by looking daggers at me, Ernest, not if you wish to cajole me into presenting her."

Carolyn looked directly at Cumberland and smiled, saying, "What must we do, sir, if he will not present me? I have heard of your great courage in battle and cannot believe that you would let so small a point defeat you."

Interest quickened in Cumberland's eyes, making her fear for a brief moment that she had gone too far and he would think her impertinent or worse. That would never do.

Lowering her gaze, she bit her lip, then said contritely, "I should not have spoken so. Forgive me. It was unmannerly. I allowed myself to be carried away by such elevated company."

York shook his head, saying, "Now, now, my pretty, don't distress yourself. If anyone's manners are at fault, they are mine, for I ought to have presented you at once. Temptation was too great to put a rub in Ernest's way, don't you know. This is Miss Carolyn Hardy, Ernest. M' brother Cumberland, ma'am.''

By the time Carolyn's attention was reclaimed ten minutes later by her godmother, who expressed herself astonished to have seen her putting herself forward in such a way, she believed she had accomplished a great deal. She had certainly stirred Sydney up even before she had actually conversed with the royal dukes, for she could not remember any other time when he had spoken so crisply to her.

Of course, she had also discovered that it was not as easy as she had thought it would be to play the coquette with him, for no sooner had she attempted to flirt than he had pricked her temper so that she had spoken to him in her customary manner. And although she hoped she knew herself better than to think, despite his warnings, that she could be led astray by a man for no reason other than his high estate, she had also discovered that there were snares to be avoided where royal dukes were concerned. She did think she would avoid the snares if she took care, but it had not occurred to her until York had invited her to walk apart with him that to refuse a royal invitation was by no means so easy as to refuse one from someone like Mr. Manningford or Viscount Lyndhurst.

York, she thought, would be fairly easy. He seemed inclined to light flirtation and she doubted he would press her if she did not encourage him to do so. And the regent was too exalted a fish to leap at any bait of her casting, but she knew also that he would be too polite to rebuff her outright if she chanced to cross his way. And, after all, she wished only for Sydney to *think* she was flirting with him.

Cumberland was another matter, for his reputation was quite as dangerous as any young lady addicted to romance could possibly wish, and Sydney was by no means the first or only person to have warned her against him. With that black patch over his eye and his menacing demeanor, his appearance alone was sinister. Certainly, no one would ever mistake him for the First Gentleman of Europe, but he had stayed talking with her for a full ten minutes by the clock on the duchess's mantelpiece, and she had got away unscathed. Best of all, Sydney had seen her, for she had observed him, standing with the regent and

Lord and Lady Yarmouth. If she played her cards right, she decided, before their visit was done, Sydney would have to acknowledge that she could manage all the gentlemen of her acquaintance without his interference or protection.

9

Carolyn had no further opportunity to practice her wiles on the royal brothers before dinner, or for the three-quarters of an hour afterward when she and the other ladies were left to their own devices while the gentlemen lingered over their port. But when the men returned to the drawing room, the regent soon joined the group of which she was a part. This was not wholly due to chance, for having noted earlier his partiality for Lord and Lady Yarmouth, she had taken care to seat herself near her ladyship, a plump woman of forty, and to engage her in conversation.

At first the group's conversation was general, but since the regent always had an eye for a pretty face, it required no great effort on Carolyn's part to engage his attention, and soon the others drew away, leaving them to themselves. She knew that he had honored her as much for her sympathetic ear as for any other reason, but that made no difference, especially when she saw Sydney, his eyes narrowed, watching them from a short distance away where he was engaged in a conversation of his own.

The regent complained just then that he had rather have been playing whist. "M' brother York's games are always amusing," he said. "Stakes are a bit high for those of us not so plump in the pockets as others, but I enjoy the company and the sport, damme if I don't. 'Tis a shame I must wait about, kicking m' heels, as I must. But 'tis always the way, waiting and waiting for things to happen, and for things that never do,'' he added morosely.

"That is tiresome, sir, certainly, but why must you?"

"Well, there's always m' father, don't you know? Being regent ain't the same as being king, not by a long chalk. But that's by the way. Tonight I'm waiting for m' daughter, and the chit's late as usual, damme if she ain't. No consideration, this modern generation, none at all."

"I did know that the Princess Charlotte was expected to arrive this evening," Carolyn said cautiously, aware that she must say nothing that might be construed as criticism of the regent, his daughter, or indeed, any of the royal family, even if it should be by way of agreement with him.

There was no need for her to say more, however, for the prince retorted testily, "Of course, she's arriving tonight. Damned ball tomorrow's in her honor, ain't it? Frederica's arranged the whole thing for Charlotte's amusement, hasn't she, all because she thinks we ought to be putting a good face on things, not letting the quizzes put about the sort of stories they delight in—daresay you know the muck I mean."

"Yes, sir."

"Damme, but it's a nuisance, fretting about what people say or even what they might think, doing the fancy, showing everyone we can be as cozy as the next family. Daresay, next they'll say I must show m'self cozy again with Ernest,'' he added, glancing at Cumberland, who was engaged in conversation nearby with Lord Alvanley, who looked for once not only as if his wit had deserted him but as if he were a trifle bored.

Carolyn made an encouraging noise, and the regent sighed, saying, "I don't like Ernest being here, I can tell you that. Bad enough when he moved into Carlton House with me, saying he needed a place to recuperate after his damned valet tried to murder him, and then followed me down to Brighton. And, damme, but his servants are as much of a nuisance as he is. There is that sneaksby Neall now, speaking to him. Dashed well ought to have sent a footman, for with a Friday face like his, he'll frighten all the ladies, damme if he won't."

Carolyn turned to look at Cumberland and Alvanley again

and saw that another man had joined them, a man wearing a plain black suit of clothes and a deferential manner. "I daresay he couldn't find a footman, sir. That man in his highness's new valet?"

"Not new," replied the regent, grimacing. "Wish he would get a new one, damme if I don't. Cornelius Neall's been with him for donkey's years. Can't think why he stays."

"But I thought you said his valet had tried to mur—"

"Well, upon my soul, Miss Hardy, a man has more than one valet, don't he? Sellis was Ernest's French valet; Neall is English. Not that there is much else to choose between them. But Ernest will have it that Neall saved his life. If you want my opinion on that matter, I don't believe Sellis killed himself afterward at all. No, no, I believe Neall helped him out a bit, if you follow my meaning, though I beg you will say nothing."

"No, sir, I won't." She looked more narrowly at Cornelius Neall and decided that he looked quite as sinister as his master.

"That pair would put a damper on anyone's party," the regent said, following her gaze. "Oh, there now, Ernest has sent Neall away again, but only look at that poor fellow, Alvanley. Daresay I ought to rescue him. Here, Alvanley, I want you."

For a moment, Carolyn thought Cumberland would accompany the younger man, for he glanced at her and took a step toward them, but then he apparently changed his mind, satisfying himself instead with a scornful sneer at his brother as he turned away.

Alvanley, only two years her senior, was of a naturally kind and affectionate disposition, but although he was good-natured, obliging, inclined to be generous, and she liked him very much, he had made it clear that he was not hanging out for a wife, and he did not flirt. Even if he had been of a flirtatious nature, she would not have encouraged him, for his habits were not all as generally delightful as his personality.

The regent greeted him cheerfully. "Ho, Alvanley, fleeing your creditors again, I hear. Ain't poverty a damned nuisance?"

Alvanley chuckled and lisped, "Curthed duns made thuch a noithe every morning latht week, I couldn't get a moment'th retht till I ordered the knocker taken off the door to make 'em think me out of town. Couldn't expect to fool 'em longer than a day or two, though, tho I deemed it thmarter to leave than to thtay.''

The regent laughed and poked Carolyn in the arm with his elbow. "There, didn't I tell you? Damned amusing fellow!" Then, to Alvanley, he added, "Told Miss Hardy here you deserved we should rescue you from Ernest, so damme if we didn't.''

"And I thank you," Alvanley said promptly. "Withkerandoeth wath more of a bore than he usually ith. I could have put up with that, I thuppose—dash it, a fellow can't tell a printh he ith a tirethome fellow—but one doeth draw the line at being polite to hith valet.''

The regent chuckled and said to Carolyn, "M' daughter named Ernest Prince Wiskerandos. Deuced good name for him, what?"

Noting that Sydney was no longer in sight, Carolyn responded a trifle absentmindedly and soon begged leave to excuse herself, pleading a long day's travel and a wish to retire. The regent chose to be benevolent, and although it was not easy to escape so easily from the company at large, she finally reached the solitude of her own bedchamber, where she found Maggie waiting to undress her. Less than an hour later, she was fast asleep.

She awoke later than usual the following morning to learn from a disapproving Maggie that most of the household was not only still asleep but was expected to remain abed for several hours longer.

"Good gracious," Carolyn exclaimed, "everyone?"

"Most of them stayed up till dawn, miss," Maggie said. Upon entering the rooms, she had set down the heavy tray to open the curtains, and she turned now from the window to fetch it and carry it to Carolyn, saying as she did so, "The gentlemen play cards, and since the duchess don't sleep much at all, the ladies feel they must do like her. Lady Skipton's woman told me even her ladyship didn't retire till after two, and you know how she likes her sleep, miss. But knowing the duchess like she does, I suppose she thought it was expected of her.''

Carolyn had long since decided that no one knew the duchess as well as the dowager claimed to know her. Her highness

seemed to be a very private person, and although she had pre-
sided over the dinner table the previous evening, she had not
so much as shown herself in the great drawing room afterward.
It was said that on such occasions she preferred to retire to the
grotto in the garden, where she might read her books and play
with her dogs. Carolyn, shifting the laden tray to a more
comfortable position, decided she wanted to see this famous
grotto.

"I'll wear my lavender habit, Maggie," she said, "for I want
to ride later, but I think I'll explore the gardens first, so you
needn't send word to the stables immediately."

"Won't do a bit of good sending word, Miss Carolyn,"
Maggie told her as she paused near the wardrobe, making no
attempt to find the habit. "The duke and duchess don't provide
horses for their guests, and since you didn't bring your
own . . ."

"No horses? I never heard of such a thing."

"Well, and that ain't all," Maggie told her. "If there's
breakfast laid out anywheres hereabouts, I've yet to learn where
it be. One of the maids I spoke to—one as lives here, that is—
told me I'd best go to the kitchens myself to say what's wanted,
but she weren't altogether sure that speaking to the cook would
do any good at all. And from what I've seen of the serving folk
in this place, royal house or not, it would surprise me to discover that the cook is not still abed and sound asleep."

Carolyn gestured to the tray on her lap. "But what about all
this? There are boiled eggs and ham, coffee, jam, toast, even
muffins—much more than you generally bring me when I wake.
I shan't eat the half of it."

Maggie said, "It was Ching Ho saw to all that, miss. He's
a wonder, that Chinaman is."

Thoughtfully, Carolyn turned her attention to her breakfast,
and when she had finished, Maggie helped her into a soft blue
velvet frock and half-boots, with a red wool, hooded cape to
keep out the chill, and she sallied forth to explore the grounds.
Leaving by way of the main entrance, she turned toward the
river and soon came to a path leading between wide, surprisingly
colorful flower beds, toward dense woodland that provided a
lush green background for the formal garden. Knowing there

must be a path through the woods to the river, she kept walking, glad of the solitude, with only her thoughts for company.

"Can you be searching for anyone in particular?"

She nearly jumped out of her skin at the sound of Sydney's voice, and although she realized who it was at once and with a surprising rush of pleasure, she did not hesitate to say sharply, "I don't know how you do that. I didn't hear a sound as you came up behind me, and we are walking on gravel, for pity's sake."

"You were lost in your thoughts," he said. "I trust you slept well."

"Yes," she admitted with a reluctant smile, "and breakfasted well, too, thanks to Ching Ho. I hope you will express my gratitude to him. Maggie tells me I would most likely have starved had he not arranged for my breakfast."

"We have stayed here before, you see," he said, regarding her lazily. "I like that cape. The color suits you very well."

"Thank you, but don't change the subject," she said. "This is the oddest house, is it not? There must be hundreds of horses in the stables, yet none for guests to ride, and hundreds of servants, yet we must rely on our own if we are to eat before dinnertime. I daresay we can all be glad that you have been here before, for Godmama would probably blame poor Puck or her own woman if she could not get her morning chocolate, and what she will say if Ching Ho had not contrived to provide her breakfast, I cannot think." She shot him an oblique look. "He will attend to her as he did to me, will he not?"

"He will," Sydney said, taking her hand and tucking it into the crook of his arm, drawing her toward the woods. "I daresay Mama knows the way of things here as well as Ching Ho and I do, however," he added, "knowing her highness as well as she does."

She looked up at him suspiciously, but she could not tell if he was joking or not. Nor did it matter much, she decided, smiling at him. "Did you stay up till dawn with the others?"

"I am not much of a hand at whist," he said gently. "Hush now. Listen to the birds' songs, and if you watch the shrubbery just along here, you may even see a red fox. The animals know they are safe so near to the house, for the duchess's dogs are so overfed and lazy, they don't trouble to chase any of them."

As they walked together in silence, Carolyn was suddenly aware that she was quite alone with him, and found herself watching him instead of the shrubbery, wondering how it was that she had not noticed before how handsome he was. Of course, she told herself firmly, one generally didn't think in such terms about men with whom one lived and with whom one had been alone countless times before. And, too, before she had come to live at Bathwick Hill, she had thought of him only as one of the grownups she knew, not as a friend or companion—or, as was now the case, one with whom she had decided to flirt. Not that anything would come of that, she decided with a sigh. She had not yet given up looking for true love, and Sydney was no one's notion of a hero.

To be sure, he was a comfortable companion, a man she could trust, and a reliable friend, but he was definitely not a hero. In point of fact, he was often rather silly, particularly when he worried more about creasing his coat or snagging a fingernail than he did about important matters. Still, she thought, turning at last to peer into the shrubbery along the path in hopes of seeing some small, trusting animal, just now, in this very odd household, his presence was a very great comfort.

When a gray squirrel skittered up the trunk of a tree only feet away from her to be greeted by a raucous, chattering diatribe from its mate, she laughed aloud. "I believe that gentleman must have been away all night. Naughty man!"

"Most likely, he came home without bringing his greedy wife something to eat," Sydney said. When she glanced up at him, she saw that his eyes were twinkling as though he waited for her to debate the matter. She stuck out her tongue at him instead and was oddly pleased when he chuckled.

She could smell the river now, and when she looked ahead, she could see it, the current moving swiftly as it flowed past Oatlands landing. A moment later they came to the towpath, and she could see Hampton Court Palace upriver on the distant shore.

"Wasn't Oatlands once a royal palace, too?" she asked. "One also belonging to Henry the Eighth?"

"It was."

"Well, wasn't it a trifle extravagant of him to have two of them built so close together?"

"He didn't build Hampton Court," he pointed out. "He merely acquired it. There are others even closer together than these, and in any case, Henry was not a king noted for his fiscal prudence. He commanded a veritable spate of royal building, you know—no doubt in rebellion against the frugality of his father's reign—but whatever his reason, there was so much of it that his nobles were unable to find craftsmen to work for them. He kept nabbing the best ones for his palaces."

"Is that when the grotto was built here?"

"No, that was much later. Have you seen it?"

"No, I thought it must be along this path."

"It isn't. You must take the path through the rose garden. I'll show you later, but now it's time we were getting back."

"I thought Maggie said everyone would sleep past noon."

"Not everyone. The Princess Charlotte arrived late last night, but she is an earlier riser and others will emulate her. Have you been presented to her?"

"No, for she's only fifteen, after all, and was never present at any function I attended. Do you know her?"

He nodded. "Met her on several occasions, mostly here, but I spoke once with her at Carlton House, when I was permitted the honor of advising her father on some Chinese soapstone figures he wanted to purchase."

"Will you present me to her, as you did to the duchess, or must I wait for Godmama to do so?"

"Don't know if Mama has had the honor herself, but it won't do for me to present you, as you must know if you would but think about it. What our amiable duchess will tolerate won't do for the heiress to the throne. Moreover, not only I am not your guardian, but I ought not to approach her on my own. Of course," he added casually, "you might ask one of your royal beaux to attend to the matter. I wouldn't recommend asking Cumberland, though. Charlotte detests him."

Carolyn looked away, hiding a smile. Although she could not accuse him of so passionate an emotion as jealousy, or even persuade herself that he was very much provoked, Sydney clearly disliked the fact that she had been encouraging the royal brothers to flirt with her, which was at least an auspicious beginning. Making her eyes wide with innocence, she said, "Why doesn't Charlotte like him? I thought him perfectly amiable myself, despite his reputation, and surely she is not so young that she is frightened by no more than a black eye patch."

Sydney was silent for a long moment before he said gently, "Perhaps you ought to consider the fact that the princess is rather better acquainted with him than you are."

Despite his careful tranquillity, she detected an edge to his voice and was even more encouraged. Shrugging with elaborate unconcern, she said, "Charlotte is very young, sir, and you must agree that family relationships do not always provide the best evidence of a person's character."

"Perhaps." They reached the garden path just then to discover that others had decided to take the air, and Carolyn was not pleased to see them, for she had found her conversation with Sydney delightfully stimulating. Nonetheless, she made no objection when he changed the subject, for she knew they could not go on in the same vein when almost anyone might overhear what they said. She set herself to be especially agreeable instead, and by the time they reached the house, she had had the satisfaction of having made him laugh again.

Inside the house, once Sydney had returned Carolyn to her bedchamber door and she had rung for Maggie, she soon discovered that, despite the arrival of even more guests to attend the ball that evening, no other plans appeared to have been made for their entertainment in the meantime. The duchess was nowhere to be seen. Sydney had diappeared after their return to the house, and the dowager, who arose at noon, emerged from her bedchamber only briefly before retiring to it again to recuperate for the evening, with Miss Pucklington to read to her before she settled down for her usual nap.

Carolyn had no intention of spending the afternoon in her bedchamber. Deciding it was an excellent opportunity to search for the famous grotto, she set out for the rose garden, managing to find a footman who did not mind indicating the way, although when she asked if he would escort her there, he looked at her as if she had spoken a foreign language. She did not press him, having made the request only to see what the response would be, and when two of the duchess's dogs ambled up to her, languidly indicating a willingness to accompany her, she laughed, declaring their manners were much better than those of the royal servants.

Others had chosen to walk in the gardens, and just before entering the rose garden, she caught a glimpse of the Princess Charlotte walking with the regent some distance away—no doubt in aid of that image of cordiality they were expected to present—followed by Lord and Lady Yarmouth and other attendants. The rose garden itself was empty, however, and there were only a few late blooms to be seen, so she did not linger.

Perceiving at once the most likely path to the grotto, she soon found herself, greatly to her surprise, in front of a large square building constructed of magnificent shellwork and nestled into the thick growth of surrounding trees. As she stood gazing at the structure in bewilderment, she heard footsteps behind her. Turning gratefully, in the expectation of finding a servant or guest who could put her on the proper path to the grotto, she found instead his highness the Duke of Cumberland.

"Beauty in distress?" he said, coming to a halt so close to her that she took an involuntary step backward.

"Not distress, sir, or not exactly," she said, standing her ground reluctantly and noting without surprise that her canine companions had abandoned her. The intensity of the duke's gaze made her nervous, but she told herself not to be foolish, that he could not be as sinister as he was painted. He was only a man, after all, and a royal prince, at that. Moreover, he was quite advanced in years, at least forty, so he was bound to be courteous to her. "I am looking for the grotto," she explained, "but this cannot be it."

"Not only can be, but is," he said, glancing at it with undisguised contempt. "Must be the first time a grotto ever found itself above the ground rather than below it, but so it is. We go up those stairs yonder to reach it," he added, indicating the stone steps ahead, leading up to a heavy wooden door.

He looked away as he gestured, and without his piercing gaze to disconcert her, she found it easier to collect her poise. "I have been away longer than I intended, sir," she said. "I ought to return if I am to be dressed before they ring for dinner."

"Nonsense, they will not ring before seven o'clock, and it hasn't even gone three yet. You have hours." He looked directly at her again and held out his hand. "Come, I'll show you. 'Tis nothing much, but once you have seen it, you can be as delighted with it as anyone else—or not, as you please."

Carolyn stood where she was.

"Are you afraid of me, Miss Hardy?" he inquired softly.

"Certainly not," she replied stoutly. "Should I be?"

"It is your choice. Come."

His forceful tone giving her to understand that she had no choice but to obey him, she allowed him to guide her up the steps to the door, hoping they would find it locked. But it was not, and a moment later they were inside.

The dim light from the few narrow slits in the stone walls had been augmented by a number of torches that burned brightly despite the lack of a single servant to see to them. Indeed, as Carolyn soon discovered, the whole place, consisting of four or five chambers, the walls and roofs of which sparkled brilliantly in the torchlight, appeared to be deserted.

"It looks as though the walls were encrusted with diamonds," she said, awed despite her nervousness, as they moved down a short flight of steps into the third chamber, the floor of which was paved with flagstone. Carolyn's gaze shifted upward to the crystal stalactites clinging to the roof high above her.

"Nothing but satin spar and a few sparkling ores, crystals, and shells," he said, adding in a tone of deep distaste, "Yonder is the pool one is expected to make so much of. No more, to my mind, than an overlarge washbasin of cold, dirty water."

Glad of an excuse to step away from him, she crossed to the edge of the glassy pool and looked down into its depths. "It does look a trifle murky, but perhaps 'tis only the light."

"Perhaps." He had moved up behind her and now placed his hands upon her shoulders. "Look at me, my pretty Carolyn."

Her breath caught in her throat as a shiver of panic raced up her spine, and she knew she had been as much of a fool as ever Miss Laura Lovelace had been. She could not step forward without falling into the pool, and she could not step backward without pressing against him, the very thought of which repulsed her, for Cumberland was Count Rudolfo come to life.

"Please, sir," she said, standing perfectly still, "I must go back to the house at once."

His grip tightened and he snarled, "Don't think to trifle with me, girl. You will not like the consequences."

"I know I behaved badly, your highness," she said, trying to keep her desperation from sounding in her voice. "I ought never to have acted as I did last night or come unattended to the grotto today—though I never for a moment thought I would be in danger so near the house," she added with more spirit. "Certainly, not from any member of the royal family."

She knew at once that she had said something very wrong, for he jerked her around to face him. "Danger, Miss Hardy?" His tone was grim, his fury nearly palpable. "Had it been my brother, you would not prattle of danger."

"Your brother?" Carolyn stared at him, as bewildered now as she was frightened. "I don't know which brother you mean, sir, but I assure you, I should dislike being treated so by any man."

"I saw how you played up to George," he said, "but you misconstrue his attentions if you think them more than fleeting. He prefers women older than himself, not little girls."

Unsuccessfully attempting to free herself, Carolyn snapped, "I am no child, sir. Let me go!"

"Not until I have taught you the danger of flirting with a true prince of the blood," he said, pulling her nearer. To her horror, she realized that he meant to kiss her. Truly revolted now, she began to struggle, but her strength was no match for his. Holding her with one arm across her back, he grabbed her chin with his free hand forcing her head up.

When he bent toward her, his eye gleaming with intent, his lips pursed toward hers, she screamed, struggling frantically, but he did not pause. His lips, dry and rough, touched hers.

"Damme, what's toward here? Ernest, whatever are you about? Unhand Miss Hardy at once. At once, I say, sir!"

"Get out, George." Though Carolyn had stiffened at the sound of the regent's voice, Cumberland did not so much as glance over his shoulder. Nor did his grip relax.

"Damme, you can't treat her so! I'll not let you!"

Her view was blocked by the breadth of Cumberland's chest and shoulders, so the first awareness she had of the regent's intent came when his hand grabbed Cumberland's shoulder. As soon as the duke was touched, he went rigid with fury.

"Take your hand from my shoulder, damn you, and get out!"

"Dash it all, Ernest, there are ladies outside! I came ahead to see if Frederica was here, because Charlotte expressed a wish to speak with her. Ought to have known she wasn't," he added. "Not a dog in sight, damme if there is."

"I doubt there is anyone at all outside," Cumberland said snidely, "but your presence does explain why Miss Hardy was waiting out there alone, does it not?"

Carolyn gasped, but the others paid her no heed, the regent saying testily, " 'Tis understandable that you could think such a thing, my dear Ernest, since she is most unlikely to have had the extreme bad taste to have been awaiting you."

The taunt nearly proved his undoing when Cumberland whirled with a growl of fury, flung Carolyn aside, and leapt at him.

She heard the regent cry out, but she was too concerned at first with the need to avoid being knocked into the pool to see what happened. By the time she regained her balance and turned, their struggle had carried them a short distance away, but just then Cumberland, with a bellow of rage, heaved the regent backward, toward her. Catching his heel on a flagstone, he fell heavily at her feet, and when the duke leapt toward him with murder in his eye, Carolyn scrambled to get out of their way. Only when Cumberland suddenly and most incredibly became airborne, flying over the regent to land with a gurgling shout and a very large splash in the icy pool did she realize that another combatant had entered the lists.

As Sydney Saint-Denis reached down to help the regent to his feet, he said over his shoulder and apparently with all his usual tranquillity, "Caro, are you hurt?"

"Sydney! What are you doing here?" Staring at him, she glanced at Cumberland, who staggered furiously in the water as he attempted to regain his footing. Then, still unable to believe what she had seen, she looked back at Sydney.

He had opened his mouth to reply to her when the regent groaned in pain and fell back to the floor. Kneeling quickly over him, Sydney demanded, "What is it, sir?"

"Damme if it isn't my ankle," the regent complained, trying to reach that member. "I've gone and sprained it, thanks to Ernest's damned insolence and Frederica's uneven floor. But you'd best get him out of that pond. How the devil did you do that trick, anyway, Saint-Denis? Pretty piece of work, damme if it wasn't, but you oughtn't to have put him in the water."

"Just something I picked up in my travels, sir," Sydney said, raising his quizzing glass to peer down at the duke, who had finally managed to get to his feet and, moving with care, was on the point of emerging from the water. Sydney dropped his glass and reached a hand out to him. "Here, Cumberland."

Starting and jerking away from him, the duke slipped again and sat down hard in the water.

"Dear me," Sydney said, raising his glass again. "I cannot think why . . . Oh, there you are, Yarmouth," he added when that gentleman appeared in the doorway. "Best keep the ladies outside, I think. There's been a bit of an accident."

Yarmouth, a slender *bon vivant* in his mid-thirties, surveyed the room with a shrewd twinkle in his eyes. "An accident, you say? The duchess won't like this much, I'm thinking."

"No," Sydney agreed, glancing from Cumberland, who had emerged from the pool at last, dripping wet and grim of countenance, to the Prince Regent. "We must tidy things up a bit, but do you keep your lady and her high—"

"What happened here?" Princess Charlotte demanded, bobbing up and down on tiptoe behind Yarmouth. "We cannot see, Yarmouth. Go in or come out."

Obediently Lord Yarmouth moved to allow the princess and his wife to enter. Lady Yarmouth cried out in dismay at the sight thus presented to her, but the princess, seeing her father sitting on the floor, nursing his swelling ankle, glared at her uncle and said, "What have you done, you vile beast?"

Cumberland, after a sidelong glance at Sydney, returned her look with one of equal dislike and growled, "I stumbled."

"Aunt Frederica will be angry if you have spoiled my party."

"Chit's right," the regent said. "Best to put a good face on it somehow. Only trouble is," he added ruefully, "don't think I can walk. Bound to cause talk if I have to be carried back to the house, damme if it won't."

Sydney had been thinking, and now he said, "If it please you, sir, I think we can contrive a tale to fit the circumstances if his highness will agree to retire to one of the back chambers until we can send the discreet Mr. Neall to him with dry clothes. With any luck at all, no one will see him, for most of those who were out walking before will have returned by now to prepare for the evening, and any who haven't can be fobbed off by telling them you and the princess were practicing for the ball when you stumbled over an uneven spot in the floor here. Perhaps the quadrille . . . No, that won't do, but perhaps—"

"Oh, who cares what you tell them," Cumberland exclaimed. "Tell them he was dancing the highland fling if you like, only get him out of here. I'm sick of the sight of you all."

Sydney said nothing, nor did he look at the duke. Instead, he gestured to Yarmouth to help him, and between the two of them they were able to get the regent to his feet, supporting him outside and down the steps to the path. In the rose garden, they hailed two of the servants who had been awaiting his pleasure, and once the regent was safely in their care, with the Yarmouths and Charlotte to follow him, Sydney and Carolyn were left alone.

"I must remember to send Cornelius Neall out before Cumberland catches a chill," Sydney said, "but since the duke's needs are hardly a priority with me, I may forget. Perhaps you will be good enough to remind me."

Carolyn bit her lip. In her astonishment at seeing the duke fly into the pool, she had all but forgotten her own part in the scene, but the memory flooded back now with a vengeance. Thinking Sydney might have things to say to her that she had no wish to hear, she attempted a diversion by demanding to know what he had done to the duke.

"He said he stumbled," Sydney reminded her.

"He did no such thing," she retorted, "and I've a strong notion that what happened to him is exactly what happened to Salas that night. Whatever did you do to them?"

Sydney shrugged. " 'Twas as I told Prinny, a trick I learned in China, no more. But, Caro—"

"I wondered why no servant ever spoke about that incident," she said. But then she could find no more words, and he was silent too, making no further attempt to say whatever it was that he had been about to say. She watched him, wondering what he was thinking, wondering if he was as angry with her as she deserved that he should be. A lump formed in her throat and at last she said in a much smaller voice, "I am sorry, Sydney, truly I am."

"It was not entirely your fault," he said. His words were carefully measured and spoken serenely, but she was coming to know him better, and she knew by the way he spoke just then that Sydney Saint-Denis was as angry as any man could be.

10

Feeling Sydney's anger and believing despite his words that much of it must be aimed at her, Carolyn had no wish to encourage him to say more. She knew she was behaving in a cowardly fashion and despised herself for it, but for the first time in her life, she was a little afraid of him and therefore grateful for his silence as they walked. When they came to her bedchamber door, she braced herself for his reproof.

He said, "I'll find Neall now."

She nodded, watching him, waiting, but he merely opened her door for her and suggested she dress quickly. "It will not do for us to be late," he said.

A moment later he was gone and Maggie was hustling her out of her dress, exclaiming over its damp skirt and insisting that she make haste. "Her ladyship rang for her woman more than an hour ago, miss, and I've been just a-waiting and a-waiting."

"I want a bath," Carolyn said as she let the maid help her into her dressing gown. "Is such a thing possible in this ill-managed house, Maggie?"

"Oh, yes, miss, for Ching Ho saw to it earlier. There's the tub all ready behind that screen there, and I've only to ring for a man to bring hot water. I don't know how that Chinaman managed it, miss, but perhaps the master took a hand."

Carolyn's mind promptly provided her with a mental image

of Sydney's elegant, well-tended hands and the thought that he must have sent Cumberland flying with little more than the flick of a finger, at most a wrist, for he had not done anything more violent. Impossible, she told herself. No one could have done such a thing. Certainly not the languid Sydney.

"Miss?"

Startled, she realized that Maggie was staring at her, waiting for some sort of response, but Carolyn had no idea what else the maid might have said to her. Collecting herself, she said, "Ring for the water, Maggie. We have no time to waste."

"But I did, miss. Just now. I told you."

"Good," Carolyn said, adding with forced calm, "Now, tell me, shall I wear my back hair in a twist tonight or curled into ringlets?" When Maggie voted for ringlets, the awkward moment was gone, and there was no time for anything after that but the preparations for Princess Charlotte's ball.

Carolyn was no sooner attired in her pink satin ball gown than Miss Pucklington arrived to inform her that the dowager was waiting, impatiently. Carolyn snatched up her gloves and lace reticule and, gathering up her demitrain, hurried to accompany Miss Pucklington, telling that lady that she looked as fine as fivepence in her pale-lavender silk gown with its matching gloves and reticule. "Although Godmama will no doubt cast us both into the shade," she added with a chuckle.

"She is magnificent, as always," Miss Pucklington agreed.

And so it was, for Lady Skipton was draped from head to toe in emerald satin and diamonds. Raising her gold-rimmed lorgnette to her eyes, she surveyed Carolyn critically. "Most becoming, my dear," she pronounced at last, "though I should have advised you to wear your pearls."

Carolyn's hand flew protectively to the flower necklace. "I prefer this, ma'am."

"Oh, as you wish. There is certainly no time to be changing your mind. Let us go downstairs."

Following her, Carolyn wondered if the afternoon's events might have led to trouble, but there was no sign of any when they joined the others in the huge dining room for dinner. And for once there could be no complaints about the service. An attendant stood behind each chair, and the sideboards fairly creaked beneath the weight of the many dishes set out upon them.

It was well after ten o'clock before they adjourned to the ballroom, and it was not until then that she remembered the regent would not be dancing, since those members of the royal family who were present at dinner had already been seated before she and the others entered the dining room.

He hobbled into the ballroom, supported by a stout cane on one side and the arm of his secretary, Colonel MacMahon, on the other. And although he laughed at something said to him by Lord Alvanley, also walking beside him, it could be seen as he took his seat that he was in considerable pain. His right leg, ostentatiously wrapped in white linen, was carefully propped on a satin stool by another attendant.

The Duke of York, coming up behind Carolyn, clicked his tongue and said, "Isn't that the very deuce of a thing?"

"Most unfortunate, sir," Carolyn said. Then, remembering that she ought to know little if anything about the matter, she said, "What on earth—"

"Ought to have known better," York said, chuckling, "than to try dancing in that damned grotto of Freddie's. And Ernest won't dance tonight either, I'm told. Sulking in his room, no doubt, on account of Georgie's ankle drawing so much attention. Just as well," he added with a twinkle. "If he did come down, he'd no doubt kick poor Georgie just for the fun of hearing him yelp."

"Indeed, sir?"

But York had recollected himself. "Mustn't let my tongue run on like fiddlestick, must I? Ernest don't like it."

The musicians struck up for the first dance just then, and recalled to his duties, the Duke of York excused himself to find his niece, for it was to him that the honor of leading her out had fallen. From his words, Carolyn realized that the tale Sydney had suggested to explain the regent's injury was the one that had been given out. No one mentioned a single detail of what really had happened, and although more than once she saw Lady Yarmouth looking at her with an expression of mischief shared, Carolyn could not in any good conscience return the look. Whether Sydney truly blamed her or not, she blamed herself for much of what had occurred.

She saw Sydney several times during the course of the ball, but since she had no more desire to flirt with him and had decided it would be best to behave with extra circumspection, even to the point of returning to her godmother's side at the end of each dance, it was easy for her to avoid meeting his gaze. He seemed to be paying her little heed, in any case, so it came as a surprise to her, when a waltz was called just before a late supper was to be served, to find him bowing before her.

"May I have the honor, Miss Hardy?"

His mother, seated next to Carolyn on one of the gilt chairs lining the walls of the room, frowned and said sharply, "Why do you address her so? I cannot recall your ever doing so before."

"Can you not, Mama?" He smiled at Carolyn. "Well, ma'am? You do not answer me."

The dowager snapped, "Don't be foolish. Of course, she will dance. She has danced only with old men and Alvanley tonight. She does nothing to form an eligible attachment."

"Poor Caro," Sydney said as he guided her with a light touch to their place in the set. The waltz, being neither so slow nor so stately as the minuet that had preceded it, was a gliding dance better suited to a more highly polished floor, and for some moments Carolyn had to concentrate on her steps, until she had adapted her movements to the uncertain surface. She had heard of a new version of the dance, performed on the Continent and even sometimes in London, where the gentleman held his partner in a near embrace throughout. Looking now at Sydney and finding his warm gaze upon her, she wondered if she would like to dance that way and decided, blushing, that she would like it very much.

He smiled at her just then and she blushed more deeply and looked away, then started when he linked his arm with hers for the allemande. When the music ended and she turned to look for the dowager, Sydney said quietly, "I had hoped you would join me for supper, but I suppose you are promised to someone else."

"No," she confessed. "No one." She had been asked twice but had not thought she would wish to stay downstairs so late.

He tucked her hand into the crook of his arm, and suddenly Carolyn was not sure she wanted to go with him, since the fact that he had said nothing yet about her part in the afternoon's events did not mean he would remain silent forever. But she could not simply pull her hand away and leave him. Deciding that they would probably join other friends, so there would be no opportunity for private conversation, she went with him quietly, only to be dismayed when he led her through the crowd to a quiet corner table and signed to a footman to serve them there.

As Carolyn took her seat, watching him warily, Sydney smiled and said, "I hope you don't mind. I have had enough chatter already tonight to last me a lifetime."

With a mixture of profound relief and quite unexpected disappointment, she said, "It is all the same to me, I suppose."

"What is it, Caro? Oh, thank you," he added when a footman placed plates laden with food before each of them. "We'll have wine, I think." Then, when the man had gone and she still had not spoken, he said, "Well? Are you not speaking to me?"

She managed a smile. "On the contrary, sir. I know you must be angry with me, and I have been waiting rather uncomfortably to hear what you will say to me."

He was silent for a long moment, and she knew by his expression that she had surprised him. Then he said, "I was vexed, certainly, though I thought I had concealed it. It cannot be necessary for me to tell you, you behaved unwisely."

Without thinking and rather sharply, she said, "Do you only do what is necessary, Sydney?"

"I have found 'tis the best way," he replied. "To do only what is necessary—no more, no less than that."

For reasons she could not have explained to herself, let alone to him, his reply incensed her to speechlessness. She glared at him, and the arrival of the footman with their wine only irritated her more. When the man had gone, she drank thirstily before resolutely turning her attention to her plate, determined to ignore Sydney. Moments later, when another footman passed by with a wine bottle, she finished what was left in her glass before signing to him to refill it.

"You will intoxicate yourself again if you drink so quickly," Sydney said gently when the man had gone.

"And if I do, 'twill be because I wish to do so and for no other reason," she retorted. "Therefore I daresay you will make no effort to stop me."

"No, Caro, I won't stop you."

Irrationally, she snapped, "You would have stopped me when I was a child!"

"But you are no longer a child," he said, "and I have not the least desire to treat you like one."

The last words came out in an odd tone, almost a growl, making her feel a little foolish but, at the same time, stirring feelings within her that had never stirred before. She stared at him as she tried to sort out her emotions, then said, finally, "I do not think I understand you, sir."

"Would you understand better"—there was a distinct edge to his voice now—"if I were to insist that you cease your flirting, perhaps avoid entirely the company of such men as Cumberland, Lyndhurst, even Manningford, until you learn to behave properly?"

Her eyes widened as resentment rose swiftly within her. "No, I wouldn't," she said tartly. "You do not have that right, sir. Indeed, this conversation is foolish and I cannot think why I stay to talk with you." Glaring, she arose from her chair.

"Sit down, Carolyn."

She nearly obeyed on the instant, so startled was she by the snap in his voice, but she caught herself and, straightening, lifted her brows in what she hoped was a fair imitation of his own manner of silent inquiry.

He responded with a wry smile. "Please sit down. I will apologize. I can't imagine why I allow you to exasperate me as you do, for anyone would think that if Mama can no longer take a rise out of me, you could not do so, either."

Oddly reassured by these words, she sat down, and when the music began again, they parted as friends. She did not speak with him again that night, but by the time she retired to her bed, she had replayed in her mind's eye every minute of their time together, hearing each word he had spoken and every reply she had made. This mild exercise only confused her all the more.

No more than she could explain why his failure to scold her had rankled could she explain her instant resentment when he had dared, mildly, to reprove her. She didn't want him to be angry. But if he was angry, she wanted him to tell her so. On the other hand, she didn't want to hear it when he did tell her so. Very little time spent with such thoughts as these was sufficient to make her bury her head in her pillow, deciding that further such contemplation was no more than pavement on the road to madness.

The following day, she awoke late to the news that the regent was ill and a large number of the guests were departing. Lady Skipton insisted at first that his illness had nothing to do with them, but by three o'clock, when it had become obvious that the duchess was no longer interested in visiting with those guests who had remained, her ladyship informed the rest of her party that she was ready to leave at once for Bathwick Hill House. They traveled to Maidenhead that day, finishing their journey late Saturday evening.

Since the weather was clement, Sydney rode, and there was no opportunity on the road or at the inn in Maidenhead for Carolyn to speak privately with him. When they reached Bath she went straight to bed, and the following day, the household returned to its normal routine. Sydney had numerous duties to attend to each day that kept him busy until midafternoon, when he generally disappeared for two hours before dinner.

Carolyn saw little of him. She was still smarting emotionally, and since there was no one to whom she could unburden herself, her guilt increased until she was certain that he must despise her for a fool. Telling herself that he could not know she had learned her lesson, and determined to show him that she had, she decided that henceforward she would behave with irreproachable propriety. There would be no more incidents like the one in the grotto, for she could be as proper as anyone if she set her mind to it.

With this end in view, she exerted herself to be of assistance by bearing the dowager company and by making herself generally useful instead of spending her days as she had before—idly reading, riding, walking in the gardens, or writing letters to her friends. She helped Miss Pucklington with those chores the dowager was constantly finding for her to perform and even assisted Maggie in finding glue to mend the hat she wore with her blue riding habit. Such virtuous behavior, though wearisome, eased her guilt until newspaper accounts of the Oatlands ball began to appear, and certain rumors began to fly.

Lady Skipton announced at supper a week after the ball that she feared for the future of the empire.

Miss Pucklington gasped. "Good gracious, Cousin Olympia, whatever has happened?"

"Why, the regent is proving to be as mad as the king, that is what," the dowager said. "What we are coming to in this country, I cannot think, to be at the mercy of a royal family tainted by madness. My father would not have approved, and nor, I can tell you, Sydney, would your father have done."

Sydney had been placidly eating, but thus addressed, he replied gently, "I must suppose that you have this information on excellent authority, ma'am."

"Well, certainly. I have it directly from Lady Lucretia Calverton, who had it from her niece in London, who had it from Lady Bessborough, who had it, I am certain, directly from the queen. Surely, Sydney, if you've heard nothing else, you must have heard about the dreadful things the regent did while we were at Oatlands."

"I cannot think of anything he did that was particularly dreadful, ma'am, but no doubt I have mistaken the matter. I pray you will enlighten me."

"Well, I certainly thought you must have known," she said with a click of her tongue, "for I saw you myself, talking with the man on at least two separate occasions."

"He asked my advice several times," Sydney said. "He does that frequently, and though I had not previously thought it a sign of madness, clearly I am biased, so you must forgive me."

Carolyn choked back a sudden urge to laugh, but Lady Skipton did not notice, her attention being firmly riveted upon her son as she retorted, "Do not be nonsensical, sir. You know I meant nothing of the sort. And while you may choose to see frivolity in the occasion, there is none, for the regent has so lost his wits that he grossly insulted Lady Yarmouth and was soundly thrashed by her husband, in consequence. Surely you have heard of the so-called royal indisposition."

"Certainly," Sydney said. "But then I . . . Did you wish to speak, ma'am?" he asked, glancing at Miss Pucklington.

Flustered, she gaped first at him and then at Lady Skipton, whose expression was unencouraging. But when Sydney said gently, "Well, ma'am?" she blinked, then hastily found her tongue.

"I did not mean to intrude," she said, "but I thought the regent injured himself when he slipped and hurt his ankle while showing his daughter how to do the highland fling."

"That is certainly the substance of what we were told at Oatlands," Sydney agreed.

"Yes," Miss Pucklington said in a gratified tone, "and it must have been a gallant effort, you know, for he is such a heavy man and his ankles are known to be weak. According to the *Morning Chronicle*, he opened the ball with the princess, and while they were dancing, his right foot came in contact with the leg of a sofa, and he sprained his ankle; however, I know that was not true, since York danced with her and no furniture was in the way in that huge ballroom. Moreover, we know the regent did not dance. But surely the truth was printed in the *Morning Post*, for that was the same tale we heard at Oatlands, though perhaps it is not precisely where I read that it was the highland fling."

The dowager had not interrupted her but had been regarding her with increasing displeasure, and said now, "Really, Judith, I cannot think when you have time to read all the newspapers, but it is not at all becoming in you to do so when there are more important matters to which you might be attending. I do not ask you to do very much, certainly, and I should think that you—"

"Godmama," Carolyn blurted, "I heard the same thing at Oatlands, and I saw the article in the *Morning Post*, too, so I am persuaded that you must be mistaken about the regent and Lady Yarmouth. He would never have insulted her, and surely Lord Yarmouth was one of those most often in attendance upon

him when it was discovered that he had injured himself more
seriously than had previously been thought, and he had taken
to his bed.''

"You've only to see the broadsides being sold in the streets
of Bath to know I am right," the dowager said firmly. "That
was no sprain. Under all that linen, I fancy, his ankle is as
healthy as my own. Perhaps you are right about the Yarmouths,
however,'' she added with an air of giving credit where it was
due. "I put little credence in what can be no more than a rumor,
since Lady Yarmouth is not likely to attract him when he is still
enamored of her mama-in-law. However,'' she added as a
clincher, "no less a person than the Duke of Cumberland has
said the illness has infected a portion of the regent's body higher
than his foot and that a blister on his head might be more
efficacious than the poultice on his ankle. And what will become
of us if our regent, like our king, goes mad? Answer me that!''

No one wished to debate the matter, but although Sydney
managed with his usual adroitness to divert her, it was by no
means the final word she spoke on the subject. Nor was she
the only one to indulge in such interesting speculation. When
the regent remained at Oatlands through the first week of
December, spurring one wit to send the newspapers a complex,
passionate ode entitled "The Royal Sprain, or a Kick from
Yarmouth to Wales,'' the rumors flourished anew, and Carolyn
thanked Providence that it had been Lady Yarmouth and not
herself who had chanced to accompany the regent's party back
into the house.

By the time Brandon Manningford, thinking the ode an
excellent bit of satire, brought Carolyn a copy one rainy afternoon in case she had not yet seen it, she was thoroughly sick
of the conjecturing. He had been shown into the library, where
he found her alone, reading a book she had previously denied
herself in the interests of conspicious propriety.

"What the devil's the matter with you?'' he demanded when
she received his offering with a grimace of distaste.

"It is only that I am sick to death of hearing about poor
Prinny's accident. We were there, you know, and nothing of
the sort transpired. Indeed,'' she added incautiously, "I believe
all the rumors originated with the odious Duke of Cumberland,

whose greatest desire in life is to make the regent look no account.''

"Even if that were true," Brandon said, "Cumberland was there, too, wasn't he? And the simple fact is that everyone else has been dashed cagey about the whole thing if all Prinny did was fall down while he was practicing some fool dance.''

Feeling warmth flood her cheeks when she realized how near she had been to telling him the truth, she said swiftly, "Where have you been? We have not seen you since my rout party.''

"In London," he said, accepting the change of subject without comment. "I was run off m' legs, and m' father refused to advance me a farthing, so I threw m'self on Ramsbury's mercy, he being a softer touch than m' sister Mally's husband. At first he said I could stay with him and Sybilla till quarter day, but I could stand it only three weeks. Daresay he didn't like it much either, because he didn't raise a whisper when I said I'd best dash back to Bath and look in on the old man. Even dug into his pockets—and right deep they are, too—so here I am.''

Laughing, Carolyn said, "How very thoughtful of you—to visit Sir Mortimer, I mean. Do sit down and don't snap off my nose when I ask if he even knows you are in town. Does he?''

"Well, of course he does," he said indignantly, taking a seat, "or so I should think. Haven't seen him m'self.''

"Brandon, it is not natural for son never to see his father. I think you ought to make it a point to visit him.''

He tilted his head to one side and regarded her for a long moment, speculatively, before he nodded and said, "Tell you what it is, Caro. You've got windmills in your head, that's what.''

"No, I haven't. What could he possibly do to you? I'll go with you if you like," she added impulsively. "I am bored to distraction, and it would be just the thing to amuse me.''

"Now, Caro, really . . .''

"Oh, come on," she coaxed. "I'll wager ten pounds that you cannot get the pair of us into his library long enough for me to have a look at him. There! Will you refuse a wager?''

He grimaced comically. "Now, dash it all, Caro, I wish you wouldn't put the matter like that. Sneaking a bear into the Pump

Room or carrying an egg on one's nose the length of Pulteney Bridge . . . now those are sensible—''

"Sensible!'' She laughed.

"At all events,'' he said with dignity, ''they are more sensible than confronting a cantankerous old lion in his den, and that's what we'd be doing, my girl.''

"Oh, pooh, I think you see Old Bogey where there is no one but a lonely old man. No doubt your poor papa hid himself away out of his desperate grief for your mother, and even if that is not the case,'' she went on hastily when he hooted with derisive laughter, ''the fact is that you're a coward, Brandon Manningford, and that's all there is about it.''

"I'll show you who's a coward,'' he said, his expression changing instantly from merriment to grim purpose as he leapt to his feet. "Get your cloak. It's cold as ice outside.''

Carolyn stood up at once, delighted. "Where are we going?''

"Don't be daft, my dear. You'll be the most-sought-after dinner guest in Bath once you can tell folks you've met the eccentric Sir Mortimer Manningford. Are you coming?''

"Now?''

"Now,'' he said severely, ''or never.''

Knowing he might change his mind as quickly as he had made it up, she didn't hesitate for a moment, snatching up her skirt and fairly running upstairs to her bedchamber, where she dragged her red wool cloak from the wardrobe and flung it over her shoulders. Then, taking a pair of warm gloves from a drawer, she hurried back down, pausing not even long enough to smooth her hair, telling herself the hood would cover it. Downstairs again, she found Brandon awaiting her in the hall.

"That was quick,'' he said, ''but where are your boots?''

She regarded her thinly shod feet in dismay. "I never gave them a thought. Oh, and it's still raining, and I left my pattens by the side door this morning.''

"Well, don't fret yourself. The rain's eased, and they're bringing my carriage 'round. Daresay I can contrive to toss you in without straining m'self, so you'll keep your toes dry.''

"Brandon,'' she said when a thought occurred to her as they were hurrying down the front steps, ''you didn't tell anyone where we're going, did you?''

He shook his head. "Just ordered the carriage brought 'round. Why?"

She twinkled up at him from beneath her eyelashes. "It has occurred to me that, uninterested as Godmama is in my comings and goings, she might be displeased to learn that I had visited your house without a proper chaperon . . . or with one, I suppose."

"Well, I won't tell anyone." He grinned mischievously. "Much better, I think, to keep mum. I believe I now know the perfect way to be revenged upon you if you ever decide to play me any of your tricks."

"I do not play tricks anymore," she informed him with dignity. "I have decided to abandon such nonsense altogether and behave always in the manner of a proper lady."

"Going with me today being but a momentary lapse, is that it?" he demanded, shaking his head at her in amusement. "What stirred this sudden desire for propriety, anyway, Caro? Something happen to teach you the error of your ways?"

She had begun to chuckle at his teasing, but the rider stopped the laugh in her throat, and before she had time to swallow it, he had scooped her off her feet to carry her down to the carriage, which was was drawn up to within a few feet of the bottom step.

The footman who was holding the door open for him suddenly looked at a point above and beyond him, giving Carolyn a scant second's warning before she heard Sydney's familiar drawl.

"Abducting the lady, Manningford?" he said. "I confess, I admire your practicality in leaving by the front door, and in broad daylight, too, such as it is."

Still holding Carolyn in his arms, Brandon swung around. "Saint-Denis!"

Sydney remained poised on the top step, his quizzing glass raised to his right eye. "Good afternoon to you," he said calmly. "Haven't you forgotten someone?"

"What? Who?" Brandon looked distracted. "Look here, Saint-Denis, this ain't what it looks like."

"No, I rather thought it wasn't, which was why it occurred to me that perhaps you had merely forgotten Miss Hardy's maid."

"Her maid! Good God, man, we don't want her maid."

"Ah, perhaps not, but I assure you that for you to carry Miss Hardy off without her is not to be thought of."

"Sydney, stop it," Carolyn begged, struggling to keep from laughing. "You don't think anything of the sort."

"I assure you, my dear, I should take the strongest exception to your driving off alone with him."

"Brandon is not abducting me," she said tartly. "Nor are we eloping. Put me down, Brandon."

"Well, then, I will," Mr. Manningford said, suiting action to words, "but I tell you, my girl, this is no way to win a wager."

Sydney turned a sharp gaze on Carolyn. "Perhaps you would care to explain this wager to me."

"No, I wouldn't," she said candidly. "In any event, the wager is off. I have changed my mind."

Sydney said, "How very unsporting of you, my dear, but I daresay he will forgive you. Do you come back inside with us, Manningford?"

"No, I don't," Brandon said, adding in a mutter for Carolyn's ears alone, "You may play this hand alone, my dear. I believe I'd be wise to return to Leicestershire for a time."

11

Sydney dared not trust himself to speak as he turned to go back into the house, for he was as much annoyed with himself for allowing his temper to flare at the sight of Carolyn in Brandon's arms as he was at the sight itself, and the combination was particularly difficult to overcome. He had made it a point to avoid close contact with Carolyn since their return from Oatlands for the simple reason that, in the grotto, he had realized that his feelings for her were beginning to have a far greater impact upon his emotions than was commensurate with the state of calm he had worked for so many years to attain.

With Ching Ho's assistance, he had advanced far beyond his natural boyish determination to annihilate all his enemies. His mind and body were rigorously disciplined, he had thought, into an inseparable entity. But now, in Carolyn's presence, although the slightest thought of her produced an undeniable effect upon his body, he could not call the response a disciplined one.

He was still determined, if not to overcome his feelings, to control them until such time as he believed it necessary to make her aware of them. It certainly was not necessary now, when she had had so little opportunity to find the hero of her dreams. He knew he was not that man. He did not so much as own a white charger, nor did he wish to pursue a career of rescuing damsels in distress. His wife, when he found her, would be content to love him, would perhaps enjoy a hand of cards of an evening or a game of backgammon or chess, if there were no more amusing entertainment at hand, and perhaps would not object to travel, for he certainly intended to visit China again. But she would not, he trusted, have the unsettling impact upon his emotions that Miss Hardy presently seemed to have.

These thoughts passed through his mind in the brief time it took them to reach the door to the library, and by then he had himself in hand again. He paused there, his hand on the door handle, and said quietly, "I am in something of a hurry. Did you wish to speak to me?"

She stared at him, clearly shaken out of her own thoughts. "I . . . I thought you would want an explanation. I know you were jesting when you suggested an elopement, but you must have wondered why Brandon was carrying me."

"I supposed he was helping you to keep your feet dry," he said. "You would both have done better, of course, to have considered how such a scene might have appeared to the servants or to anyone else who might have observed it."

"Not to you, however," she said, the tension in her voice making it clear that her temper was on a short rein.

"No, not I," he said, ignoring an urge to draw her into the library and tell her precisely what he thought. "Is that all?"

"You don't want to know where we were going?"

"That is not necessary."

"Not *necessary*!"

"You didn't go," he said matter-of-factly. "Now, if you don't mind, I was on my way to the stables when I saw you and only came back for a book I promised to take to Sir Percival Melvin, with whom I am dining tonight. He is also a collector and wants my advice regarding some articles he is thinking of selling. In any case, you must be longing to take off your cloak. The smell of damp wool does not become you."

A moment later, Carolyn found herself alone, glaring at the library door, which had closed rather abruptly behind Sydney.

"Is something wrong, Miss Carolyn?" It was the footman Abel, and he drew back in haste when she whirled abruptly, without altering her expression.

Seeing his reaction, she strove to compose her countenance and said in a tolerably mild tone, "No, nothing. You may go."

Why, she wondered as she turned toward the stairs, had she thought Sydney was angry with her? And why, thinking him angry, had she not been distressed, but rather stimulated instead? And why was she angry now, rather than relieved to discover that he was not angry? Having set herself to flirt with him, behaving as foolishly as ever Miss Laura Lovelace or any other of her ilk had done, she had compounded her error when she had turned her wiles upon the royal brothers in order to show him she could manage any man. Then, when she had failed dismally at that venture, was it any wonder that she had expected him to be vexed? But he had scarcely noticed her activities or cared much when he did.

And that, she thought shrewdly as she made her way up the second stairs, was most likely what had cut her to the quick—that, added to the sad fact that he had not so much as commented upon her exemplary behavior since their return from Oatlands. It was not, she assured herself, that she had any particular need or desire for his approval. It was just that he might have said *something* to show that he was at least aware of her efforts.

These thoughts did nothing to pacify her temper, nor did the fact that he had not seemed to care in the slightest when he found her practically being carried off by Mr. Manningford. Indeed, that last thought acted upon her in such a way that by the time she reached her bedchamber door, she was seething and determined by fair means or foul to make Sydney react in a more predictably male fashion. It was not until she saw Ching Ho moving down the corridor, the hat and coat he carried indicating his immediate intention of going out, that she had any idea of what she meant to do, but that sight affected her in precisely the same way that years before at Swainswick, on holiday from school, she had been affected by the knowledge of Sydney's bedchamber, an arena ripe for mischief, was empty and waiting.

On the thought, she sped down the corridor, pausing only long enough at Sydney's door to listen for any sound that might mean another servant was still within. There was none.

Cautiously opening the door, she saw at once that the room was empty, and she tiptoed swiftly to the doorway into the adjoining dressing room. It too was vacant. Pausing, she glanced first around the larger room and then the smaller, wondering what she might do that could not fail to stir him, either to merriment or to fury. At that moment, all emotions were as one to her.

Her gaze came to rest at last upon the dressing-room commode cabinet, and she remembered his admission, only weeks before, of his vexation that night years ago when, as a mischievous child, she had pasted his slippers to the floor. If that prank had vexed him, she reflected, perhaps something of a like nature would distress him even more.

Unlatching the little front door of the cabinet, she opened it and gazed with profound satisfaction at the floral-patterned Sèvres chamber pot that resided there. She had no need to lift the lid to know that the pot would be empty and shining clean, for even if the chambermaid had been remiss in her early-morning duties, Ching Ho would never have allowed his master's commode to go untended for long.

Before her mischief could be accomplished, however, it was necessary for her to go to her own room to throw off her damp cloak and fetch the glue that Maggie had used to repair her hat, but once she had found the glue and returned, it was but a few minutes' work to achieve her purpose.

At last, with a final glance around the dressing room to assure herself that she had left behind no sign of her visit (other than a slight, lingering scent of damp wool that she trusted would soon dissipate), she slipped into the corridor again, closing the door behind her. Stifling an incipient bubble of laughter, she told herself as she hurried back to her own room that he would surely be unable to ignore what she had done this time. The thought that he might come to her bedchamber in the middle of the night did not distress her in the least, even though it also occurred to her that if he should so exert himself it might be for the sole purpose of wringing her neck.

Sydney had not returned from his dinner engagement before she retired, and throughout the night, each time she awoke thinking she heard a noise in her room, she was visited by a sense of mixed fear and anticipation. But by the time she had broken her fast the following, gray morning and learned from Abel that Sydney had ridden out earlier and had not seemed the least out of sorts or disturbed, her feelings changed from a surge of exasperation to the dismal belief that he didn't simply care what she did. From that point it was but a small step to the restive awareness that she had allowed herself to be carried away by an impulsive, childish desire for revenge and the belief that he must now despise her all the more for behaving so stupidly.

She would have been surprised to learn that Sydney, while not despising her in the least, had certainly been thinking about her and had ridden out early that morning for the sole purpose of avoiding a confrontation. The discovery during the small hours of the night that not only had the lid been glued to his chamber pot but that the pot itself had been glued to the shelf upon which it rested had very nearly overcome his careful patience.

As he had made his way to the commode closet at the end of the dark, chilly corridor, he had seriously considered visiting Carolyn in her bedchamber to express his displeasure. Only the knowledge that such a late-night visit to a chaste young woman living under his protection could not, under any circumstances, be justified had dissuaded him.

He had made no effort that morning to conceal what she had done, either from the chambermaid whose duty it was to empty the pot, or from his valet, when that worthy entered to set out his clothes for the day. Ching Ho had observed dispassionately that it would be difficult to preserve the shelf and impossible to preserve the chamber pot, but that he would attend at once to the matter of replacing the latter, an attitude that had succeeded in exasperating his sorely tried master.

By the time Sydney finished his ride, his disposition was fairly tranquil again, and he returned to the stables safe in the knowledge that he could now meet Carolyn without affording her the satisfaction of knowing her prank had vexed him. It was a distinct annoyance, therefore, to learn that the carriage had been ordered out a bare half hour before his return to carry his mother and Miss Carolyn into town to visit the Pump Room.

Frustrated, Sydney went directly to a room behind the stables, where he knew Ching Ho might be found at such an hour. Ching was there, wearing a loose cotton tunic and baggy pantaloons and seated cross-legged on one of several large mats that lay on the floor, his hands resting lightly upon his knees, his eyes narrowed to slits. It was a moment before he responded to his master's presence, but when he did, he rose smoothly to his feet and made a slight bow.

"You wish to take your exercise so early, my master?"

"I'm in no mood for duty this morning," Sydney said casually. "I had thought we might have a go at the new way we devised for defending against an attacker with a weapon."

Nodding, Ching Ho helped him change into garb similar to his own, but as he moved to hang up his master's buckskins and coat on the rod provided for them, he said over his shoulder, "Do we practice for a particular assailant, my master?"

Sydney grimaced. "The only one assailing me at the moment is unarmed, Ching, though I cannot say she has no weapons. I just wish that a few hours of practicing Wu Shu on a mat could teach me the right way to deal with her."

"Yes, my master."

"What the devil does that mean—yes, my master?" Sydney demanded, taking his place opposite him. "Sometimes, I swear, talking to you is like talking to myself, which—now I come to ponder the matter—is no doubt why I talk to you at all about such personal stuff as this. It is not generally my nature to gabble, you know." He bowed.

"No, sir." Ching Ho returned his bow and watched critically as he began a series of stretching and limbering movements, speaking only once to suggest that Sydney lunge a little more to the left in order to center his body.

Straightening a moment later, Sydney said, "I wish you may tell me why I allow that young woman to exasperate me so."

Holding his hands out at waist level, Ching Ho moved toward him. "Knife sharpens on stone," he said. "Man sharpens on man."

"I'm talking about a woman," Sydney said testily, moving to his left without taking his eyes from Ching. " 'Tis an altogether different matter."

"I do not know that, sir." Ching Ho likewise began to move, keeping the same pace, his gaze fixed upon his master's eyes. Feinting with his right hand, he countered with his left when

Sydney responded. The brief flurry of hand movement that followed did not alter their steady, circling pace. When their hands were still again, Ching Ho said, ''I think perhaps it is not only the lady's mischief that disturbs your senses, my master.''

''No?''

''No.''

The pacing continued as Sydney said grimly, ''I damned nearly lost my senses altogether because of her flirting at Oatlands. When I saw that devil Cumberland with his hands on her, I wanted to kill him. Daresay that disappoints you after all you've taught me about self-control, but it was damned fortunate for him the pool was there. A fine thing it would have been, killing a royal duke right in front of the regent. Oof!'' This last remark came as he went down hard on his back, on the mat. As he drew a long breath to regain his wind, he glared up at Ching Ho.

Reaching out a hand to assist him up again, Ching said gently but with a twinkle in his eyes, ''A man should not allow himself to feel hate or to seek revenge when evil is done to him, my master, but neither should he isolate himself from *all* feeling lest when passion comes, it should overwhelm him and thus prevent his observing that which it is necessary for him to see.''

''You are absolutely right,'' Sydney said as he got to his feet and faced him again.

The edge in his voice brought a glint of wariness to Ching's eyes as he feinted again and said softly, ''A man must be grateful for all experience, my master. Without bad people and bad relationships, how can we appreciate fully the good peo—'' His voice broke off with a cry when, like twin streaks of lightning, Sydney's right hand and foot flashed out, simultaneously catching his wrist and his knee. An instant later, the Chinese servant lay as his master had lain before him.

Sydney looked down at him and said in a measured tone, ''I don't believe I have yet reached that state of blessedness wherein I can properly appreciate the good Cumberland has done me, Ching. Shall we try that move again?''

Although Sydney had put little force behind the blows, Ching Ho was a little slow to rise, and conversation between them after that confined itself to the exercise. Sydney emerged from the session refreshed and calm of mind, and when he met Carolyn later in the day, he was able to treat her in the politely affectionate manner that had become habitual with him. Noting, throughout the evening that followed, that she cast him a number of speculative looks, he decided that being left to wonder what he was thinking was doing her a great deal of good. Knowing that his behavior was frustrating her and hoping the lesson would prove to be a salutary one, he yet guarded his flank, lest she resort to behavior even more outrageous than before.

This state of affairs lasted but two days. On the third, while sorting through his morning post, which had been delivered to him in his library, Sydney discovered a letter bearing what appeared to be the royal seal. Opening it, he read a flowery announcement of the regent's intent to arrive at Bathwick Hill House the day after Christmas for a visit of undetermined length. Sydney stared at the missive for a long moment before he grinned appreciatively and rang for Ching Ho.

Showing him the letter, Sydney said with amusement, "The lady surpasses herself."

Ching scanned it quickly and said, "This is not genuine?"

Sydney laughed. "Prinny coming here? I wish I may see the day. He detests Bath. When he desires my advice, he sends for me, as you very well know. 'Tis a good trick, but that wench wants a lesson, and I believe I am the man to teach her one. We are expected to spend Christmas at Swainswick with Skipton's family, and I doubt my sweet Nemesis has realized that I shall be unable to escort them if I must cater to Prinny's whims. No doubt she meant only to throw me into a dither by this little prank, but I'll show her the error of her ways."

Thus prepared, he bided his time for the rest of the day and joined the family at the supper table, anticipating sweet revenge. He had no intention of mentioning the matter too soon, knowing Carolyn must be wondering how he had taken the news of the royal visit, so he waited until someone else brought up the subject of Christmas. Not much to his surprise, it was Carolyn herself who did so, saying she hoped the intermittent, drizzling rain would cease before they left for Swainswick.

Seizing the opportunity, Sydney said casually, "I shan't be

able to go with you, I fear.'' He watched Carolyn's face, but all he saw was a shadow of surprise, perhaps even disappointment.

Before she could say anything, the dowager said, ''I cannot think what could be important enough to prevent you from escorting us, Sydney, but if you believe that the journey will inconvenience you, there is really no reason for us to go at all. 'Twas only the fact that you have always joined the family there in the past that decided me to put myself to the trouble of going this year. But I believe it will suit us better to invite Skipton to bring Matilda and the children here instead. I shall write to him directly after supper.''

''What!'' Sydney's aplomb evaporated without warning, and he turned from gazing pensively at Carolyn to stare at his mother in shock. ''You cannot mean to invite them all here.''

She lifted her lorgnette to peer at him. ''And why not, may I ask? He is your brother, after all, and while I do not approve of Matilda, I must suppose that she has every right to accompany him. What is more, I believe the children will be delighted to have this opportunity to see all your little treasures.''

''I am persuaded, ma'am,'' he said, paling at the thought, ''that you have lost your mind. What can you be thinking of even to consider inviting such an invasion of this house?''

Although Carolyn stared to see him so unsettled, the dowager was made of sterner stuff. She straightened ominously and, without even resorting to her lorgnette, looked down her nose at him with such an expression as would have withered a lesser man, and said, ''You will surely not be so selfish as to attempt to prevent their coming here.''

He was silenced, but he took the first opportunity after the covers were removed to demand a few words with Carolyn.

''In the library,'' he said, making it clear by his tone that he would brook no argument.

She went with him without speaking, but when he had shut the door, she said at once, ''Whatever is the matter, Sydney? I believe your mother was only awaiting an excuse to invite them here, you know, for it will be a great deal easier for her to bear with Matilda in this house than in the one that used to be her own. And, truly, you will not mind—''

"Not another word," he said, adding with grim determination, "Basil and his brats are not coming to this house if you can help me prevent it, my lass. 'Tis the least you can do after precipitating this whole mess."

"Me!" She stared at him. "Whatever do you mean?"

"Enough, Caro. I know the letter I received this morning was only one of your pranks. When I said I wasn't going to Swainswick, it was to teach you a lesson. I don't want Basil and his family running roughshod over this house, but I've no wish to betray you to Mama either, so we must think of a plan."

"But, Sydney, I didn't—"

"Don't make it worse! I know you meant only to stir me up, as you put it, but even the notion of turning this house into a battleground between Mama and Matilda makes me queasy. I don't wish to sound selfish, though very likely I do, but you know exactly how it will be with the pair of them under this roof. At least at Swainswick I can plead business elsewhere on nearly any day but Christmas itself, and the children have their nursery and schoolroom. Here, I shan't know from one moment to the next what mischief they have got into, and nothing will be safe."

"Sydney," she said, eyeing him as though she feared he had taken leave of his senses, "I'll willingly help prepare for their visit, and we can put away those things you are most concerned about, but there is nothing dreadful in such a visit and—"

"No, there isn't." He steadied himself with an effort. "I suppose I sound as if I've lost my wits, but this house has always been a sanctuary to me, even before I inherited it. Uncle Henry never cared much for the conventions, so I could be myself here and not behave according to all the petty rules laid down by the *beau monde*. I shall detest having them here."

Without warning her eyes filled with tears. "As you have detested having us here, I suppose. No wonder you have taken such care to hide your—"

"No, no!" He was shocked. "Good God, Caro, don't cry! I only wanted you to help me persuade Mama to go to Swainswick as she originally planned to do. I never meant for you to think you were unwelcome here. No one was ever more welcome."

"Then I do not understand why you are so upset," she said with a sniffle as she drew her lace handkerchief from her sleeve to dry her tears. "You mentioned a letter, Sydney. Is it a matter of business that prevents your going with us to Swainswick? Surely, it cannot be Trust business at such a—"

"If you do not want to experience the full force of my temper," he said severely, "do not persist in this nonsense. To pretend to have no notion why I said I can't go to Swainswick is doing it up too brown when I've told you I know you wrote that damned letter warning me of the regent's visit."

"The regent? Coming here! But why? I thought—"

"So help me . . . Yes, Shields, what is it?" he snapped when the door opened to admit his butler. At the sight of a second man, following closely behind him and wearing dark-blue livery trimmed with gold lace, Sydney put up his quizzing glass and said, "I believe I gave orders that I was not to be disturbed."

"Yes, sir," the butler replied, adding in his stateliest tone, "but this man is a royal equerry, sir, and he has orders to see his message delivered into your hands."

Sydney glanced suspiciously at Carolyn, but her attention was fixed upon the visitor. Surely, he thought, if this was more of her mischief, she would be watching for his reaction. Doubt assailed him. The equerry's livery was correct right down to the gold-filigree buckles on his black shoes, details that Sydney doubted Carolyn would remember from her few brief contacts with the royal family. Lowering his glass, he silently extended his hand to take the message.

Opening it, he scanned it rapidly, glanced at the equerry, then back at the letter. The second time, he read more carefully, realizing at last that there could be no doubt of its authenticity. Looking ruefully at Carolyn, he murmured, "I owe you an apology. Shields, we are to prepare for a royal visit on Boxing Day. Oh, and Lord and Lady Skipton and their children will be spending Christmas here, and no doubt a few days before and after. See to those arrangements as well, will you?"

"Certainly, sir." The butler bowed and left the room.

Sydney turned to the equerry. "I received formal notice of your master's intent this morning. I am surprised to receive another message so soon as this."

The equerry nodded. "His royal highness desired that you have plenty of time to change any plans that might conflict with his, sir, and so he sent formal word at once by last night's post. But wanting to assure himself that you knew precisely what it is he hopes to accomplish here, he took care to send a more personal message by hand. Will you wish to write a reply, sir?"

"Yes, of course. I shall inform his highness that he is right welcome and assure him we will do our best to accommodate him in every way. There is no need for you to rush off with it tonight, though. My people will give you dinner and put you up. I daresay you will make better time after a night's rest."

"Yes, sir. Thank you, sir." He bowed and left the room.

Sydney turned to Carolyn. "You are entitled to a sincere apology, I believe, for I thought you sent the first letter and ought to have believed you when you denied it, but after the last trick you played me, it was only too easy to doubt you."

She colored. " 'Tis I who should apologize, sir, for acting on a childish impulse, which I have sincerely regretted and dared hope you would not mention. I daresay the mischief came out of having foolishly resolved after our visit to Oatlands to behave as a model of propriety, then failing miserably in the attempt."

"Good Lord, Caro," he exclaimed, amused, "you ought never to have made such a resolution!"

"No," she agreed with a sudden impish grin, "I know. Fatal! I thought I had outgrown that childish need to do what I have been forbidden to do, but you see how it is, sir, even when I myself do the forbidding. I am a sad case. But I collect we truly must expect the regent to arrive the day after Christmas."

"We do. It seems that he wishes to examine some of the *objets d'arts* that Sir Percival Melvin means to sell, and fears that if it becomes widely known that they are for sale, the price will be driven up. He must still be concerned with his public image if he means to concern himself with price," he added, smiling. "I am sure certain members of Parliament, at least, will be pleased to learn of it. Nonetheless, since he wishes to have my opinion on the authenticity of the items and since Melvin's house lies in Queen Square, he is coming to Bath."

"But surely he might save himself a trip by having you act as his agent," Carolyn pointed out.

"He has a second motive," Sydney admitted, "which he did not wish to trust to the Royal Mail, believing, probably with reason, that some of the carriers are hand in glove with the newspapers. In any case, he writes that he hopes to gain a respite from the constant public speculation about him. Not only has Cumberland continued to follow him from pillar to post, harassing him to give up his Whig friends in favor of the Tories, but even his own mother is pricking at him. It appears that his sisters desire to have their own residence, a scheme that Prinny approves but the queen abhors, and since he is still not entirely recovered from the illness that followed hard upon his injury, he says he cannot tolerate all the brangling. In other words, my dear, Prinny is running away, and he wishes to find sanctuary in this house. I cannot deny him that, can I, however much I might wish him, Skipton, and the rest of them at Jericho."

"Well," Carolyn said with a sigh, "you would not be out of line in laying the blame for this at my door. If I had not behaved like a noddy at Oatlands, his highness would have no need now to escape public speculation. All those rumors are flying about because of what happened in the grotto, and nothing at all would have happened if I had not managed to draw the attention of the odious Duke of Cumberland."

Sydney protested. "Though you did not behave with wisdom, my dear, that was no excuse for Cumberland's behavior, nor is it reason now to blame yourself for the regent's plight. No, listen to me," he added, taking her gently by the shoulders and giving her a shake when she looked as though she would debate the matter. "You are not to hold yourself responsible for any of this. Cumberland and Prinny have been at odds since they were children, so their mutual animosity can have nothing to do with you. Cumberland has always coveted the throne, and it is that fact above all others that makes Prinny fret and stew about his own safety. He sees threats behind every bush and fears Cumberland above all others, because he knows Cumberland or his minions to be capable of any dastardly deed."

"You are right, of course, but I—"

He shook her again, less gently. "I tell you, you did nothing to warrant what Cumberland attempted to do. Rumors would fly in any event, for the royal family live in the public eye and men will always speculate about them, though it must drive many of them to distraction. Prinny is the most at risk, of course, not only because of his profligate ways but because he is the heir. That fact also makes him the greatest target.''

She was gazing at the top button of his waistcoat now. ''You know, Sydney, you have never said anything about what happened that day in the grotto. I know you were angry with me. You never said so, of course, but I could see it all the same.''

He was quiet for a long moment, then said evenly, ''I was never angry with you, so you may put that thought straight out of your head. Do you understand me?'' When she met his gaze with a searching look, then sighed at last and nodded, he said, ''Good, then we may be comfortable again, so sit down and help me think of what must be done before the royal party arrives. My people are capable, but they have never entertained royalty before.''

''Well, I have not done so either,'' she pointed out, sitting in a chair near his desk.

''No, but you have visited houses where royalty has been entertained, as I have. Between us, surely we can think of certain things that were done primarily to accommodate them.''

''Not at Oatlands,'' she said. ''The service there was nothing special, certainly, and it is a royal house.''

''True,'' he agreed, smiling, ''but I do not think we can be as casual as the Duke and Duchess of York. The regent will expect more at Bathwick Hill House, and we will not disappoint him.''

Glad to be able to help him, Carolyn allowed him to draw her into a discussion of his plans, but by the time she retired that night, her thoughts had begun tumbling over themselves in her head untli she did not know what she was thinking. Sydney, whom she had thought she knew well, was beginning to seem like a stranger to her, and she was even more rapidly coming to believe she knew herself no better.

To have flirted with him when she believed him impervious to her wiles had seemed safe and even pleasant until his apparently impenetrable calm had stimulated her to behave in an unseemly manner, resulting in the unfortunate events at Oatlands. Then, after their return to Bathwick Hill, when she had exerted herself to behave impeccably, she had ended by doing something more reprehensible than all the rest, and childish to boot. Why, she wondered, did she do such things? What on earth was wrong with her, that she must continually appear to be seeking in Sydney's responses some reflection of her own self-worth?

12

Deciding at last that she must cease to look to Sydney for approval and begin to act in a manner more properly befitting an adult female, Carolyn began the following morning by throwing herself into the preparations for the Christmas visitors, thus giving herself no more time to brood. Indeed, in the days that followed, with all the preparations necessary to house the party from Swainswick as well as a royal entourage, there was no time to spare for anyone, except of course the dowager, whose greatest contribution to all the activity was her consistent criticism of any suggestion that she could not mistake for her own, and her casual, if misguided, assumption that any visitor to Bathwick Hill House must be so gratified to find himself there that he would notice nothing amiss. She failed to understand why the upheaval should result in inconvenience to herself or any change in either Miss Pucklington's or Carolyn's habits.

"I have been told," she informed them both on an occasion when Miss Pucklington had so far forgotten her duty to her benefactress as to offer to assist the housekeeper with a final check of the arrangements being made for the royal party, "that it is well known of the Prince Regent that wherever he goes, although he expects such attention and respect as he thinks is due to him, when this has been shown, he dispenses with any such continuance of it as would affect the comfort of those about him. It is not so with others of the royal family, who, as I know from my own experience, delight in subjecting the persons where they visit to such tedious attention to ceremonious personal respect as must make everyone uncomfortable. We need not concern ourselves with that, however, since his highness comes alone to us, and therefore Mrs. Shields can very well attend to the details of his comfort without your assistance. You may fetch my shawl now, Judith, for it has become a trifle chilly.''

Miss Pucklington did not have the termerity to debate the matter, nor did Mrs. Shields object to seeing to such details as pertained to the royal entourage; however, as she had explained apologetically to Carolyn, she had had little experience in providing for a nursery party and would not turn down assistance in that regard from any quarter. Carolyn, having agreed to do what she could, saw no reason to explain her decision to Lady Skipton and avoided having to do so by the simple expedient of not telling her anything about it.

By the time Lord Skipton ushered his family into the drawing room, two days before Christmas, she had arranged for two experienced nursery maids to be added to Sydney's staff, and had, she hoped, arranged a sufficient number of activities to amuse the children and to keep them away from Sydney's treasures if not altogether out of his way.

Had she been asked for her opinion, she would have said she did not dislike Lord Skipton's family. Indeed, though she had small opinion of his lordship, a stout man nearly ten years Sydney's senior, who took his duties as baron and landowner rather too seriously for her taste, she rather liked Matilda and was frequently amused by the children. Though she did not care for Nurse Helmer and could not look forward to such disputes as might be expected to arise between Matilda and the dowager, for a time she basked in the hope that the three of them would contrive to be as stiffly polite to one another as they had been before the estrangement. However, she realized the moment the family entered the drawing room that her hope had been a vain one.

Matilda, a tall, thin woman with straw-colored hair and a sallow complexion, having bent to kiss the dowager's cheek, stepped back to allow each of her three children to do likewise, saying astringently, "I cannot think what you are about, Mother Skipton, to have allowed the gardeners to leave all those shaggy seed pods on the rhododendrons lining the drive. My own dear Feathers would have lopped them off weeks ago and would have raised the mulch as well. I shall ask him if he has a cousin or some such nearby who can see to the gardens properly for you. Stephen, make your bow correctly. Do not merely bob your head in that unmannerly way to your grandmama. She will think you to have been raised in a back slum."

The dowager, raising her cheek to one supposedly adored grandson while nudging the other out of her line of sight and doing her best at the same time to deter a toddling, tow-headed granddaughter determined to climb into her lap, raised her eyebrows and said to Matilda, "Your Feathers does well enough in his own way, I suppose, though he is certainly not as capable as our Murphy was before Skipton pensioned him off. I believe Feathers was only an undergardener then. And since, here at Bathwick Hill House, dear Sydney employs a head gardener, a second gardener, and no fewer than fourteen gardeners' boys—"

"Surely not so many as that, Mama," Sydney said, entering the room just then to greet the arrivals. "Well met, Basil. Matilda, are you reorganizing my staff? I should have thought you would require at least a day or so to look the place over before attending to that onerous chore."

Watching as he shook Skipton's hand, Matilda showed not the least sign of discomposure. "I daresay you wish I had waited to speak my mind," she said, "but I cannot abide slovenliness, and your garden needs attention."

"I don't mind," he said calmly. "Pray, do not hesitate to speak to my head gardener. His name is Frachet. I have always admired the gardens at Swainswick, and I give you *carte blanche* to amuse yourself here, or as much as you can at this season."

"Can we look for slugs, Mama?" demanded the younger of the two boys, a fair-haired gentleman of nine. Grinning at Sydney, he confided, "Mama lets us put salt on them, Uncle Sydney, and they boil. It's beyond anything great to watch them."

His eyes atwinkle, Sydney said, "If you find any slugs,

Stephen, you must ask Frachet what he wants done with them. I daresay he will be willing to listen to all your suggestions.''

The dowager said ominously, ''Many persons particularly admire our gardens here at Bathwick Hill House, Sydney, and I cannot think that so clipped and shaven an appearance as that now displayed at Swainswick is what we should choose to admire.''

''Can you not, ma'am?''

Lord Skipton, shifting the heavy book he carried under his arm, said ponderously, ''Not shaven, ma'am, dear me, no. Shouldn't stand for that. Not that I know anything about the garden, of course. Matilda's province, that is, and she don't spend her time just snipping dead heads off the violets either. Daresay the gardens at home are the best in the county, and Matilda goes right to work with Feathers, gloves, trowel, and all her ten green fingers.'' He beamed proudly upon his wife.

The dowager retorted, ''Those gardens were well-established long before you met Matilda, Basil, and she would do better to be spending more time looking after her children than her violets. Stephen is looking a little pale to me.''

''Why, ma'am, there couldn't be a better mother,'' Skipton said. ''Furthermore, we've got Nurse Helmer, just as you had, to look after them. She wanted to look into the arrangements made for the children, but she's with us, right enough, and you won't tell me you don't trust her, I fancy, not after she raised your own two sons so admirably.'' Laughing at his own humor, he added, ''Here she is now. Say good day to her ladyship, Nurse. You need stand on no ceremony here, as I hope you know.''

Nurse Helmer, a stout, formidable-looking woman of sixty, dressed in dark-blue wool with a white cap perched on her crisp gray curls, smiled grimly at the dowager. ''How do, ma'am. Good to see you in such health. You three, come along with me now,'' she went on as she removed the toddler's clutching hands from the dowager's skirt and picked her up. ''Time for your supper. And Master Sydney,'' she added in the same firm tone, ''I'd take it kindly if you'd explain to that cook of yours that I won't have mince for the children. You ought to have remembered that, I'd think, but the nursery maid tells me she's been sent up a cottage pie for their supper. I've sent word down to the kitchens, but I'd prefer you to explain the matter to the cook yourself.''

Only Carolyn noticed that Sydney stiffened slightly before he smiled at the nurse and said, ''I'll see to it, Nurse.'' When she had departed with the three children in train, he turned to his brother. ''What's that book you've got there, Basil?''

Skipton looked shocked. ''Why, 'tis the family Bible, of course. Good Lord, man, you wouldn't expect me to have left it behind, would you?''

''Why not?''

''Well, I presume that your parson will want the lesson read in chapel on Christmas Day, and I always do the thing at home.''

''Well, I know you do, but you won't do it here. Dear fellow, you must know we attend Sunday services at the abbey. And even if you are such a gudgeon as to believe you might be asked to read the lesson, does it not occur to you that there will be a great heavy Bible right there on the lectern?''

''I shouldn't feel right reading from any but our own,'' Skipton said, adding with a sigh, ''I suppose if it is to be the abbey, the bishop will take the service.''

''With a canon to read the lesson,'' Sydney said firmly.

Skipton did not seem entirely convinced, but he did not press the matter beyond commenting now and again, bleakly, that he had expected to read the lesson on Christmas Day, since it had been his habit for many years to have done so in Swainswick.

Their arrival having set the tone for the entire visit, Carolyn began to think even before Christmas dawned that the days had somehow managed to double in length. If the children were not into mischief, they had disappeared altogether and had to be searched for, and if the dowager was not complaining about their behavior, she was complaining that she had seen too little of them. The opening skirmish with Matilda having but whetted her appetite for more, she did not allow an hour to go by without more of the same, including a fierce dispute over the Louis-Fifteen table, which was ended only when Lord Skipton said flatly that Sydney was welcome to the ugly thing. By then both

Carolyn and Sydney had begun to look upon the regent's impending arrival as a providential circumstance.

Christmas Day was hectic, for it had snowed in the night and the children clamored to go outside. The discussion over whether they might do so or not nearly brought their mama and the dowager to daggers drawn before it was time to depart for the service. Leaving Harriet in Nurse's care, the others joined all Bath in the abbey, where the boys were awed to silence by the majesty of the towering architecture and his eminence's bellowing voice. The respite was brief, however, for they were in such tearing spirits afterward that Carolyn volunteered to take them into the hedge garden to build snow persons, but even with that interlude, which was none for her, there was scant repose for anyone. Thus, by the time the regent and his party arrived the next day, despite the fact that the children and Nurse had departed a full hour before, the entire household was worn to a frazzle.

Carolyn felt as though she had been running for a week, and the announcement that the royal party had arrived only made her want to climb to the topmost attic of the house and hide. Taking herself firmly in hand, she smoothed her skirt, took a final glimpse at herself in the mirror, and set off down the corridor toward the grand stair.

A chambermaid intercepted her there. "If you please, ma'am, you must come at once to the kitchen."

"What is it, Dolly? You must know I cannot come now. The royal party is at the door."

"I know, ma'am, but he did say you're to come at once."

"Who said that?"

The maid looked around quickly and lowered her voice. "He says, tell you it's Salas, miss, and I think he's a gypsy, I do, really, though what in the world a gypsy can have to say to a lady in this house is more than I can imagine, and so I told him, but he said you would want I should fetch you to him right quick, and so I thought I'd best, miss, and so I have."

"So you have, Dolly. Take me to him at once." Hurrying after the maid, she wondered what on earth could have brought the gypsy back to Bathwick Hill.

Salas had not changed. Standing just inside the scullery, near the door to the yard, he looked the same as he had looked the first time she had laid eyes upon him in the gypsy camp. His flashing white smile was the same and his dark eyes twinkled with the same mischievous merriment. But Carolyn was in no humor to be amused. Well aware that every ear in the kitchen was bent in their direction, she said, "come outside, if you please, though I cannot think why you insist upon speaking to me."

His smile widening, Salas said, "A man does not require a reason to speak to a beautiful woman."

"Stop that," Carolyn said. "I have many things to think about, and I do not wish to waste time with nonsense."

"Telling a beautiful woman that her beauty is appreciated is not to speak nonsense, lady. I but—"

"What do you want, Salas?" she demanded.

"Salas comes only to request some small assistance," he said. "He would prefer to speak with the master but is told that the master is occupied with your king who is not yet a king."

"If you mean he is entertaining the regent, that is so," Carolyn said. "What do you think I can do for you?"

"You must speak to him, lady, tell him Salas requires help. Remind him that it is in his interest, since he will not wish Salas to say certain things to certain people regarding our previous encounter. Indeed, one thinks it will be good for all if Salas is to leave England for a time."

"Good gracious, what have you done that you must leave the country? And why come here, of all places? I thought your camp had long since moved to the south."

"The others are near the town of Salisbury," he said, "a town of small-minded persons who lack understanding. It is most inconvenient of them to wish to lock Salas up, but so it appears they wish to do. One does not understand this."

"Lock you up? Then I collect that, not being content with attempting to steal from Mr. Saint-Denis, you have continued to make such attempts elsewhere. And now you dare come to us for help?" She shook her head at his effrontery. "I must tell you, Salas, that if they only lock you up, it will be too good for you. And Mr. Saint-Denis will say the same thing. Or he would," she amended, "if I were to agree to disturb him merely to ask for his opinion, which I assure you, I will not do."

"Then you cannot be considering the consequence to yourself and to the master if Salas is taken. It is true that he has borrowed things, but only such few things as ought by rights to belong to all and to be used by those who have the greatest need of them. This is law among the Romany, for we do not live by the foolish, selfish laws of you English."

"Since you chose to live in England, I should think it only sensible to live by English laws," Carolyn told him severely, "and if you choose to flout them, then you must not be indignant when those laws say you must be punished. And why, may I ask, should there be any consequence to us, in any event?"

"Your words are perhaps logical to you," Salas said, shoving a hand through his dark curls, "but it is not the Romany way to think one man should own that which can benefit many. And as to consequences, you cannot have reflected, lady, or you would have no need to ask. The master did not call for a constable that night because he had no wish to have it known that Salas sat at his table, pretending to be a foreign count, to deceive others. Deception is also better understood by the Romany than by the English, but is it not so that if Salas tells this tale, many besides the master will be displeased? He will be better pleased, one thinks, if Salas goes out of England instead."

"Well, you are wrong about that," Carolyn said indignantly, "if you think he will let you force him to help you esc—"

"No force, beautiful lady. English constables be most persistent and will catch Salas if he is here to be caught, so it be more practical that he disappear for a time to the Continent, where he has friends to look after him. It was Salas's thought that the master would aid this venture to avoid having others know of attempt to trick people with Salas pretending to be foreign royalty. Perhaps," he added musingly, "even to trick a king who is not yet truly a king. Word of such can fly like bird, one thinks, all over England."

Aghast at this unexpected turn in the conversation, Carolyn began to think she was no match for the gypsy and to wish

Sydney were at hand to deal with him. That Sydney could do so easily she did not doubt, but by the same token, she had no wish to disturb him while he was with the regent. It would be better, she thought, to delay Salas until she could find time to think of a way to get rid of him herself, or else—lacking a plan of her own—until she could at least select a more convenient time to bring the predicament to Sydney's attention.

"Look here," she said at last, "you must realize that the master cannot take time just now to consider your difficulty. It will be better, I think, if I find you a place to hide until he can put his mind to your problem. There must be a room in the stables where you can hide out, and I'll have someone bring you food there." She regarded him with sudden suspicion. "Look here, you haven't borrowed anything in Bath lately, have you?"

He grinned. "No, lady. When the master said we must depart at once, Salas was in no way to borrow anything, for not only was Salas's father enraged but Salas had no wish to further displease a master who can turn him upside down only by touching him. Salas would like to learn that trick."

"I daresay," Carolyn said dryly, "but since you do recall how easily he bested you, you might take time now to consider whether you wish to displease him again."

"One does not wish to do so," Salas said flatly. "One has come only to do him the courtesy to warn him of certain consequences to himself should Salas be taken. One wishes him no harm, lady, truly. But Salas likes to talk. It is a—how you say—a fault that he has never properly overcome." His eyes twinkled merrily, his expression inviting her to share his joke.

She grimaced. "You know perfectly well that you mean to exaggerate your story well beyond the truth, and you ought to be flogged even for threatening such a thing. I will not stay now to debate the rights of it with you, but I think I can promise you that Mr. Saint-Denis will be most displeased. Here, Dolly," she called, seeing the little maid come out of the scullery, "do you know a room in the stables where this man can sleep until our guests have departed and the master has time to deal with him?"

"Oh, yes, miss," Dolly responded, regarding the gypsy with

wide eyes. "There be a room as won't be used for a day or two that even has mats on the floor, so he can be right comfortable."

"Good," Carolyn said. Then seeing the way Salas looked at the little maid, she quickly added, "See that he has food and a couple of warm blankets, but you get one of the stable boys to help you. No doubt one of them will be glad to do so."

"Oh, yes, miss, my brother Danny works in the stables. He'll look after this man well enough."

"Excellent." Seeing the gypsy's grimace of annoyance, she shot him a triumphant look and returned to the house, smoothing her skirts as she went and hoping both that her hair had not been mussed too much by the breeze in the yard and that the dowager would not have become incensed by her prolonged absence.

She found the family and their chief guest in the drawing room. When she entered, she saw the dowager's lips fold together alarmingly, but Sydney smiled at her from his place near the fire. Lord Skipton, who had agreed with his wife that their departure was inconceivable with the regent in the house, nodded in a friendly manner, and the regent, looking pale and sitting at his ease in a large wing chair near the fire, said, "Damme, there she is! I have just this minute been asking Saint-Denis where he had hidden you, Miss Hardy. Pretty as ever, I see. And how have you been keeping yourself since Oatlands?"

She was shocked to see how worn he looked, but she hid her feelings as well as she could and replied, "Very well, thank you, your royal highness. I hope your journey was a comfortable one."

"It was, damme, it was. Looking for a little peace and quiet now, don't you know. Not an easy task for a man in my position, but couldn't think of a better place to find it than Bath. Sleepiest damned town I know."

Matilda, seated next to Miss Pucklington on the opposite side of the hearth, said briskly, "The city is thought by many people to be a trifle flat, sir, but there are many others who enjoy its amenities, as I am sure you must know."

The dowager, sitting on her favorite sofa, stiffened enough at the first word of criticism to disturb the little spaniel curled in her lap, but her tone was complaisant when she said, "I am persuaded, sir, that Bath is well-known for its fine culture and excellent history. Indeed, I do not know another town with such a remarkable history as Bath."

"A damned long history, if you ask me," replied the regent, "and folks always wanting to tell one about it. London is much the same, you know, more history than one wants to hear. But I have come here to rest, you know, so I daresay I will like the place well enough. Better than London, at all events, just—"

He broke off when the drawing-room door opened and Shields, visibly shaken from his customary stately hauteur, entered to announce, "If it please your royal highness, his royal highness, the Duke of Cumberland begs to be announced."

"Well, it don't please me," the regent declared, clearly appalled. "Send him away, man, send him away! I won't see him."

But Cumberland, not waiting for permission, strode past the butler into the room, with the faithful Neall at his heels. "You needn't talk to me, George," the duke snapped. "Indeed, I've no wish to hear your prattle, but I damned well intend to talk to you. What's this nonsense I've been hearing?"

"Ladies present, Ernest," the regent said weakly, waving a hand in the general direction of Lady Skipton, who was sitting rigidly upright and stroking poor Hercules hard enough to make him glare at her in profound disapproval.

Cumberland, who was for once attired in a plain coat and pantaloons, snatched off his hat, practically flung it at Neall, and glanced irritably at the others. "Beg pardon," he snapped, adding unnecessarily, since no one had moved, "Don't anyone get up. George, I want to be private with you."

"Well, I don't want anything of the kind," the regent said plaintively, "and after the dreadful things you've said of me to anyone who'd listen, you ought not to expect I should. Go away!"

"I have said nothing at all, damn you, and if I ever discover the gabblemonger who has set these lies afoot, I will destroy him with my own hands. I don't doubt, however," he added, looking grimly from Sydney to Carolyn, "that you have been encouraged in this house to see the devil wherever I walk."

"Damme, I won't listen to such stuff," the regent told him. "I don't need encouragement, and Saint-Denis wouldn't speak against you, in any event. Well, God bless my soul, Ernest, he's a gentleman, ain't he, which is more than folks say of you."

"Perhaps the *gentleman* will not object to housing me for a day or two until I can prevail upon you to listen to me," Cumberland said, with a challenging look at Sydney.

Sydney said gently but nonetheless firmly, "As to that, your royal highness, if the regent objects to your pres—"

"Oh, let him stay," the regent said wearily. "He will only prevail upon one of your neighbors to house him if you do not. He nettles me till I cannot bear it, but damme, he's the most persistent man I know. You won't want to be burdened by all his people, though. Tell him your house is too small."

"He would have to have an exaggerated notion of its size to think otherwise," Sydney said. "This house is not Oatlands."

"Never thought it was," Cumberland retorted, flicking a contemptuous glance at the regent. "I know the sort of entourage George trails about with, so I've got only Neall and two other body servants with me. The others have gone to the nearest inn." He curled his lip. "Do you mean to house me, then?"

"Shields will show you to a room, sir," Sydney said calmly.

As the duke turned abruptly to follow the butler, Matilda said, "It is a pity we did not know he was coming, for he might have had the suite of rooms Skipton and I are occupying, which is much nicer than any that will be left now."

Skipton nodded agreement, but the regent paid them no heed. As soon as the door was shut behind Cumberland, he pulled a white handkerchief from his waistcoat pocket, mopped his face with it, and demanded, "Why has he come? Damme, I'll tell you why, to plague the life out of me, that's why."

The dowager, ruffling Hercules' ears, said, "I believe you have never got on well with him, sir. 'Tis often the way with brothers, you know, and of course, that unfortunate eye patch of his does tend to make the duke appear rather sinister, but surely . . ." She broke off, sniffing the air suspiciously. "Good gracious me, what an odor! Judith, surely you—"

"Oh, no," exclaimed Miss Pucklington, coloring up to the roots of her hair and looking quickly away.

The regent, looking from one to the other and then at Hercules, who was licking himself in a way generally not approved of in polite circles, suddenly shouted with laughter. "Blame it on Ernest, ma'am! Damme, if he don't leave a smell wherever he goes." Having laughed himself into a better humor, he said to the dowager, "You must know that he has amused himself of late by initiating rumors of the most malignant sort about me. Tellings folks he fears the same ailment that afflicts our unfortunate father has got its hold on me. Poppycock, of course, but damme, people believe him because he is my brother."

Matilda said, "His highness has said he did not say any such thing, sir, if you will pardon my reminding you. Perhaps you ought not to blame him without more evidence of his guilt."

The dowager clicked her tongue. "Indeed, I cannot imagine why any man's brother would tell such lies."

"Ernest wants me declared unfit," the regent said flatly, "so that he can take over the throne. He is the most cunning fellow, you know, forever looking for one's weaknesses and then pouncing upon them. I must watch what I eat, I daresay, even here. Wouldn't put it past the damned fellow to poison me."

"He will not do so in this house," Sydney said quietly, adding as Hercules began to scratch himself, "Cousin Judith, I believe it is time someone took that animal for a walk. He has provided enough amusement for one day."

Miss Pucklington got up at once and took the spaniel from the dowager, who made no objection and occupied herself for a moment or two with brushing dog hairs from her skirt.

Lord Skipton, who had followed his own, rather slow train of thought, now said pensively, "I do not think it possible, sir, that Cumberland can expect to take your place, for he could not become regent after you. Surely the Duke of York is the eldest after you, and Cumberland but one of your father's younger sons."

"True," the regent agreed, "but Ernest ain't deterred by that. Wants to be king, and I doubt he would cavil at a few murders along the way. Damned shame we can't just give him some small spot on the map like Hanover to rule. Make him perfectly happy, I daresay, for he dotes on the place and would just as lief live there as here. Can't think why, but then I've not spent the time there that he has."

Sydney deftly turned the subject, and the conversation became general after that, but although they chatted amiably about any number of other things, the Duke of Cumberland still occupied more than his share of everyone's thoughts.

13

No one could deny that Cumberland's arrival strained the hospitality of Bathwick Hill House to its limits. The royal duke, while continuing to insist upon his innocence with regard to the rumors about the regent's mental condition, made not the least effort to conceal his contempt for him when they met again at the dinner table that evening.

Whether the duke had sinister intentions toward his brother or not, everyone could see that his sly references and innuendos were making the regent miserable. When Lady Skipton gave the signal to withdraw, Carolyn hoped that the men would linger long over their port, but she was not entirely surprised when they entered the drawing room less than half an hour later.

Skipton looked disapproving, the regent harassed, and Cumberland looked saturnine. Only Sydney appeared to be his usual self. In fact, as Carolyn noted, there was even a glimmer of amusement in his eyes.

The regent's wiry secretary, Colonel MacMahon, drew a chair nearer the fire and fussed over his master as he settled himself. Mr. Neall hurried to do the same for Cumberland, and when the two attendants had effaced themselves at last, the dowager turned to Carolyn and said placidly, "No doubt their royal highnesses would like to hear you play for them, my dear."

Carolyn paled, saying hastily, "Ma'am, you know my skill

is nothing superior. I would prefer not to inflict it upon them.''

"Nonsense, you have been well taught and play quite tolerably. Do not be difficult, my dear. It don't become you.''

Without thinking, Carolyn looked imploringly at Sydney and was immeasurably relieved when he said at once, "I will play for you if you like. His highness appreciates a pretty voice and will enjoy hearing you sing a ballad or two.''

Though knowing her voice was likewise nothing beyond the ordinary, Carolyn acquiesced at once, feeling as though she had been spared a dreadful ordeal, and when the regent said that it would not matter what she sounded like so long as they might simply sit and watch her, she was able to grin saucily at him and say, "You may change your mind, sir, if I miss a note. I know you are famous for having a fine ear for music.''

While the regent preened himself and settled comfortably back in his chair, Cumberland looked compellingly at Carolyn and said with intent, "George is known for his excellent taste not only in music but . . . in many other things.'' Then, finding Sydney's eyes suddenly fixed upon him, the duke added casually, "I daresay we shall all enjoy your singing, Miss Hardy.''

"Thank you, sir.'' She went hastily to the pianoforte after that and helped Sydney select some music, but she was still nervous, for she was guiltily aware that she had practiced infrequently since leaving school. When she moved to take her place, he stopped her with a light hand upon her arm, and when she looked up at him, he smiled reassuringly. Carolyn felt herself relaxing at once, as a warm feeling of confidence spread through her, and she smiled back, no longer nervous at all.

The first song was a simple ballad, one she hoped would not betray her lack of skill, but she need not have worried, for no sooner had she finished the first verse than Sydney, who played as well as he did most things, joined his pleasant baritone voice with hers. By the fourth verse, the regent, who did indeed have a great love for music of any kind, had moved up beside her to sing along, and so much did he enjoy himself that the songfest continued until Cumberland had had his fill of it and excused himself in disgust to retire to his bed.

Nor did the evening end with his departure, for by then, Matilda and even Skipton had joined in the singing, and the dowager was heard to assure Miss Pucklington that she was enjoying herself very tolerably, very tolerably indeed. Only when the singers had entirely exhausted Sydney's collection of music did she ring for the tea tray.

"Damme, ma'am, but I cannot think when I have enjoyed myself so much in a single evening," the regent informed her as he accepted his cup. "It is just as I thought—a Bath cure is what I needed. I daresay that after a good night's sleep, I shall be in plump-enough currant to get a very good price from Melvin for those of his things that I choose to admire."

It appeared the following day that he was indeed feeling well, for Sydney bore him off directly after they had broken their fast to visit Sir Percival. Carolyn, learning that Cumberland had likewise gone into town upon business, and that Lord Skipton had ridden out to look over Sydney's estate, left Matilda to the dowager's mercies and went to the stable, where she learned to her dismay that Salas had decided to make himself useful by helping to tend the royal horses. When she demanded what he meant to say if anyone questioned his presence there, he informed her cheerfully that the royal servants assumed he served Sydney while Sydney's servants assumed he served the regent.

"No one will object," he added confidently. "You forget, lady, that Salas has magic in his hands for all *grees*."

"Well, don't get to thinking you are going to live here permanently," Carolyn said with asperity, "for it won't happen. You must be patient until the regent leaves, Salas, but then you will have to go, too."

"But that is what one wants, no? It would not suit Salas to remain here, lady. He prefers to live with his own."

Not sure if she believed him, she left him and returned to the house, where she occupied herself with a few of the many errands the dowager had assigned to Miss Pucklington. When one of these took her late that afternoon into the kitchen garden, she was astonished to discover the regent, quite unattended.

Standing on the gravel path, peering down into a radish bed, he raised his head at the sound of her footsteps and greeted her with a rueful smile, saying in a more sober tone than was usual with him, "Daresay you are surprised to see me here."

"Very surprised, sir," she admitted. "I did not know you had returned from town, and one does not, in any case, expect to find the ruler of one's country gazing at radishes in the kitchen garden. I hope your visit to Sir Percival was a successful one."

"Oh, yes, some devilish fine pieces." He paused, grimacing. "MacMahon and the others have been flitting about me like flies since we returned, and Ernest . . . well, the fact of the matter is I came here looking for some peace. Don't see much of that, you know, but I thought this would be one place no one would think to look for me. That cursed brother of mine has been telling me I ought to make a few public appearances in London if I wish folks to believe me fit to rule. Damme, but he says it as though he still believes I ain't fit. And the worst of it is, I know if I do return to London, he'll have been before me with his little hints and jealousies. Fact is, I'm sick of it, damme if I ain't. What I need is one of them clever magician fellows to make Ernest disappear with a flick of his magic wand, damme if I don't."

Carolyn bit back a smile, for he looked more like a chubby boy, disappointed at some turn of fate, than like a grown man with the fate of a nation resting on his shoulders, and she found to her amazement that she felt sorry for him. She wondered what it must be like for him to have fought for power in the face of strong opposition and general lack of public confidence, and nearly to have won it all, only to discover that the burden was heavier than he liked to carry.

"It must be difficult," she said, putting her thoughts into words, "to be always in the public eye, and to know the world is watching and criticizing everything one does."

He straightened. "Can't blame them for that," he said in a tone more like his normal one. "I'll be king one day, after all, damme if I won't. Near enough now, for all that—nearer still in six weeks when all the restrictions are gone. Can't wonder at them wanting to know every move I make. Daresay, being female, you might not realize how it is, but even the *Times* notes where I go every day and what I do. Today it will report that

I am visiting Bathwick Hill House as the guest of Mr. Sydney Saint-Denis. Might even mention Miss Carolyn Hardy. How would you like that, m'dear? Daresay it would be a feather in your cap.''

Carolyn, thinking she was coming to know him better, said gently, ''I do not believe I should like it at all, sir—everyone wondering over his tea if I should succeed or fail and grumbling at every turn as though he could do better. It seems that every man is entitled to his privacy, except a royal prince.''

''Regent, m'dear, not merely a royal prince anymore. Aye, and that's the rub, damme if it isn't.''

''It must be a very great responsibility, sir.''

''That it is,'' he agreed. ''Not a day passes by but someone or other is demanding something from me. It was less arduous being only a royal prince, I can tell you. Then, it was only my debts that annoyed them. As if a fellow in my position could live on the paltry allowance they provide! But here, we have talked too long about me, m'dear, and a kitchen garden is no place for beauty like yours. Let me take you away from here.''

She had no objection to letting him make her pretty speeches, but instead of allowing him take her from the garden, she indicated a bench under a bare apple tree and suggested that they sit down instead. ''I came out here looking for one of the gardeners, sir, to tell him my godmother wants some late bulbs planted, but there is no great need for me to find him at once, and you will not wish to give up your peace so soon.''

He agreed at once and set himself to charm her with such good effect that in no time at all she was laughing with him and regaling him with certain details of her history that she usually kept to herself, knowing they would make him laugh. He was quick to admit equally mischievous episodes in his childhood, and since she knew as well as any other citizen of England that that childhood had been much more severely restricted than her own, she encouraged his laughter by describing pranks she had played on Sydney at Swainswick.

''You made Saint-Denis the butt of your jokes!'' He laughed heartily. ''Damme, even after watching him floor Ernest, I find it hard to imagine him with a hair out of trim, so I do.''

''Well, he was younger then, of course,'' Carolyn said, not

feeling at all inclined to admit more recent activities, "but even so, sir, he rarely lost so much as an ounce of his self-possession, and I must own that to stir him out of that calm became a near madness with me. His mother has told me that he was used to have the most devilish temper, but I cannot believe her. I ask you, sir . . ."

The regent shook his head. "Don't see that m'self. Daresay the old lady was making it up to be interesting.'

"Yes, so I thought; however, after that, I wanted more than anything to see him put out of countenance, but the plain fact is that Sydney never is put out. The most I could hope for, when I was particularly annoyed with him, was that the prank itself would relieve my irritation."

He nodded vigorously. "I believe you, damme if I don't. Just now, I should very much enjoy being able to get back at Ernest for all he has done. Things were simpler when we were boys. Not," he added with a sad, reminiscent air, "that one ever really got back at Ernest, even then. He is the sort who always can think of something worse to do. It was much better to hoax him several days later and hope he never found out who had done it. In any event, one is an adult now, and regent. It would not do." He sighed. "It would be a fine thing nonetheless if something so simple as a hoax could free me from Ernest's damned mischievous tongue, damme if it wouldn't."

Carolyn sighed too, for he sounded so wistful that she found herself wishing that such a thing were not impossible to contrive. If only she were a truly clever person, she mused, she would know how to make undesirable persons vanish with no more effort than it took to nod her head. But since she was not such a person, she was unable to think of a way to make even Salas the gypsy disappear, let alone the odious Duke of Cumberland.

Had the regent spoken to her at just that moment, no doubt her thoughts would have taken an altogether different turning, but as it was, he was lost in his own meditations and remained silent for quite a little time, doing nothing to distract her, so that what had begun as the tiniest seed of an idea had time to take root in her mind and flower there until it actually began to seem possible. Doubts set in at once, for the plan was too simple and depended too much upon small but essential details.

She looked speculatively at the regent, who chose that very moment to recollect himself.

"I say," he said ruefully, "I've fallen into a brown study, which is not at all the thing to do, damme if it is. Shocking, in fact. Only goes to show what Ernest's mischief has done. Not my style to sit in silence beside a beautiful young woman."

"Never mind, sir," she said. "You told me once that his highness has a certain fondness for Hanover, did you not?"

"Aye, he was at university there for four years and then entered the army there—well, you've seen for yourself that he always wears his damned uniform. One would think that losing his left eye at Tournay would have given him a distaste for miliary life, but it didn't. Still thinks himself a fine soldier. Not but what I'd like nothing better than to see him off to battle again, damme if I wouldn't, but he ain't taken a military turn since they made him Duke of Cumberland nigh onto eleven years ago, so I'm afraid it won't answer."

"What if he were called to duty in Hanover?" Carolyn asked.

"Now, that would be a fine thing," the regent agreed, looking at her hopefully. Then his face fell. "But it won't happen, you know. Bonaparte's in control there, you know."

"I think it could happen," she said thoughtfully, "but he might not believe the messenger, you know, and if he were to question him too closely, the plan could fail."

He stared at her intently. "What plan?"

She swallowed and took the plunge. "I know a man who might easily pose as a messenger from Hanover. He could arrive here, his horse all lathered, and announce an emergency of one sort of another in Hanover. He will insist that the duke's presence is being demanded there. We shall have to put our heads together, of course, to determine the exact nature of the emergency, for I know absolutely nothing about Hanovarian politics. But you will no doubt be able to think of something. What do you think, sir?"

For a moment a light of pure mischief gleamed in his eyes, but then he shook his head. "I doubt that Ernest would believe it," he said, "and even if he did, I have learned to my cost that it does no good to take unknown persons into one's confidence in such schemes. They nearly always turn up later and want more for their trouble than they are worth. Your messenger could prove entirely too costly, my dear.''

She grinned. ''If that is your only concern, sir, I can put your mind to rest, for the messenger I have in mind wants only to reach the Continent without anyone else's knowing he is leaving the country. He would be willing to disappear once he reaches Belgium or Holland, or wherever they make landfall. By the time the duke realized he had been duped, I can promise you, our messenger will have disappeared. What do you think now?''

But it was not the regent who said grimly, ''I think the time has come to put an end to your foolish pranks, Carolyn.''

Startled nearly out of her wits by the sound of Sydney's voice so close at hand, she whipped her head around to see him emerging from the nearby shrubbery. Though she had no notion how much he had heard, there could not be the least doubt this time that Mr. Saint-Denis was blazingly angry, and though she leapt to her feet, she could think of nothing whatever to say to him.

Making no effort, for once, to conceal his anger, he snapped, ''I will speak privately with you at once, Carolyn, if his royal highness will excuse us.'' He looked steadily at the regent. ''Your secretary has been looking for you, sir. A courier has arrived with letters from London.''

Getting up with less haste than Carolyn had displayed, the regent said nervously, ''Nothing in our little *tête-à-tête*, you know, Saint-Denis. Just came out to get away from everyone for a few minutes, and Miss Carolyn chanced to find me instead of the gardener she was looking for when she came into the garden. Nothing in it to make you take a pet, nothing at all. Damned clever notion she's taken into her head, damned clever, but nothing's amiss, man, nothing at all.''

''I am sure there is not, sir,'' Sydney said through gritted teeth. ''There can certainly be nothing amiss in Miss Hardy's bearing you company in so open a place as my kitchen garden, but I hope you will bear me no ill will when I insist that she go with me into the library now.''

''No, certainly not, no ill will at all,'' the regent said, favoring him with a narrow look from under his brows. ''However, I should like to say that we would not take it kindly if you were to use her harshly, Saint-Denis.''

Sydney said evenly, "I have not that right, sir."

"Well, damme, man, you sound as though you regret that!"

"No, sir. Shall I send MacMahon to you here?"

"No, don't send him, dammit. He'll find me soon enough. In any case, it's becoming chilly out here. I shall go into the house with you."

They entered the house in a strained silence that lasted until they encountered the royal secretary in the hall, at which time the regent favored Sydney with one more long, pensive look before he nodded dismissal and turned away. Carolyn, feeling oddly bereft by his departure, decided after one look at Sydney's face to hold her tongue a bit longer. Thus it was not until they reached the privacy of the library that anything at all was said between them, but then, as soon as Sydney had shut the door, he demanded furiously, "Have you lost your wits?"

She spun to face him, her heart pounding as it had never done before, even when she had been called to account for some misdeed at school, and a frisson of fear raced up her spine when he stepped away from the door, toward her, for he looked more menacing than she had ever imagined he could look.

Never before had he seemed so tall, so powerful, and she was suddenly, uncomfortably, reminded of the ease with which he had dealt with the gypsy and Cumberland. This was not Sydney as she had always perceived him, for there was no kindness in his expression, none of the languid indolence that was so much a part of him. His eyes were narrowed, his mouth taut, and when she could no longer meet his angry gaze and looked away, she saw that his hands were clenched into fists against his thighs. Indeed, every muscle—and she wondered irrelevantly why she had never before noted how hard they all looked—was rigid with fury.

The silence grew and deepened, for she could think of nothing whatever to say.

"I am waiting for a reply, Carolyn." His tone was flat, uncompromising, and when his right fist twitched against his leg as though he had had to restrain it, she jumped, her gaze flying again to his face. Still, a stranger looked back at her.

"I . . . I don't know what you want me to say." Hearing herself and despising the weakness in her tone, she struggled to regain her rationality, to sound less like a frightened child and more like a woman with a mind of her own. Telling herself that it was absurd to let him unsettle her only because he was behaving strangely out of character, she said more forcefully, "I have not lost my wits, sir."

"Then I must have misheard you in the garden." His words were measured, spoken still in that inexorable tone, and he exerted such visible control over his body that she could not doubt for an instant that he longed to shake her. He added, "I am certain that my hearing is as acute as ever it was, but I'll attempt to believe you if you say you were not plotting one of your mischiefs with the regent against, of all people, the Duke of Cumberland."

She swallowed hard, for the violence of his tone was such that she felt each word like a physical blow. "I cannot deny it," she said, fighting to keep her voice steady. "That is, I cannot say we were not discussing the duke, for you must know we were. You see, the regent had expressed a desire to—"

"You admit it, then," he cut in impatiently. "You have been foolhardy enough to plot against one of the most dangerous men in the kingdom! You—"

"Surely, he is not so dangerous as that," Carolyn said, interrupting him in turn and adding recklessly, "What do you think he will do to me, for goodness' sake? Murder me?"

"The thought has certainly crossed my mind," he retorted. "Are you so sure he will not? He is said to have murdered his own valet, after all, and while the truth of that tale has certainly been taken into question, his reputation is such that many persons of sense still believe it. Do you dare to believe he could not at least contrive to remove from his path one insignificant young woman who offends him?"

"I am *not* insignificant," she said, "and I should not be in danger, since there is no reason that he should ever know of my association with this plan. Moreover, sir, I'll have you know it is a very good plan, in that it not only rids his highness for a time of his loathesome brother but it also rids us of—"

"Enough!" Glaring, he covered the short distance between them in one step to grab her by the shoulders and give her a rough shake as he snapped, "You don't know what you are saying. Your idiotic plan can never succeed. Don't you realize Cumberland will immediately discover that there is no emergency in Hanover? Pray, just what sort of emergency were you planning to offer him, anyway? No, don't reply to that. I won't answer for my actions if I hear you spout any more nonsense. Even if he should not realize at once that you had had a finger in this pie, if he should *ever* discover it, your reputation, if not your very life, wouldn't be worth the snap of my fingers."

Carolyn stood perfectly still, so aware of his hands on her shoulders that she could not have stirred had she wished to do so. In all the years she had known him, Sydney had never touched her in anger, but at that moment, she had a strong notion that if she were to say the wrong thing, or even speak in the wrong tone, he might box her ears, or worse. Oddly, the thought of such brutality did not distress her, any more than did the fact that she was certain she would later be able to see the imprint of his fingers in the soft flesh of her shoulders. On the contrary, she felt very much protected, and even more to the purpose, that feeling steadied her mind and made her processes of thought more acute than she could remember their ever having been before.

There was a long moment of silence before Sydney relaxed his grip. He did not take his hands from her shoulders, however, nor did Carolyn attempt to step away from him. Instead, she looked steadily up into his eyes and said quietly, "I believe you, sir."

"Well, that's something, at least," he muttered. He still did not release her.

"Yes, but it does not change the fact that my plan can work," she said. "No, please don't fly into the boughs again," she added quickly when his fingers tightened. "Truly, sir, I shall have bruises there for a sennight. And you don't know the whole of it, anyway. Salas is back."

"The devil he is! What the devil does he want?"

She bit her lip ruefully, then looked at him with mischief dancing in her eyes. "I'm afraid he thinks you will willingly repay him for keeping silent about his imposture as a foreign count. Oh, Sydney, I'm sorry about that, truly I am, but it was you who decided not to haul him before a magistrate, after all, and he has somehow got it into his head that you will therefore do anything to keep him from putting it about that we meant for him to deceive everyone, even the regent."

"I'll teach him. Only give me ten minutes to see if I cannot convince him it will benefit him more to hold his tongue."

"That will do no good," she said with a sigh, adding quickly when his mouth tightened, "I don't doubt that you could frighten him. He thinks it was magic that allowed you to best him, and indeed, I must say that I cannot think how you turn people upside down as you do. But it will not answer, you know, for even if you can make him hold his tongue for a time, he is bound to be revenged upon you later, and you will not ever want him telling his tale to all the Bath quizzes. I cannot help but think it would be wiser to aid him in leaving the country."

"Perhaps he will not wish to leave," Sydney said, "and in any event, I cannot think what any of this has to do with the matter at hand, which is your—"

"But don't you see," she said impatiently, "he does wish to leave. That is why he came here. The authorities in Dorset are after him because of his thieving habits, and he fears to be apprehended if he cannot get out of the country. I thought it would be an excellent notion if somehow we could get the Duke of Cumberland to take him away with him. And since—"

"No," Sydney said sharply, reverting to the stern demeanor that had seemed so out of character. "I utterly forbid you to have anything to do with Cumberland, Carolyn, or with any plot against him. You are not to think about that again."

"But I must, Sydney. I told the regent—"

"I don't give a damn what you told Prinny, you—"

"Damme, but that's treasonous talk, Saint-Denis!" The regent, pushing open the library door and entering without more ceremony than that, kicked it shut again behind him and stood scowling at the pair of them. "Daresay you'll forgive me for intruding. One of the few real advantages of my position is that most everyone does forgive that sort of thing, damme if they don't. Except m' mother, of course,'' he added conscientiously.

14

Sydney snatched his hands from Carolyn's shoulders and said, " 'Tis I who beg forgiveness, sir. I spoke in heat."

"Never know you to do that before," the regent said, shaking his head as he took out his snuffbox and opened it. "Daresay you had reason. Pretty little thing."

Carolyn, blushing, said quickly, "Sydney says we mustn't hoax the Duke of Cumberland, sir. He fears for my safety."

Looking reproachfully at Sydney, who met his gaze calmly, the regent took a pinch of snuff between his forefinger and thumb, released it while gracefully pretending to inhale it, then dusted his fingers on his waistcoat and said, "Daresay you think Ernest is a bad man." When Sydney continued to look steadily at him, he shrugged. "You're right, he is a bad man. Wouldn't do at all for him to get wind of Miss Carolyn's part in any of this, but dash it all, man, she's got a good plan. No reason it oughtn't to take the trick. God bless my soul, you can't think I would give her away." He glared at Sydney. "Or do you?"

"No, sir," Sydney said. "I don't think it. But you and she are not the only parties concerned, you know. There is a third."

"So there must be," Prinny agreed. "The messenger. You had someone in mind for that role, I believe, m'dear."

"Yes, sir," she said, looking at Sydney, who had withdrawn his own snuffbox from his waistcoat pocket and was staring at it thoughtfully. "I do not think Salas would betray me, Sydney, for he has his own skin to consider, and I'm convinced he will play least-in-sight the moment he reaches the Continent.''

Returning his snuffbox to his pocket without opening it, Sydney said, "It would be better if Salas had no knowledge whatever of your part in this scheme.''

"But who will explain it to him if I do not?''

"Damme man, you cannot think I will speak to the fellow,'' the regent exclaimed. "It would not be at all the thing. Who is this Salas person, anyway? Damned odd name if you ask me.''

Relaxing, Sydney showed amusement for the first time since he had interrupted them. "He's a gypsy, sir, a damned insolent gypsy. Having had the gall to try to steal from me and the wisdom thereafter to leave the county, he has now had the audacity to return, hoping that because I once let him go, I will help him escape the authorities again. But if he is willing to hoax Cumberland, I daresay he is one who could turn the trick.''

"To convince Ernest that he's from Hanover, he'll have to be a clever fellow,'' the regent said, "for my brother spent many years there. Does this gypsy of yours even speak German?''

"I don't know,'' Sydney admitted, "but I doubt it will signify. His Romany heritage, not to mention his unholy cheek, will stand him in greater stead than speaking German would do.''

"I suppose you're right,'' the regent agreed. "Damned Romanies are everywhere. Now we've only to consider what message he must carry, and the deed is as good as done. I tell you, I'd look forward to being free of Ernest's vicious tongue even for a day; if we pull this off, he'll be away a fortnight or longer. Damme, Saint-Denis, it will be worth anything you care to name.''

"Not Carolyn's safety,'' Sydney replied. "I appreciate your desire to rid yourself of such a nuisance, sir, but I cannot allow her to run the slightest risk.''

"Well, damme, didn't I say there would be no risk?''

"Since Hanover has been fairly peaceful since Napoleon made it part of Westphalia, you can scarcely expect a genuine uprising to aid your scheme,'' Sydney pointed out. "Cumberland will soon learn that he's been made the dupe.''

The regent shook his head. "Damme, that don't signify a whit. Suppose he does discover it's a hum? If you think he'll lay the blame anywhere other than at my door, you don't know him. But I'll keep a sharp lookout then, just as I do now—sharper, I expect, for having had the respite—and if Boney should chance to nab him in the meantime, I shan't weep any tears.''

Sydney smiled. ''It would be as well for you, nonetheless, if we can contrive it so that he doesn't suspect you either.''

''Yes, well, if you can contrive that,'' he retorted with asperity, ''then you are a clever man. Don't think you can, m'self, and in any event, it won't matter. Wants to murder me already, don't he? Haven't I been saying so these past six months and more? What difference if I give him more reason to work his mischief? I tell you, Saint-Denis, all I want is some relief from the fellow. Get him out of the country for a sennight, and I won't count the cost.''

''Very well, sir, I'll agree to help, but only if Miss Hardy does not come into the matter.''

Carolyn said indignantly, ''I won't be kept out of it, Sydney. Moreover, I don't believe you really mean to help at all. You can scarcely say our prank is a necessary thing, no more, no less; yet, you told me—''

''Surely, my dear, I have frequently said that if a thing is to be done at all, it should be done properly,'' he said, looking down his nose at her in a fair imitation of the dowager.

Carolyn, recognizing the imitation, could not repress a chuckle, but the Regent, interested only in the fact that Sydney had agreed to help, took his seat with an air of getting down to business and demanded briskly, ''What tale will we give this gypsy fellow to tell Ernest?''

Sydney motioned Carolyn toward another chair, and when she had seated herself, he said, ''Must it be Hanover, sir?''

''Well, damme, where else would we send him?''

''I don't know. I thought perhaps you knew something about conditions there that had put the notion into your head.''

''Well, I don't. For a dashed long time one never knew what would become of the place. After that upstart Bonaparte invaded, he kept dangling it before Prussia like a carrot before a donkey. A bargain was made after Austerlitz to join it with

Westphalia, as you must know, but Boney's no gentleman, and he took it back again after Jena. Damned French have been there ever since, one way or another, for all he still calls it Westphalian.''

"Cumberland *is* known to be partial to the place," Sydney said thoughtfully.

"Damme, we all are, aren't we? Ernest and the others even went to school there and served in the military there. Daresay they're even popular there, for all we know," he said gloomily, adding on a crisper note, "and where the devil else would a message to Ernest come from that would do us a lick of good?''

"There is that," Sydney agreed. "Very well, sir, Hanover it must be. Now, what shall he be told?''

"He is said to be a very fine soldier," Carolyn said with a weather eye on the regent, for she knew it was a sore point with him that as heir to the throne he had never been allowed to enter the military.

"Trained for it, wasn't he?" he observed morosely. "Not all of us had his opportunities, damme if we did.''

"But you did tell me once he was an even better soldier than the Duke of York or the Duke of Clarence," Carolyn reminded him.

"So I did, so I did." He sighed.

Sydney had been thinking, and now he said, "I have a notion. Suppose he received a message from someone or other bent on rebellion against the occupation? I daresay there must be any number of Hanovarian factions that object strongly to being called Westphalian, or whose members simply hate the French. Perhaps if it is suggested to Cumberland that he is the only leader who can unite them all, then . . .''

"Damme, but you're as clever as Miss Carolyn," exclaimed the regent. "Rebels with different objectives, eh? The very thing. Ernest will think them very knowing sorts to have demanded his leadership, and your gypsy fellow will be an excellent messenger in such a cause. Who else, I ask you, but a damned Romany could move easily from group to group through an occupied land?''

After that it was only a matter of talking out the details, and ten minutes later, Sydney turned abruptly to Carolyn and asked where he could find Salas. Learning that the gypsy was so close at hand did not please him at all.

"In my own stables! Good God, Caro, what if Cumberland has already seen him before, or one of Cumberland's henchmen?"

"Well, they haven't done so," she said reasonably, "because all the duke's people except Neall and two other body servants are housed elsewhere, and those three are too toplofty ever to view a visit to the stables as part of their duties. You needn't think they might visit in a spirit of friendship, either, for the regent's servants aren't even on nodding terms with them."

"Very true," the regent put in. "Some of his fellows, like that Neall, are damned sneaksbys and might have pretended to have chores there only to spy, but since Ernest's got no cattle in your stables, they wouldn't get away with it for a minute."

"Very well," Sydney said. "Then I'll find Salas and see what he thinks of all this. We've concocted a tale that ought to draw Cumberland off, but it will be as well for us to be sure that Salas can be trusted. That is by no means a certainty."

"He won't give us away," Carolyn said confidently. "He enjoys mischief as much as anyone and badly wants to get to the Continent. I daresay his latest exploits have been very serious ones, since they have brought him here, for no matter what he says to the contrary, Sydney, he cannot have been certain that you would agree to help and not simply have him clapped up."

Sydney nodded and just then the library door opened and Colonel MacMahon entered, followed by a minion carrying a stack of papers. The regent greeted them, saying with cheerful aplomb, "Well, damme, there you are, MacMahon. Come in, come in. We wondered where you'd been hiding yourself."

Sydney and Carolyn, accepting a jaunty wave from him by way of dismissal, left at once, and in the hall, when Sydney had shut the door on the secretary's indignant excuses, Carolyn said, "You might think you are going to keep me out of all this, Sydney, but I've no intention of missing all the fun. I'm going with you right now to talk to . . ." Seeing his gaze shift significantly to the porter, sitting in his chair near the door, she ended lamely, ". . . to go to the stables with you."

"No, you are not," Sydney said. He glanced again at the porter, but with a grimace this time, as though he wished the man at Jericho. "Look here," he said, "we'll talk more later, but—"

"I want to go with you and hear what you say," she said stubbornly, adding in a whisper, "and what he says in reply."

"I'll tell you all about it later," he said, not whispering but speaking low, "but believe me, you can do no good by going, and may do harm. If I go to the stables to talk to one of the men, there is nothing particularly unusual in it, but if you go with me, curiosity will be aroused in more than one quarter."

She considered this argument and, against her will, saw merit in it. "Very well, then, but I ought to tell you that if you cannot find him at once, Dolly said she had put him in a room with mats all over the floor. I daresay they were put there to accommodate all the extra—"

"I know why they are there," he said with a sudden glint of laughter in his eyes. "With as many guests as we've had, I haven't been next or nigh to that room in days, but if I do find him there, it will be one more count against you, my dear."

Though she did not know why he was amused or understand the meaning of his words, she was glad to see that he was no longer vexed, and when he called for a footman to fetch his cloak, she left him and went up the stairs feeling very relieved. It was odd, she thought, that such a small thing as watching a cloud lift from his expression could so easily affect her, but she had been noticing that fact more and more often of late. Halfway up the stairs she paused and looked back.

He was watching her, and he waved, then turned to allow the footman to place his cloak around his shoulders, and stepped toward the door. The porter jumped up to open it for him, and a moment later, the door was shut again behind him and the hall seemed suddenly, despite the fact that both servants were still there, very empty.

Giving herself a shake and telling herself not to be absurd, that he was only going to the stables and not to the end of the earth, she turned back and continued her way up the stairs, but the interlude had given her pause in more ways than one. When was it, she wondered, that Sydney's very presence had somehow become essential to her peace of mind? Was the phenomenon a recent one, or had she always responded this way?

She turned down the corridor toward the stairs to the upper floors, turning these thoughts over in her mind. Certainly, her visits to Swainswick had always been more pleasant when he was there than when he was not, but always before she had put that down to the fact that it had been fun to dream up pranks to play on him. The two of them had not really become companions until she had moved here to his house.

Climbing the second set of stairs, she remembered how eagerly she had looked forward to the move, but she could not convince herself that that fact had had much to do with Sydney. Swainswick had become unbearable by then with her godmother and Matilda continually sniping at each other. Leaving the manor had been essential; the fact that they might leave it for Bathwick Hill had meant only that they did not have to go to Dower House, a fate that the dowager appeared to view as only slightly less disastrous than lingering death. And Sydney, as she had perceived him then, had been only a pleasant, foppish, rather congenial, and definitely unquarrelsome host.

Therefore, Carolyn decided as she entered her bedchamber, she had not cared so much for him then. Her feelings had developed gradually as she had come to look upon his departures—when he left to attend to his duties with the road trust or to visit the auction rooms in London or a friend's home, to look over some latest acquisition—as black spots in her life, and his return from each journey with the delight of knowing that they might all be comfortable again.

Indeed, she concluded, shutting her bedchamber door behind her and moving to stand by the window, comfort had become something she equated with his presence; discomfort, with his absence. But it was more than that, too. Comfort had come when he had paid heed to her, talked with her, joked with her, played cards or backgammon or chess with her; discomfort, when he had ignored her or seemed not to care what she had done.

She had been fooling herself all this time she had thought she was attempting nothing more than to stir him enough to make him display emotion, for once, instead of concealing it beneath his practiced patina of elegant manners. Why had she never seen before that it was not merely his approval she sought or his displeasure she avoided? Each time she had resolved to make him react to her, had she not really been flirting with him, trying to attract his notice, attempting to discover if he might love her as much as she had come to love him?

The last thought startled her, for she had not realized the direction her thoughts were taking, but standing there, staring blindly out the window, she pondered the last thought carefully. She did love Sydney, not as an elder brother or cousin, and certainly not as she would an indulgent father or uncle. Indeed, that view of Sydney made her want to laugh. Being eight years her senior scarcely made him paternal, nor did the fact that he was as different from such suitors as Brandon Manningford and Viscount Lyndhurst as chalk was from cheese. In their own ways the others were more like the heroes in her favorite books, particularly Lyndhurst with his penetrating glances and his aura of danger, but Sydney's slim elegance and graceful manners were much more to her liking. In fact, now that she came to realize it, she had consistently compared all other men to him and found them wanting.

A sharp rap was the only warning she had before Miss Pucklington opened the door and said, "My dear, I have been searching the entire house for you."

Collecting herself with an effort, Carolyn said, "Have you, indeed, ma'am? I fear I've been wool-gathering."

"Well, his highness the Duke of Cumberland has been asking Cousin Olympia this past half-hour and more what had become of you, so I finally took it upon myself to suggest that I look for you. They are in the drawing room, and she and dear Matilda have been telling him all about the Saint-Denis family."

"Good gracious, not all, ma'am, surely?"

"Oh, no, it is only about how wonderful the family is, and you know, my dear, on that subject, at least, they are very much in accord—not that they would ever think it right to come to cuffs before him on any subject—but I am afraid, you see, that his royal highness might be growing just the teeniest bit bored."

Carolyn grinned at her. "I do see, ma'am, and I hope he may be bored to death, but I will come just as soon as I change my dress and tidy my hair."

Miss Pucklington, expressing herself anxious that Carolyn should lose no more time than absolutely necessary, pulled the bell for Maggie and helped Carolyn until the maid arrived, so that it seemed no time at all before they were ready to go down.

In the drawing room, the dowager and Matilda appeared to have taken advantage of having the duke all to themselves to impress upon him the great importance of the Saint-Denis family over the centuries, for as Carolyn and Miss Pucklington entered, Matilda was saying in a consequential way, "I believe my husband's family must be connected with well nigh every noble family in England, you know."

"I don't say that is true," the dowager declared, "but I am certainly not the first earl's daughter to marry into the family, nor even the first Beauchamp, for there was Mary Beauchamp who married Thomas Saint-Denis in the early part of the last century, and a Beauchamp, you know, may look as high as she chooses—or nearly so," she added with a slight inclination of her head that might or might not have excepted present company. She paused, evidently harboring a belief that her chief listener might choose to assure her that a Beauchamp might certainly look *quite* as high as she chose, and only when he remained uncooperatively silent did she acknowledge Carolyn's entrance, saying, "There you are. We have been wondering this age where you had got to."

"Oh, yes, indeed, Cousin Olympia," Miss Pucklington said hastily, "as I have only just been telling her. She was changing her gown, don't you know, for I daresay she has been seeing that all is in readiness for their royal highness's dinner."

Before Carolyn could think of a comment that would not contradict this statement, Matilda chuckled. "I'm sure I can't think why she should. This household appears to run itself with commendable efficiency. I wish I might know how Sydney contrives it, for I am persuaded that my own does not run so smoothly."

"Well, one cannot wonder at that," the dowager said tartly, "when you insist upon leaving everyone to get on without your supervision. I think it most ill-advised of you to have sent the children back to their governess when they might just as easily have remained here in Nurse Helmer's charge."

"Nurse spoils them," Matilda said placidly, "and Miss Rumsey does not. Children need a firm hand."

"How right you are," Cumberland said, taking her side, Carolyn was sure, only because he disliked the dowager. "My parents would certainly agree with you that the best way to teach a child is with a firm hand, as I know to my cost. My father believed in a whip for his sons, a good sound smacking for his daughters. Indeed," he added in an altered tone, with a speaking look at Carolyn, "I think wayward women need the same firm hand when they err against those set above them. They must be made to see . . . What, come to fetch me already, Neall?" he exclaimed, seeing his valet on the point of entering the room. He arose at once, and apparently unaware that he had offended all four women by his previous comments, said blandly now, "You must excuse me now, ladies, if I am to be dressed in time for dinner."

When he had gone, the dowager and Matilda, apparently forgetting their brief dispute, immediately embarked upon a mutual and spirited annihilation of the duke's character. Miss Pucklington occupied herself with her knitting, and Carolyn remained silent, relieved that the other two seemed to be no longer at loggerheads with each other.

There was no time to speak to Sydney before dinner, but afterward the gentlemen lingered even more briefly over their port than they had done the night before, and joined the ladies in the drawing room. When the regent suggested another night of singing, Carolyn promptly invited Sydney to help her get out the music and under cover of this activity demanded in a hushed voice to know if his mission had prospered.

"He's agreed," Sydney murmured, casting a glance toward Cumberland, who with barely concealed distaste had plumped himself down in a chair from which he could observe Carolyn without being expected to converse with the dowager. Making certain the regent was likewise beyond earshot, Sydney added, "He'll bring his message tomorrow before noon."

"So soon?"

Sydney said gently, "You and our chief tormentor wanted him gone at once, I thought."

Shooting him a speaking glance, she was surprised to detect

laughter in his eyes. Flushing and suddenly more than ordinarily conscious of his nearness, she stepped away from him and quickly invited the regent to join them at the piano.

Though she tried more than once, she could make no further opportunity to be private with Sydney that night. Nevertheless, she was determined to learn the precise details he had arranged with Salas, and retired to bed as soon as she reasonably could, hoping that since no one else was likely to put in an appearance before ten or eleven the following morning, she might tackle Sydney while he ate his breakfast at nine, as was his custom.

He, in his turn, was determined to avoid just such a meeting and warned his valet, as that worthy helped him prepare for bed, to order breakfast served in his bedchamber.

"Miss Carolyn tried three times tonight to ask me damned fool questions about what Salas means to tell the duke, Ching," he said as he shrugged out of his coat, "and I don't put it past her to try to winkle it out of me tomorrow if she can."

"But it is her plan, my master, or so you told me," Ching said as he took the coat and then Sydney's breeches and went to lay both on a chair, to be taken away later.

"Only the framework, and if you think I want her getting herself into mischief or having that devil Cumberland suspect her involvement, you've got the wrong sow by the ear, and that's a fact. As it is, our dearest duke stsared her nearly out of countenance tonight, until I wanted to throttle him. Dammit," he added as he pulled off his sock, "I've got a hangnail, Ching."

"I have no wish to speak out of place, sir," Ching Ho told him, finding a pair of small scissors and kneeling to deal with the problem, "but if you wish Miss Carolyn to stay away, you perhaps would do better to keep her occupied yourself."

Sydney could think of a number of ways to keep Carolyn occupied, but none of these thoughts acted upon his temper as they ought to have done, and it was with a touch of asperity that he said, "If you can tell me how I'm to do that, with Prinny demanding that we go over the list of things he purchased from Melvin, I wish you will do so. I'm certain she intends to have some part in the mischief if only to make certain Cumberland gets that damned gypsy safely away."

Ching Ho got to his feet again and fetched the warming pan

that had been left on the hearth. Sliding this beneath his master's covers, he said, "Surely you can prevent that, sir. If you were to tell her she must not do so, and perhaps explain—"

"No, no, Ching," he said, waiting only for the pan to be withdrawn before climbing into bed, "to give the lady an order like that would be fatal. As to explaining, I'd as lief not discuss it with her. Confound it, I don't want to talk to her at all until Prinny and the others are gone. I tell you, I'm beginning to find it dashed hard to . . ."

But here his words trailed into silence when it suddenly occurred to him that he had reached a point where he could no longer discuss his every feeling with his henchman. He certainly had no wish to tell Ching Ho that he was finding it nearly impossible to be in the same room with Carolyn without catching her up in his arms and kissing her thoroughly.

"Never mind what I was saying," he said when Ching Ho set the pan on the hearth and looked back at him. "Leave my candle. I'm going to read. But mind you remember I'll want my breakfast here. I'd order up a horse and ride out for the day, but I can scarcely do that with the regent still here, so I'll just stay here until he's up and about and then slip into the drawing room or wherever he is. MacMahon will be with him, of course. That will fix Miss Caro, right enough."

The following morning, when Carolyn discovered that Sydney intended to breakfast in the privacy of his bedchamber, she was sorely tempted to do to him as he had done to her, and invade his room. Only a minute's reflection was necessary, however, to show her that she could do nothing of the sort, especially with guests in the house, without creating a scandal.

Possessing her soul in patience until he came downstairs was difficult enough, but to discover then that he had no intention of being alone with her was maddening. She was forced to sit in the drawing room, watching while he and the regent discussed each item the latter had purchased the day before. Colonel MacMahon took notes on their conversation, and the only other people present were the dowager and Miss Pucklington, for Skipton had retired to the library with the papers, and Matilda had taken advantage of the first sunshine in days to go for a long walk.

The dowager kept up a stream of placid small talk, but Carolyn paid her no heed as she tried unsuccessfully to catch Sydney's eye by such subtle methods as were available to her under the circumstances. He was blind to her efforts, however, and for a brief moment she actually hoped Cumberland would join them, so that Salas would have to deliver his message where she could hear what was said. A second thought reminded her that even if the duke did decide to join them, no message could be delivered while the dowager or Miss Pucklington was present, since both would remember Salas only too well.

Cumberland put in no appearance until shortly before noon, but when he did enter, looking important and a bit self-conscious, Carolyn knew even before he spoke that Salas had once again successfully carried off an unlikely imposture.

"Know you'll all be disappointed to learn that I must take my leave of you," the duke said in a sardonic tone, "but a matter has come to my attention that demands that I depart as soon as my bags have been packed. Neall is seeing to that now, so we'll be leaving in an hour. By the bye, Saint-Denis, I've a wish to travel swiftly and without folks making a great to-do about who I am. Since you're a road trustee, I daresay you can write a pass that'll get a pair of plain coaches through all the turnpikes in a hurry without my having to identify myself, can you not?"

"Certainly," Sydney said. "I'll inscribe it so you may use it for as many coaches as you like." Ringing for a footman, he sent him to fetch paper from his desk in the library, and when the man returned, he wrote out the pass and gave it to the duke, who left the room at once.

This interruption having drawn the dowager's attention to Matilda's continued absence, she spoke sharply on the unwisdom of a young woman's striding about the countryside with no more than a gardener's boy to accompany her. And when Matilda still had not put in an appearance twenty minutes later, her comments became so pointed that Miss Pucklington, setting aside the frock she was mending, offered cheerfully to go in search of her.

"For she might very well have come in, you know, and not knowing you wanted her, be in the library with her husband.

Or, if she has not come in, I can send someone to look for her.''

Carolyn, who had been nearly consumed with curiosity by that time and wondered how Sydney and the regent could so calmly continue to chat, promptly offered to assist in the search, hoping by this ploy to escape without drawing Sydney's attention to her real reason for wishing to do so.

In the hall, telling Miss Pucklington that she would look in Matilda's bedchamber, she hurried upstairs, took a cursory glance inside the empty room, and then, determined at least to witness the duke's departure, ran to her own room, flung her red cloak over her shoulders, and hurried down to the hall. As she was on the point of leaving the house by the front door, however, the dowager, carrying Hercules in her arms, called to her from the top of the grand stair.

"Carolyn, 'tis the most ridiculous thing, but Judith appears to have gone out to find Matilda herself and never thought to take dear Hercules with her. Sydney thought you would not mind taking him out, and though I told him I was sure you had not meant to go anywhere, here I find he was perfectly right, though I am sure I don't know why you should go. Matilda does not require a searching party to find her.''

"I was not . . . that is, I can't possibly . . .''

"Surely, you do not object to taking him.''

Suppressing a sigh of annoyance, Carolyn said, "To be sure, I'll take him, ma'am, although I believe he would not object on so fine a morning if one of the footmen were to do so.''

"He bites footmen,'' the dowager reminded her, adding, "Here is his lead, so you may take him at once and be back in a trice.''

Resigned to her fate but not without fondly visualizing Sydney's head on a platter, Carolyn went up and took the dog, setting him on his fat little legs before descending the stairs again. Abel, entering the house just then, saw her and said, "Miss Carolyn, I've brung a message for you.''

The dowager, still on the landing, said, "Indeed, young man, and what sort of message might you be bringing in from out of doors, if one may inquire?''

With an apologetic glance at Carolyn, he replied, " 'Tis from a gentleman, m'lady. One of the gardener's boys met him on the drive and brung this to me when he saw me helping to put his highness's valises into the second coach.''

"And why, pray tell, does he not come to the door like a Christian?" demanded the dowager.

Abel so far forgot himself as to chuckle. "The lad was told he'd just returned to Bath and would as lief come nowhere near such company as we've got beneath the roof just now, ma'am. Says it fair gave him the fidgets just to be at the gate. Said he'd meet you in the hedge garden, miss.''

"Very well, Abel, thank you." She scanned the note and found that although the message was couched in more elegant terms, the message was much as Abel had described it. The note was unsigned, just a scrawled, undecipherable letter at the end, but she had no doubt who had written it.

"Just one moment, Carolyn," the dowager said. "It is not at all becoming in you to be meeting unknown young men in the garden. You must think of the very odd notions our guests may take into their heads, should they learn of such behavior.''

Carolyn smiled. "He is not unknown, ma'am, for 'tis Brandon Manningford. You need say nothing about him to our guests, or perhaps,'' she added with a chuckle, "you might tell them that I have Hercules for my chaperon. If he bites footmen, I daresay he would also bite Mr. Manningford." Taking the dowager's silence for consent, she hurried out the door.

There was no sign of Cumberland's carriage, but since she had no way of knowing if the duke had already departed, she decided that walking Hercules would provide her with an excellent excuse for going toward the stables just as soon as she had found Mr. Manningford. Indeed, she mused, seeing her there with Brandon, the duke would be most unlikely ever to suspect her involvement with the plot.

Hercules was not cooperative, for he wished to visit the stableyard directly and had no interest in side trips. Having involved herself in a tug-of-war with him, which she was by no means certain of winning without strangling him, she finally picked him up and carried him. By the time she reached the hedge garden, his growling and struggling had put her severely out of temper, and when she did not at once see Mr. Manningford, she called his name out in annoyance.

"Really, Brandon, I am in no mood for foolishness. Come out at once where I can see you."

When the heavy, dusty cloak descended over her head, blinding and choking her, she dropped the dog, and as her assailant scooped her up and flung her over his shoulder, she had the deep satisfaction of hearing his muffled but unmistakably human cry of pain. Utterly furious with him, she hoped Hercules had drawn blood.

15

Her captor made such haste that Carolyn was bounced on his shoulder until she ached and could scarcely breathe. The ordeal lasted only minutes, the worst of which came when she was dragged willy-nilly through the hedge to the gravel road beyond and thrown heavily into a waiting coach. As she struggled to free herself from the stifling blanket, the coach rocked with the weight of her captor's entrance, then lurched forward with enough force to fling her against the squabs.

"Wait till I get my hands on you, Brandon Manningford," she muttered, trying again to free herself, only to have her efforts circumvented when her captor grabbed her and began to wind a rope around her arms and chest. "Don't! I can't breathe."

There was no answer, and once tied, she was pushed ignominiously off the seat onto the floor. Finding that her struggles only bruised her arms and made it more difficult than ever to breathe, she soon grew quiet, and a moment of logical reflection then convinced her that her captor could not be Mr. Manningford, for she was certain that not in his most outrageous mood would he treat her with such roughness.

Her second notion was that Cumberland had somehow, and for reasons best known to himself, arranged her capture as a way of being revenged upon her for her part in the episode at Oatlands. But this thought, too, vanished after a moment's thought. No matter how vicious his reputation, the duke had never once been accused of defiling a woman of quality. He could have no reason to abduct her and every reason not to present the regent with the fact of such folly as a weapon to use against him.

Sydney would never do such a thing to her, nor would any other gentleman she knew, except possibly, she realized with a start, Viscount Lyndhurst. Upon consideration of this last possibility, she decided that that gentleman was entirely capable of such a deed. It was quite likely, in fact, that having been ordered off by Sydney, Lyndhurst had decided to take her by force, from under Sydney's nose, so to speak. Congratulating herself upon clear thinking under duress, she decided it was, after all, the exact behavior one expected of the villain in all good romances, and Lyndhurst—though she had generally chosen to view him as a potential hero—was completely acceptable to her as a villain. No doubt, she concluded, following her train of thought to its logical end, Sydney would soon ride to her rescue.

There was, she realized, only one problem with that last assumption, in that Sydney had no way of knowing where she was. She did not think she ought to depend upon Lyndhurst having written a second note, gloating over his intention. Nor did she think the dowager would mention the first note. By the time anyone realized she had been gone too long—for Hercules would certainly tell no one what had happened—the coach would be miles away with no one having noted its direction. By and large, she decided, she would do better not to emulate any of the storybook heroines who waited patiently for their rescue. She would do better to attend to the matter herself.

This decision, made, she set herself to devise a way by which to accomplish it and soon realized that her trussed-up condition rendered nearly any plan impossible. By this time, the bouncing of the coach was bruising her and she was rapidly becoming cramped by her position. She had just decided that her best chance lay in the hope that they were on a post road, where an observant turnpike-keeper might note her struggles when they had to draw up at the pike. If he could not effect a rescue himself, at least he might set Sydney on her trail.

Having reached this depressing conclusion, she did what she could to ease a growing crick in her neck, and had begun to wonder how long it would be before Lyndhurst revealed himself, when with a loud cracking sound and a hideous screech, the coach toppled onto its side and came to a wrenching halt. But for the heavy blanket and the fact that, somehow, she had managed to land on her captor, she might well have been injured. As it was, she nearly suffocated before, muttering curses, he struggled free of her weight. Even then, he seemed to pay no heed to her, and it was only through her own efforts that she was able at last to find a position that allowed her to breathe with any ease again.

Telling herself that the viscount would rue the day he had dared do this to her, she waited grimly for further events, listening for what she could hear of the conversation outside the coach. For the most part, she could hear no more than horses neighing in protest and men shouting at one another.

The coach rocked, and she heard a voice exhorting someone to "Get her out of there." Strong hands grasped the ropes binding her arms and she was heaved painfully upward and out of the coach, certain she would be covered with bruises, but otherwise unhurt. When the hands drew her upright, she found she could stand, and on that thought she collapsed, trusting to the blanket to break her fall once again.

"Good God, sir, she's bad hurt."

"Get that blanket off her. And get her off the highroad, damn you! Someone could come along at any moment."

Carolyn did not recognize the voice and wondered why Lyndhurst was not giving the orders, but she did not dwell on the matter, for she was heaved up again, yanked through shrubbery for the second time that day, set down again, and at last felt hands loosening her bonds. She kept perfectly still until the blanket was pulled away, then opened her eyes and looked scornfully up into the grim face of Cornelius Neall.

"You!" She spat out dust with the word and breathed in fresh air as she tried to sit up.

He sneered at her. "I ought to have known you were having a game, but you'll gain nothing by it, girl, for my master wants you taught a lesson and he won't care how I teach it, so don't rile me." Seeing her peer through the leafless, straggly hedge at the coachman and two guards, all of whom appeared to be none the worse for the accident, he said, "They won't help you. They know who butters their bread. Get those horses free," he shouted to them, "and get that coach righted again. If the wheel can't be fixed, you'll have to do what you can to get the thing clear of the road. If anyone asks, remember you're naught but lackeys. That is not a royal coach." Then, turning back to Carolyn, he grabbed her arm and pulled her toward a nearby thicket with dense shrubbery, saying, "You come along with me."

She seemed to have no choice, though she was still shaken and her arms and legs did not want to obey her. She went with him as best she could, stretching her limbs and trying to work the crick from her neck. She did not want to think about what she must look like, and when she reached to rub her neck and felt wisps of tangled hair everywhere, she indulged herself in a brief, foolish hope that Sydney would not ride to her rescue until she had managed to tidy herself a bit.

She felt no fear for the simple reason that it was all too much like a scene from one of her books to seem real, and when they had reached the thicket, she jerked away from Neall and grabbed the trunk of a birch tree to steady herself as she said, "You can't get away with this, you know. They'll come after us."

"Who do you think will try to stop my master, that fop Saint-Denis? Or perhaps the old lady? Now the younger Lady Skipton, she's another matter," he added insolently. "Might have some gumption, that one—not enough to take on a royal duke, of course, but some."

Carolyn stared at him. "But you must know that Mr. Saint-Denis is quite capable of coming after me."

"Don't be daft, girl. He's no more threat than what you are yourself. He might whine a bit to the regent, but that will do him no good, for Prinny don't make any attempt to bridle Cumberland, as anyone in England knows full well."

Carolyn said grimly, "The regent might not, but Sydney will. He has done so before and he will not hesitate to do so again.

Don't you recall what happened to your master at Oatlands? I know you must, for Sydney went to fetch you himself after he threw your precious duke into the grotto pool.''

Neall laughed. ''Won't do you a lick of good to make up tales like that one, girl. Do you think my master did not tell me the truth of it—that the regent interfered with his friendly little interlude with you, and while teaching him the error of his ways, the duke slipped and fell into that damned pond? The regent suffered a good long time afterward for his mistake. Aye, but you laughed when my master fell, girl, and that was your undoing, for that is why you are here now. And your damned Mr. Saint-Denis dared to laugh as well, I'll wager, but you'll both be laughing out of the other sides of your faces now.''

Carolyn's jaw dropped. ''Is that what he told you?''

''It's the truth.''

She opened her mouth to contradict him, but even before she had decided it would be of little use, she became aware of new sounds on the road. From that distance, the hedge obscured her view of the wreckage and the men working to clear it away, but it was not so high that she could not see the horsemen approaching from the opposite direction to the one in which they had been traveling. Only the top of his head was visible, but he was not wearing a hat, and his hair was thick, black, and curly.

She nearly shouted for Salas to come help her but remembered in time that she must not give him away. A moment later, she was rewarded for her restraint when he spurred his horse through the hedge and cantered across the field toward them.

Though she knew he had recognized her, he scarcely looked at her, riding directly toward Neall and sliding down from his horse as it came to a halt.

Neall regarded him with displeasure. ''What do you want?''

''Your master sent Salas back to discover why second coach has not yet caught up with first. You were to travel swiftly to catch us before first turnpike. Only one pass was written, he says, and you must be with him for it to include you. Am I to tell the master you cannot obey his command?''

''We'll be along as soon as we can,'' Neall said, disgruntled.

"The men are looking over the damage now. I can't be blamed for losing a wheel off such a damned ill-kept coach, can I?"

"There will be much delay if you must pull up at each pike," Salas said. He allowed his gaze to drift to Carolyn, and his appreciative smile was not, she knew, assumed merely for Neall's benefit. "Why do you bring the pretty lady? Does she travel to the Continent with us?"

"That will be for his highness to decide," Neall said in quelling accents.

Salas shrugged. "Salas does not care if you bring your lady, but you must tell those men on the road that they will have to find one new horse. One has hurt his leg and must be tended before he can pull carriage again."

"They'll see to it. Tell his highness to go on without us. I've enough cash by me to pay our shot, and we've nothing to identify us. One way or another, we will catch him before he makes the south coast."

"With the lady?" Salas raised his eyebrows. "Does she then go willingly? Salas thinks lady might fuss or scream, or—"

"Very well," Neall retorted, goaded, "tell him . . . No, dammit, *ask* him to write out a copy of that damned pass he's got and you can bring it back to me. No one will know the difference. And you needn't say anything about the girl, either. She's a little surprise I've got for him."

Salas grinned again. "Lady will be a very big surprise, I believe, not little at all." And with that, he wheeled his horse and galloped back toward the hedge and the road beyond.

Carolyn watched him go, wondering if she had been wise to keep silent, hoping he did not think she was there as anything but a prisoner. Surely, he would ride for Sydney or do something else to help her. He could not wish to be part of her abduction. None of these thoughts having done much to reassure her, she decided she had best get on with her own rescue attempt.

"Mr. Neall," she said blightingly, "I collect from what you said to that man that his highness is not a party to your plan. Not that I thought he could be, for I think you will find he will not be pleased by what you have done. He has respect for Mr.

Saint-Denis, even if you do not, and will not want it known
that you have abducted me, so I should recommend that you—"

"Be silent," he snapped, and to her shock, he yanked a pistol
from his coat pocket and leveled it less than a foot from her
bosom. "I don't want to listen to you. Even if you should chance
to be right and his highness don't want you, just remember
there's a simple way to ensure that you cause neither of us any
grief. . . if you understand me."

She understood only too well, and the instant, blinding terror
she felt nearly overwhelmed her. Suddenly it was not difficult
at all to remember that she was not living in the pages of a book.
In books, heroines did not get themselves murdered by stupid
little men in fields near a highroad. And unfortunately, she could
hear no thunder of hoofbeats in the distance to herald the arrival
of her hero. Furthermore, she could expect no lightning bolt
on such a depressingly brilliant day, or depend upon the ghost
of some adoring person who had passed on, to return for that
one, brief moment necessary to save her. Such things, as she
knew—and indeed, had known perfectly well even when she
had read about them—simply did not happen in real life.

Neall glowered at her and she glared back, determined that
he should never guess how dreadfully he frightened her. That
determination steadied her. Reminding herself that he would
not shoot unless he believed the duke didn't want her, she racked
her brain for a way to save herself before that moment came.

She feared from what she had seen of him that Salas would
be no help to her. Not only had he expressed greater concern
over the injured horse than over her abduction, but he would
no doubt continue to put his own skin before hers. And while
she thought she could depend upon Cumberland not to cheer
her abduction, she could place no dependence upon his vetoing
her murder. If only, she mused, she could be granted one small
stroke of luck.

A rattle of hoofbeats and shouts from the roadway diverted
Neall's attention just then, and Carolyn seized her opportunity.
Remembering what Sydney had taught her, she made a fist with
her right hand, hoisted her skirt above her knees with her left,
and leapt forward, jabbing him twice in the throat with her
knuckles. Then, as he grabbed for his throat with his free hand,

she elbowed the pistol aside and brought her right knee up hard between his legs. The pistol exploded harmlessly as Neall collapsed, moaning and clutching himself, at her feet.

Carolyn spared no time to look down at him, let alone to congratulate herself, for the hoofbeats she had heard had come from the wrong direction. Holding her skirt high, she turned and dived deeper into the thicket, but as soon as she knew she could not be seen from the field, she wriggled into a space between two evergreen bushes and peered back through the foliage.

To her profound satisfaction, she saw that Neall still lay writhing where he had fallen, but she jumped back involuntarily when Cumberland rode through the hedge into the field. The sight of Salas behind him was slightly reassuring, but she decided to remain where she was.

Dismounting, the duke strode to where Neall lay, and it was evident at once that he was angry. "Get up, you dolt," he snapped, his gruff voice carrying easily to Carolyn's ears since most of the noise on the road had stopped. "Where's the girl?"

Neall made only a token effort to rise, and she couldn't hear what he said, but when Cumberland looked toward the thicket, she held her breath. The gypsy, still mounted, said something to him, but he shook his head, and she heard him say clearly, "No, no, she must be found at once. Go call the others."

Salas said something else, and thinking furiously as she watched and tried to hear them, Carolyn decided that running would do her no good, and unless she was willing to leave her red cloak behind, she would be easily visible to anyone coming nearer than Cumberland was now. She had nearly decided to stand up and hope that, between them, she and Salas could prevent her murder when there came a fresh disturbance as Sydney Saint-Denis mounted on his sleek bay hack, trotted through what was now a rather wide gap in the hedge.

He appeared to be alone, and when he drew to a halt near the gypsy and raised his quizzing glass to look down with faint interest, first at Cumberland and then at the still-moaning Neall, Carolyn leaned forward to gete a better view, choking back a sudden, nearly overpowering urge to laugh.

The duke evidently saw nothing humorous in Sydney's

attitude. "I knew nothing of this, Saint-Denis," he snapped.

"No?" Sydney drawled. "How intelligent of you not to pretend that nothing has happened, Cumberland, and for that, I shall reward you by believing that you are, if not innocent, at least not actively involved. But what, if I may be so bold as to ask, have you done with Miss Hardy?"

"Neall tells me he thinks she ran into the thicket," Cumberland growled. "She, and not I, must take the credit for his present painful condition."

"I am glad to hear that," Sydney said, adding, "She was, I suppose, in that coach yonder?"

"She was," Cumberland admitted. "This fool thought . . . Well, it is of no purpose to say what he thought, but—"

"Oh," said Sydney gently, "I daresay he thought you might wish to be revenged upon me, and perhaps upon Miss Hardy as well, but I cannot think why he took no more care than he did with his abduction. Surely he must have known I'd be hard on his heels."

Neall struggled up, glaring at him. "I can't think what you'd have done, you spineless fop. That little bitch is wor—"

"Shut your mouth," the duke snapped, kicking him.

"How wise you are, Cumberland," Sydney said softly. "I should dislike doing more harm to Mr. Neall than has already been done to him, but I find my temper a trifle uncertain, so perhaps, having shut him up, you will make certain he stays that way until I have got Miss Hardy safely out of here. And, Cumberland," he added in that same soft tone, "I should make all haste to leave the country if I were you. I feel sure that your mission must keep you away for several weeks at least."

Cumberland looked at him sharply. "I am beginning to think that perhaps this mission—"

"You would be wiser not to finish that statement, sir, and to continue in the belief that your immediate presence on the Continent is of grave import. No, no," he added as the duke cast a shrewd glance at Salas, "do not think that like the ancient Caesars you can, with impunity, expend your ill humor on the messenger. I've no doubt his friends on the Continent look daily to see his safe arrival there, and it is never safe to betray the

Romanies, for their reach is long and their respect for authority capricious at best. Do you understand me?''

"Damn you, Saint-Denis, you know too much. Do you dare to threaten me, sir?''

"Oh, I shouldn't think of it as a threat, your royal highness, but surely you must understand that when the regent learns, as he certainly will if he has not already done so, that you have most foolishly dared to abduct a gentlewoman—''

"I didn't abduct her.''

"But you, sir, of all people,'' Sydney said with a faint smile, "know the power of a delicately placed rumor, particularly when there is a modicum of truth upon which to base it.''

Cumberland glared at him, silenced.

Neall growled defiantly, "They might the both of them be made to disappear, highness.''

Sydney smoothed a wrinkle from his sleeve. "I doubt you would be so stupid, Cumberland, but I ought perhaps to warn you that I've got men with me, beyond the hedge. I thought it as well that they hear none of this, but that can be altered if you prefer it so.''

Cumberland said grimly to Salas, "Get down and carry that fool back to his coach, and we'll go on ahead.'' He paused, then looked thoughtfully up at Sydney and said in a milder tone, "I'd take it kindly, Saint-Denis, if you would do what you can to sort this out with George. It won't do him the good you think it will to have it noised about that I had aught to do with this.''

Sydney pretended to give his words consideration before he said, "I suppose that if I can assure him your mission will keep you away for a fortnight, Cumberland, or maybe even three weeks, I might perhaps see my way clear to smoothing over the rest.''

"Very well, damn you.''

"Then you may leave me to find Miss Hardy on my own,'' Sydney told him. "You will understand that she may be reluctant to look at you or that pond scum Neall again anytime soon.''

Cumberland stiffened. "You would do well to remember who I am and not be so quick to flaunt your disrespect, Saint-Denis.''

"I have a lamentable memory, I believe,'' Sydney murmured.

Cumberland scowled but said no more, turning on his heel to follow Salas, who had dismounted and was supporting the hunched-over Neall back to the road.

Sydney waited until the others had passed through the gap in the hedge before he said, "You can come out now."

Carolyn stood up and stepped forward, pulling her cloak more tightly around her. "You saw me?"

"Red is rather a noticeable color," he said apologetically, swinging his right leg over the pommel and sliding down from the saddle. "You did well to get away. Did they harm you?"

She shook her head, watching him, as her heart began to pound. "How did you know?" she asked. "Did Godmama tell you about that stupid note?"

"Hercules told us," he said, regarding her with a warm glow in his eyes that sent the blood rushing to her cheeks.

"Hercules?" She hardly knew what she was saying.

"Yes, Hercules."

Carolyn gave herself a shake. "Sydney, that's nonsense. Hercules is a dog."

"A very rude and obstreperous dog. Matilda was returning from her walk when she came upon him, trying to keep my head gardener confined to his shed. The silly clunch was afraid Hercules would bite him. When Matilda brought the little monster into the house, we knew something had happened to you. Neall must have thought no one would bother to follow."

"Cumberland never told him the truth about what happened at the grotto," Carolyn said. "And Hercules bit Neall."

"Good for him," Sydney said. "I never said he wasn't intelligent. It was fortunate for him that Matilda came along when she did, however, for she was able to deter Frachet from bashing him with his shovel. Matilda has thus redeemed herself in Mama's eyes by saving Hercules' life. Mama demanded that I sack Frachet, of course, but I don't think I shall." He opened his arms to her. "Come here, my love."

She went to him, and when his arms closed around her, she sighed with contentment. "Oh, Sydney, say that again."

"I shall say it many times, no doubt." He tilted her face up and kissed her on the lips. "I don't doubt I shall regret this to my dying day, but I believe I must ask you to marry me, Caro. Do you think you can bring yourself to do so?''

''Why should you regret it?'' she demanded, trying to pull away and finding, to her great satisfaction, that he would not let her do so.

He kissed her again and then said as though he recited a litany, ''Emotional upsets, apple-pie beds, very expensive chinaware that has to be thrown into the dustbin—''

''No, did you really have to throw it out? I thought hot water would dissolve that glue.''

''It doesn't. Ching Ho did the unhappy deed. 'Twas a very fine bit of Sèvres, but I prefer Chinese porcelain and no doubt it was never happy in its ignoble role and was just as glad to meet its end at your fair hands.''

She chuckled. ''Tell me, sir, is this your notion of a properly romantic proposal and the sweet talk that ought to accompany such a moment, because I must regretfully inform you that it is not mine. Only look at me. And at this place.'' She gestured toward the barren, weed-filled field around them.

''I see nothing amiss,'' he said, looking down into her eyes. There was no laughter in his expression now, nor the least sign of affectation, and she found it suddenly a little difficult to meet his steady gaze. ''Must you have roses and candlelight to answer my question, Caro?''

''No,'' she whispered. ''I was only teasing. Oh, Sydney, I knew you would come, but when you did, it wasn't in the least like I imagined it would be.''

He smiled at her. ''What did you expect?''

''I don't know. I don't suppose it would have been at all the thing to have knocked the duke down again—''

''No.''

''But you might have done so to Neall.''

''My dearest love, you had already completely incapacitated the poor fellow. What would you have had me do?''

She grimaced. ''I know, it was not necessary.''

''More than that, you unnatural woman, it would have been viciously and most needlessly cruel.''

''Well, I don't care for that. He is a dreadful man.''

"You," Sydney said shrewdly, "wanted a knight on a white charger." He glanced at the hack, grazing placidly nearby. "My poor fellow's not even the right color. How dismal for you!"

She laughed. "You are a wretch. I won't deny that over the past weeks, I have frequently felt as though I were dwelling in the pages of one of those books written by my gentlewoman of Bath. Whoever that industrious lady may be, I should like to pull a few caps with her, for she most grossly misled me."

"And how is that?" he inquired, bending to kiss her again.

"Sydney," she protested, "there are no doubt any number of persons watching us from the other side of that hedge."

"I don't mind if they watch. Do you?"

His arms were tight around her, and she realized she didn't care a whit who was watching, for delicious new feelings were running rampant through her body, and with each new one, she looked forward to the next. When his right hand moved beneath her cloak and gently over her breast to her waist, she caught her breath but made no attempt to move away from him. Indeed, she moved closer, placing her hands at his waist and standing on tiptoe to encourage him to kiss her again.

"Tell me how were you led astray, my love?"

She blinked at him. "Led astray? Oh, well, I thought love must be the way it is in books, or not be at all."

"Isn't it?"

"No, of course not." But she paused, and when her lips parted, he kissed her again, much more thoroughly than before. When she could speak, she looked at him, bemused. "At least, I didn't think it was. I kept waiting for true love to strike me like a lightning bolt, but it never did. The books didn't say it could start with just liking and trusting someone, and finding comfort in being with him, and then grow until one day when he frowns or goes away—even if it's just out of the room—one is miserable until he comes back again. Love isn't a great flash, Sydney. It starts small and grows and grows, sometimes where one least expects to find it."

"Like a weed?" he suggested, grinning at her now.

"Don't be rude. You certainly won't tell me that you just saw me and fell flat."

"No, only the time you pasted my slippers to the—"

"Sydney," she said, striving to sound very firm, "if you mean to talk nonsense, I think we should go home."

"I don't have to talk at all," he said, kissing her again, "but I do agree that we will be more comfortable at home. I shall carry you back in true heroic style, my love, upon my saddle-bow. Just don't muss my coat."